GHOST TOWN

by Charity Blackstock

GHOST TOWN

Charity Blackstock

Ursula Torday

COWARD, McCANN & GEOGHEGAN, INC.
NEW YORK

First American Edition 1976

SBN: 698-10735-7

Library of Congress Cataloging in Publication Data
Ghost town.
I. Title.
PZ3.T6306Gk3   [PR6070.065]   823'.9'12   76-6906

Printed in the United States of America

GHOST TOWN

Chapter 1

I HAVE BEEN ILL.

In my advice column, which I run under my maiden name of Elizabeth Ingram, I am always sensible, sound and calm: indeed, I have to be, so appalling are the problems that confront me. Now it seems that I have to sort out my own difficulties, and that is unreasonable. I am not really sure if I have been ill at all, but that is what they all tell me, in varying tones of sympathy, curiosity, resignation and perhaps contempt. They say I have had a nervous breakdown. "You've had a nervous breakdown, Elizabeth, and frankly, I'm not surprised, you've been over-working." I have not been over-working, and I don't think I've had anything of the kind. But then I am never sure what a nervous breakdown really is. It is, I suppose, the ultimate retreat from an intolerable world, one immures oneself within one's symptoms, whatever they may be: mopping and mowing, violence, a plucking at oneself, an inapproachable stillness and silence. I have done none of these things. I have never mopped or mowed in my life, I don't even know what it means. As for stillness and silence, I talk interminably about whatever happens to me and, unless this counts as a disturbed symptom, I believe that I have remained as sane as I am ever likely to be. Indeed, as I spend my entire life on the verge of a breakdown, I believe I might almost be reckoned as immunised. It is the hearty, jolly, sane people who crack, like the man in the Father Brown story: neurotics like me are so neurotic anyway that an odd breakdown here or there makes no perceptible difference.

But it is true that within the last year or so I have endured a certain number of shocks, some big, some trifling, all of them

5

were shocks, they all piled up, and somehow my hairdresser and Timmy Hills, who is a very odd character indeed, were the combined last straw: it was then that the strange symptom appeared.

I discovered that I could not walk. Well, it wasn't quite as dramatic as that, but within the space of a few minutes, for no understandable reason, I became tottery, like an old lady. I am not yet an old lady, I am forty-eight. This sometimes seems to me an immense age, but nowadays when old girls dash around on television and elderly politicians retain all the vigour of their youth, it counts almost as the prime. The whole business was not only frightening to me, but utterly shameful. I find all illness a matter for shame — in myself of course, not in other people. It must be some atavistic throwback. Even when I have 'flu, or something quite mild, I have immediately a deep, inner conviction that it is a punishment for my sins, I am unclean, I must keep away from the world. And to become in an instant a weak, wambling, dependent creature who could only just make it to the bathroom, was appalling and terrifying: I realised at once that I must have been very wicked to deserve such punishment.

I am really all right again now. I am still easily tired, and the journey to the Grand Canyon, when I at last visited my ghost town, was something of a nightmare, but I can move around, even if occasionally I still fall down and have to be picked up by complete strangers who invariably, with no doubt the best of intentions, pull me in different directions so that I feel as if I am being torn apart by wild horses.

All this then — and thank God for it — is in the past, but I could never forget it, indeed, I must remember it, for without it I would never have felt compelled to try to find Steve again.

It lasted — nervous breakdown, psychosomatic nonsense, whatever you like to call it — for five long months, and Steve of course was one of the shocks. I think in a minor way Daniel's marrying Vanda was another, though on its own it would hardly have counted. And of course that beastly little Timmy Hills. How strange it is that one can take catastrophe and survive, yet crumple up entirely before something trivial and unimportant. I cannot call my hairdresser anything but trivial and certainly Timmy is the most trivial little horror imaginable, but the two of them combined that September afternoon to hit me like a sledgehammer. Nothing I could do in any way helped me, though in the end I survived, presumably by some strange mental process of my own, the realisation that Daniel still needed me, and a chance remark from a silly woman who had no idea what she was doing.

Certainly my own feeling of shame helped me. Not at the beginning, but in the end. It was after all perfectly ridiculous, and I live in a world where we go in for self-analysis, where we pride ourselves on dissecting everything within the walls of our little minds. Not, I must admit, that it makes much difference to our general behaviour. We say triumphantly to ourselves, I am jealous, I am weak, I am vindictive. We analyse it carefully, it sounds wonderful, then we go on being jealous, weak and vindictive, with as it were a kind of divine intellectual dispensation so that it no longer matters, so that wrong somehow becomes right.

In this case I had at last to do something about myself. I could not spend the rest of my life in a wheelchair, advising other people to pull themselves together. The days of elegant invalids are long since vanished with the servants who used to wait on them, and it has to be faced that the incapacitated are nothing but a confounded nuisance to other people. And I found that I was beginning not to want to get better. I no longer wanted to see people, the thought of going out was a nightmare, and my outside journalism, which is after all my living, was dying on me for lack of fuel. Harry left me a small income, but it only just pays the porterage in my new flat. It would soon be the wheelchair and the geriatric ward and this, though of course exaggerated, shocked me back into life again. Steve has been dead for a year now, Daniel has his own life, and I was I, I was not going to be completely done down, especially when the instrument of disaster was someone like Timmy Hills. I loved Steve, I love Daniel, but Timmy was nothing to me, just a poor, spiteful creature, with no other mission in life than drinking my whisky and putting a period to my powers of resistance.

My affair with Steve finished a long time before he died, last year. He said, "You don't imagine we'll ever marry, do you?" No, I did not really imagine it; though he did marry twice, he was in no way a marrying man. Marriage with him would have been a disaster for both of us. A love affair with him was a disaster too, but at least he was not bound down, and the realisation that one can walk away takes the edge off things. It was not so amusing for me, there was nothing I would have liked better than to bind him down, especially as my brief marriage with Harry Waterman had been so happy, but I knew in my heart that if we were tied together, we would kill each other, it would have been utterly impossible.

So Steve was gone, after our two fighting years, he married Joanna, and that marriage went the way of the first one. He was constitutionally unfaithful, he drank too much, and his writing, which was in a different class from mine, drifted away into boredom so that there was not much left for him. He must always have felt himself far from home. He always considered himself an American, though he was born here and a British subject. He even spoke with an American accent. His parents went to live in America when he was twelve, leaving him in the charge of an aunt, but later he too crossed the Atlantic, to spend a large part of his life in a place called Flagstaff, which is in Arizona. I do not know why he at last left his adopted country, but somehow this disfranchised him, there seemed nothing to keep him here in London except his own bitter and contrary spirit.

I saw him for the last time two years before his death. I do not even know the girl he married, though of course I heard about her, from both enemies and friends. We are like actors, we live in a small, enclosed world, everybody knows everybody else. I suppose everyone knew about Steve and myself, we were not important but we provided an interesting gobbet of gossip, especially as we finished so publicly and in such ugliness and bitterness.

He sent me a copy of his last book. It was like a hand reaching out, but I knew that hand would be snatched away if I even made a gesture towards it. There was no inscription. The book simply arrived. I did not acknowledge it. I excused myself by saying that I did not know his address, but that of course was nonsense, I could always have written to his agent or publisher.

It was not a good book. He wrote the one splendid, moving and magnificent book that made his name, and after that almost everything was a smudged carbon copy, black with sex and violence and self-disgust, with little of the tenderness and compassion that still lay deep within him. It was only once, just before we finished, that he broke all tradition by showing me the typescript of this latest novel. I was first flattered then

8

horrified. It was bad. I have just said it was not a good book. That is not true. It was out-and-out bad, b-a-d. It rambled, it had no sequence, the characters were dummies, it bore the unmistakable imprint of a book that the author himself despised. Any writer will know what I mean. If we write at all, we go on writing, for it becomes a kind of compulsion, and if we have been in the profession for some time, we usually produce something reasonably competent. But if the heart is not in it, it is no use at all, and it should be torn up and thrown down the rubbish chute. I do not write as well as Steve, and I am a journalist, but the number of articles I have torn up in my time would feather a bed for a legion of down-and-outs. Steve did not tear his novel up, he rambled on for four hundred pages, and towards the end it was so incoherent that I had to force myself to finish it. I was inextinguishably bored, and if you can say this of someone you love, it is boring indeed.

He said, "What do you think of it?"

What should I have answered? It's rotten, tear it up. It will do you no good. It will probably be published because of your name, your faithful readers will read it, for old sake's sake, but I doubt if they'll finish it, and the next one they will leave on the library shelves.

Well, put yourself in my place. What would you have done?

I said, "It's marvellous. I loved it."

He flushed with pleasure. We are all the same. Don't ever be taken in by a writer who asks you for your candid opinion. He doesn't want your opinion at all, he wants to be told he's a genius. When I was younger and sillier, I tended to give that candid opinion, and my writer friends dropped from me like leaves in the fall. Besides, Steve and I were in a sense rivals. He seldom had a good word for my own articles, damning faintly in the way he knew so well how to do: he offered me a contemptuous criticism, intimated that all the parts I myself liked, should be cut out. He made great fun of my advice column, sometimes chanting the letters at me. He always contended that these cries for help were phoney, that the magazine staff sat there laughing to themselves and making it all up. My God! If he could only have seen the innumerable letters we dared not print, all of which were answered privately, even if stamps were not enclosed. There was no need to invent problems. Such problems exist that a psychiatrist in a nightmare could hardly fathom, and these arrived on our desk, written in fear, desolation and desperation: the world, we all began to think, is full of sad, lonely people who have no one to confide in, who turn in anguish to a faceless woman they have never met, never will meet. Elizabeth Ingram and her staff are permanent travellers on the train: our companions pour out their woes, get out at the next stop and we never see them again. Sometimes — for I do most of my work at home, going to the office only once a week — I feel weighed down by the sorrows of the young whom I do not know.

Of course I made more money than Steve, and he knew this: it was one of the barriers between us. He implied naturally that my stuff was popular, and my readers therefore mentally sub-normal. I accepted this. I accepted everything. It was immoral of me to do so, for there is no justification for self-depreciation. If I had really believed that my writing was so shoddy, my broadcasts so stupid, I should have stopped immediately and taken up collecting postage stamps. I had no more right to run myself down than to tell him that a bad book was good. But so I did, and I have never quite forgiven myself. I lied to placate, poor dogsbody that I was, and Steve was satisfied, he loved me for a brief while longer, while the typescript went to his publisher who, I imagine, was secretly appalled.

The book did not sell. How could it? The public will often accept the second-rate, even the third-rate, but there must be heart and sincerity, and in Steve's book there was none of this, there was nothing. He wrote two more after this, then turned to magazine serials because he needed the money. I suppose I could have laughed, only by this time there was no laughter left in me. One of the books I read, with the utmost difficulty, and the other lies unopened on my shelf. I bought it for some personal masochistic reason, but I could not bring myself to do more than flick the pages over: it would have been like meeting an old friend whom one once passionately admired, only to find that now there was nothing in common.

I do not know why Steve sent me his book. We never saw each other again after that final scene in the B.B.C. pub, we did not even speak on the phone. I retreated, because there was nothing else to do, and after all, there was Daniel, friends, my own work, a life that was at times confused, even blocked, yet which in the way of lives went on.

I did not read the book again. I looked at the poor jacket, read the blurb, and saw that Steve was described as the author of his one best-seller, which had been written five years back. "By the author of — " It was a sad give-away, and I cried for Steve, not for our love, but for the vanished glory, for the pity of his producing something so cheap, bad and dull. I did not write for the simplest of reasons: I did not dare. He might have answered. He might have come to see me. The thought of this made me shake with fear: it was like the burnt child confronted with a blazing fire.

Once, I believe — I always will believe — he did call. I don't know, of course. It might have been some idiot playing games, for the bells outside the door of my old flat were illuminated, and it was great fun for passers-by to play them like an xylophone, ping-ping-ping, and sometimes if they were feeling really merry, they would wait for me to answer on the inter-com and shout derisive messages back.

The bell went about half-past nine. It was the time when he liked to call, and for a long while that hour would be zero hour for me; even though the pain had lessened, it was a kind of Pavlov reaction. The bell went loudly, and was repeated twice. I found myself cold and sick with terror. I suppose I was watching something on the television, it was an ordinary evening, I was feeling perfectly happy, Daniel was coming down for the weekend. I did not move in my chair. I must have gone white, for I felt faint, and I am not the fainting kind. I could not have answered that bell if my life had been at stake. Perhaps this was a foretaste of the strange paralysis that was to come upon me. I am a great coward, and in moments of fear and danger I freeze as a rabbit is supposed to do before a snake. I simply sat there through the three rings, and each time the bell sounded it was as if I were stabbed, so that the pain was unendurable.

I suppose it could have been anyone. My own friends do not usually call so late without warning me, for they assume that I may be working, Daniel has a key, but his friends sometimes use my flat when they are in town as a lodging for the night: the young seldom bother to let you know in advance. Whoever it was simply went away, and nobody phoned, though I listened carefully for the telephone in my bedroom. If it were Steve, he departed, he never called again, and a few months later he was dead. Only that evening he was there with me, his

11

presence was in every corner and cranny of my flat, and I would still swear that he came for help and comfort as he used to do, as Daniel used to do and still sometimes does.

I did not answer. And now he is dead.

But I no longer mourn over this. I am not a mourner and, until everything descended on me, I have always contrived to remain in the present — even when Harry died, even with the difficulties over Daniel's marriage. I do not like ghosts. I did not know how much ghosts would mean to me, until I came to Jericho City, though of course Steve in a way was responsible for that: even though it was not really his own, he adored the country he had abandoned: he was always with one hand tearing the States to shreds, and with the other prepared to murder me if I spoke one derogatory word.

"You don't know how beautiful the country can be," he said. "Of course your kind of holiday is in Southend. You're like all Britishers, you wouldn't dream of going far afield."

I have never understood why Southend is synonymous with the lowest depths, but then I have never been there. I always visualise it in terms of whelks and comic hats and vulgar postcards. I think I might enjoy it. In any case this remark of Steve's was a pure fantasy: he was in a good mood and trying to be funny. I have travelled possibly rather more than he had, though of course he was a prisoner of war in Germany, and had fought in various parts of Europe. But as far as holidays went, he seldom went away at all, though occasionally he went to France, where he always seemed to end up in some extraordinary adventure, entangled with a French girl so beautiful that even then I was not quite sure if I believed in her.

I remember the odd tale of the landlady at some provincial auberge. Steve was there with a friend: the friend slept with the daughter and Steve with the middle-aged landlady: apparently his prowess was so remarkable that she refused to charge him anything for his lodging.

I think that even in my bemused state I regarded this as a sexual fantasy, especially as he related it in such a Maupassant manner. But I was not thinking of lies or ghosts then: it was one of our happy times, I was grateful to be with the living.

"One day," Steve said dreamily over his beer — he was a great beer drinker and deplored my preference for shorts — "One day, my girl, I'll take you to the Grand Canyon. I'll even introduce you to Paul Ducane."

"Paul Ducane!" I repeated, amused. "The film star? It's a long time since I've seen him. He must be quite an old man."

"There's a ghost town about a hundred miles out. You could do an article on it. It's called Jericho City. You would know Paul Ducane, wouldn't you? You and your bloody Westerns — "

Me and my bloody Westerns! But I still watch them, mainly on the box, and never nowadays with Paul Ducane. I no longer like his primitive kind of movie, with dead Indians falling around him, but when I was younger I went to every film he made, for he was going strong when I was up at college. I did not say this to Steve, but I thought he must be dead. He was not really a good actor. He always played the same role, indeed unkind critics said he always played Paul Ducane. But then critics always slam such actors, and it makes no difference at all: his box office ratings must have been among the highest in the world. He never acted in anything but Westerns. He was tall and spare and handsome, with a magnificently boned face that never really showed any expression but which was so beautiful that it did not matter. He was swift on the draw, rode his horse as to the manner born and, so they said, did all his own stunts. He must have ridden away into the sunset some fifty times or more and, when he was not galloping away, was walking grimly down an empty street, hands swinging at his sides, to meet the bad man at the other end. His love scenes were mostly disastrous, unless he had an unusually dominant producer, but he had married three or four times, lived on his ranch and in Beverly Hills, and his only other claim to fame was his fanatical hatred of Reds, whom he appeared to see round every corner. I know all this, because I once read an article on him. From time to time some paper would print an outburst against the Commies but as otherwise he was a harmless man, no one paid the least attention. He was, I suppose, not really an interesting person at all, but he possessed that curious, unmistakable glamour on the screen that is nothing to do with looks or brains or even acting ability: once before a camera he gripped you, so he went on making old-fashioned films for a long time and, though no longer the hot property he once had been, I daresay he continued to draw in the audiences.

I no longer watched Paul Ducane, but Steve was quite right. I did like Westerns, and so of course did he, for all he professed

13

to sneer at them. I can see him even now sitting on the edge of his chair, thumping his fist into his other hand as the villain was knocked out cold by John Wayne, somehow it always seemed to be John Wayne. But then Steve was a great one for fighting: he always seemed to be embroiled in some kind of brawl. I think he would have been very much at home in the old Western days.

Certainly he would not have murdered Indians. He was a great protector of the weak and persecuted: it was a pity that this did not apply to women. It certainly didn't apply to me.

He died in a ditch on a country road. It was just over a year ago. He was not found until the morning. They said it was a heart attack. He was something of a hypochondriac, but no one seemed to know that he had a weak heart. His marriage was already on the rocks, though there was a child, a little girl whom he adored. He was good with children, it was his most endearing aspect. He died in a ditch, as I read in the paper next morning — he was accorded one very small paragraph, with a reference to the one magnificent book — and I imagine he was coming back from the latest girl-friend and almost certainly drunk. Various people told me this: people enjoy retailing such things. So Steve was dead and, do you know, I think he would have liked to die like that, it would have suited his sardonic humour. I could never visualise him on a conventional death-bed, with the sun slanting through the curtains and weeping friends around. I am sure his last word would have been a four-letter one. He was a great one for four-letter words, and my vocabulary increased enormously during our acquaintance. I don't swear very much nowadays but when I do, Daniel disapproves. I don't blame him. Swearing is a foolish habit, but once acquired it is, like smoking, difficult to break.

So Steve is dead, and Harry of course died a long time ago. We were only married for two years, and they were the happiest two years of my life, though everyone prophesied disaster from the very beginning. He was more than twenty years older than me, he was a widower and he had a son of fifteen while I was then thirty. It won't work, how could it — He is fifty-six, he is old enough to be your father, and the boy is just the age when he will bitterly resent a stepmother, and one so young at that. You're completely crazy, you are simply asking for trouble, surely you could marry someone nearer

14

your own age, and why be encumbered with a stepson when you should be having children of your own — Etcetera, etcetera. Fortunately, I paid no attention to any of this, and they were all wrong: it worked, I was incredibly happy; Daniel and I got on very well and, being a practical boy, he did not waste time in resenting me, as Vanda did at the beginning, but treated me as a friend, and even made use of me as a confidante in his innumerable love affairs. As for children of my own, it seemed that I could not have any. I tried desperately, and I tried with Steve too, though he would have been horrified to know it. It was not that I wished to blackmail him, for that I regard as the lowest, meanest feminine trick in the book, it was simply that I always wanted children, especially Steve's. I was very grieved that I could not manage it, but at least I could be grateful for Daniel who was after all the nearest approach to it that I could ever have.

Harry died of a stroke. He died instantly. And Daniel, who loved his father, instantly took charge: he was and is the type of masculine male who likes to be in a position of authority and, despite his youth, he coped with everything including myself, all the miserable arrangements that accompany death, notices in the papers, notifying friends, cremation, and it was only long afterwards that I realised with a pang of conscience how much I had laid on the shoulders of a seventeen-year-old.

Vanda has found herself a good husband, however bad the first one was. He is solid and dependable, if rather lacking in a sense of humour: within his limited vision he possesses compassion, and if he tends to view everything from the scientific point of view, that is because he is a doctor. I don't think he possesses much imagination, yet sometimes he startles me with the odd flash of intuition, and he is at times disconcertingly observant. He is also very good-looking in his pink-faced, ginger way, and a great many girls drifted in and out while he was up at college: it was one of the red-brick ones and it suited him very well, though I would have loved in my snobbish way for it to be Oxbridge, especially as I was up at Oxford myself.

I knew Vanda before I met her. Daniel had started a small partnership practice and had found himself a small house near Amersham, where he still lives. He arrived at my flat one weekend, rather pinker-cheeked than usual, tending to laugh in a nervous way: he suddenly produced her photo from his notecase.

15

Oddly enough, I had been thinking for some time that he was due to find himself a wife. He was thirty then — this was three years ago — and that nowadays is considered quite old to be still unmarried. He is by nature — though he would be furious with me for saying so — a good, respectable, middle-class young man, with a passion for children, and I think in his heart he has always wanted to settle down. Naturally he accepted the permsoc. with a vast enthusiasm, and liked to give the impression that he slept joyfully with dozens of girls: Daniel, thus wandering from flower to flower, always reminds me of an elephant, and I feel that all the beds he swore that he leapt into, must have been heavily weighed down at one side. However, I accepted all this debauchery without much comment, invited pretty girls to tea and supper, and pretended not to notice that Daniel was bored to death with most of them. As well as indulging in this sexual orgy, he plodded solemnly to all the more outspoken plays and films, and sometimes when I pictured him sitting there, reverently absorbing scenes of copulation, perversion, vomiting and violence, I had to smile — gently because I loved him, but I could not entirely restrain myself. I would have loved to know what he really thought about it, but he never discussed such matters. Occasionally he took me with him, but not often — "You're a wee bit old-fashioned, Elizabeth, you know, I don't really think you'd like it. There is one scene where all the men are completely starkers — "

"I've seen naked men before, Daniel."

"Well, I suppose you have." A stiffness in the voice, a turning away of the head. Daniel prefers not to think of me seeing naked men. He knew about Steve of course, and with the utmost disapproval, but he only knew because it was impossible to keep it from him. I didn't want him to know, I never spoke about it, but Daniel is not after all a fool and, whenever you turn up at your stepmother's flat there is a tall, gangly American — for so he would seem — lounging there with his jacket off, drinking her beer and obviously owning both her and the place, you cannot entirely deceive yourself. He was very stiff and pompous with Steve, and palpably jealous: this entertained Steve, but he liked Daniel and on the whole let him down lightly. But his way of speaking, his attitude to life and, above all, his patent possessiveness with me, antagonised Daniel bitterly, and I did my best to keep

16

them apart. We never of course mentioned the matter: indeed, as far as I could manage it, I never mentioned Steve's name.

Only when Steve was dead did Daniel permit his feelings to show. He must have seen the paragraph in the paper. He is after all both observant and inquisitive. It was shocking to me to see how secretly overjoyed he was. There was almost a radiance to him, of which I am sure he was completely unaware. But even then he never referred to it. I sometimes think there is an odd, almost puritan, vindictive streak in him. He does bear grudges, and deep in his heart thinks that by taking a lover I have let the family side down. I am not sure. He may have forgiven me for Steve, but I think that even now he would trample on Steve's grave.

However now, this winter afternoon — it was just before Christmas — he was not concerned with me at all, except for once in a motherly role. There was no more Steve to disturb him. The affair had just ended, and once again Daniel knew about this very well, but made no mention of it. He took the photo out and put it in my hands. He was careful not to watch me as I looked down at it, only wandered over to the record-player, and put on some songs of Nana Mouscouri, wearing the air of one to whom all this was utterly unimportant, just something incidental, don't you know, nothing to create about.

And I saw Vanda for the first time. "She's Italian. She comes from Rome." I didn't like very much what I saw. Perhaps I too was jealous. But though jealousy plays a part in all this, there was something else, and I wish that Vanda could have seen this too, for it would have made the first stages of our uneasy relationship much better.

It was a set kind of photo, the sort that is not often taken these days. In my early times, when I needed a press photo, I had to go to the photographer, usually with my hair newly done, sit on a high stool and smile carnivorously into the camera. Nowadays the photographer comes to me, I don't have my hair done or change my clothes, and he wanders about, chatting me up and taking innumerable small photos from every conceivable angle. The result is about fifty prints, and usually half a dozen of these are presentable. Vanda had plainly sat herself down on the high stool. The rather heavy, pale face with its huge dark eyes gazed unsmilingly upwards: I suppose "cheese" in Italian would not provide the right effect, but presumably the photographer had tried unsuccessfully to make her smile. In those days she wore her night-black hair long and straight: I remember that she was always pushing it behind her ear, twisting it round her finger, or even passing it through her lips as if she were sucking it. I knew at once that she would like me as little as I liked her. I was shocked at myself, especially as it seemed to me that she was far too old. I had always liked Daniel's girls, and I had a presentiment that this one whom I did not care for, was serious: I had never known him carry photos around before, it was usually the other way round with lovelorn young women putting Daniel's picture under their pillow.

"She really has a lovely voice," said Daniel. He has not much ear for music, but he is a little ashamed of this and tries to cover it up.

I said, trying not to laugh, "Does she sing too?"

"Sing too? What do you mean? Oh. Oh, Vanda. No. Why on earth should she? I was talking about Nana Mouscouri."

"Oh come off it, Daniel!"

He flushed a glowing crimson. Like many redheads he flushes easily. He snatched the photo back from me, and made a great business of putting it back in his notecase.

"Tell me about her," I said. "And I don't mean Nana Mouscouri."

"Well — Can I have a drink?"

"Help yourself. You can give me one too. I think the sun is over the yard-arm, but it doesn't matter anyway."

I sometimes wonder if Daniel drinks too much and, if so, whether it is partly my fault. At the beginning, not only did he hardly drink at all, but he was quite censorious about people who did. He would deliver me little lectures on alcohol and nicotine, telling me sternly that I was cutting down my life-span, that I didn't need these drugs which were far more lethal than marijuana. Indeed, at one point he developed all kinds of diet fads, and when he came to see me I had to cook brown rice for him, cut out meat, make sure there was not too much starch and even, at one point, cut out butter too. Nowadays he eats everything with a cheerful appetite and, though he doesn't smoke, packs away quite a lot of whisky. It is true that I have never seen him remotely the worse for it, but there always is drink in my house, and he helps himself freely, which in a way is as it should be. I cannnot help feeling that

18

Steve set a bad example, though I myself am reasonably restrained: after all, if I drink I can't work, and if I can't work I die.

I said, as we drank our whisky, "Is this serious? You sound as if it is."

"Oh no, of course not. She's a bit older than I am, you know. She's married and getting a divorce. Her husband's a real swine, just walked out on her." Then he said, studying his whisky glass, "She has three children."

"Oh, Daniel!"

"They're lovely children. I get on very well with them. Mario's nine, Sophy's five, and little Federico is just two and a half."

I was not at all taken in by the offhand denial, and I was a little shocked to hear of the three children. Daniel is only just starting up, he has very little money, and a ready-made family seemed an intolerable burden. However, as one repeatedly tells oneself, it was none of my business, so I asked how he had met her.

It was at a friend's house. Her husband, Martin Salvatore, was a business-man from Milan, who was trying to set up a London branch. They had a small house in Amersham. When he left her, she stayed on, working during the day in a canteen. "She's really terribly nice," said Daniel. "We got on at once. I know you'll like her. She's longing to meet you. I've told her all about you." He laughed, rather self-consciously. "She said the other day that you made her quite jealous."

I made no comment on this, but I was to find out that those few careless remarks summed up the whole unhappy beginning of our relationship, though this, thank God, has now changed. Daniel is less innocent these days, but I think he will never entirely understand women: perhaps few men do. I only said, trying to sound enthusiastic, "When am I allowed to meet her?"

"Oh, as soon as possible. You will be one of the very first. I'll bring her along when I come back from the conference."

"That will be lovely. Why don't you bring her here for Christmas dinner? I could have a nice little tree for the children, and we could make it a real party. I haven't had a proper Christmas for a long time."

He flushed up with pleasure, and at that moment I decided that I must like Vanda or burst. But matters were rather taken out of my hands, for I met her in a sense long before the official meeting. Daniel went off to his medical conference — in York, I think — and I made my arrangements for Christmas, enjoying myself childishly with the tree and the candles and buying gifts for the children, even though I did not know them — a charm bracelet for Sophy, books for Mario and coloured bricks for the little boy. I think, however cynical we may pretend to be, we all enjoy a family Christmas, and I decided that I would even decorate the flat.

The telephone call came in the second week of December. I did not of course know the strongly accented, rather deep voice. When she said, "I am Daniel's Italian girl-friend," I realised who it was, and was both touched and pleased. I exclaimed — perhaps to her it sounded gushing — "You must be Vanda. Oh how nice of you to ring me. I've heard so much about you."

"I have heard about you too." In that deep voice it sounded almost menacing. There was a pause, then she said, "Daniel is very fond of you, isn't he?"

I was a little disconcerted, but I said as lightly as I could, "Oh well, I'm his stepmother. I was his father's second wife. I daresay he told you."

"Yes, he did."

I felt somehow that we were not getting anywhere. The voice was far from friendly. I said, "I do hope we'll meet soon. Daniel is obviously very fond of you, whatever his feelings for me. He carries your photo around everywhere."

"Oh, does he?" For the first time there was genuine warmth, a crack in that abrupt, deep voice. I realised that she really was in love with him, so perhaps it would work out after all. She said, "I love him so very much. I wish to marry him."

I could not think quite what to say to this, for it was a little unusual to hold such a conversation before we had even met. She went on, her voice grown harsh, "I am married. Did he not tell you?"

"Yes, Vanda, he did."

"I have three children."

"I think you must have had a very difficult time."

"I will of course divorce my husband. I was going to go back to him and try to make the best of it, but now I've met Daniel I know I will spend the rest of my life with him. My husband is completely mad."

I don't quite know what I answered to this. It seemed to me that the conversation was running entirely out of control.

"He is a terrible man. He has always been unfaithful. He beats me. He brought his mistress into the house. I have been so unhappy. I will be happy now with Daniel." Another pause. "I am older than he is. Did you know?"

"I think he did just mention it. I don't really think that's at all important if you love each other." This was beginning to sound more like my advice column every moment. Then I said before I could stop myself, "How old are you?"

"Thirty-two." The snap of the teeth was almost audible. I knew she was lying and that therefore she must be a great deal older.

I said, "I don't see why age should matter. My husband was old enough to be my father, and we were terribly happy. Well, Vanda, it's lovely to talk with you. I gather you are all coming to me for Christmas. I am very much looking forward to — "

"What do you mean?" The voice was stiff and cold. Vanda did not seem to possess much of the natural graces.

I said, my voice trailing, "Didn't Daniel tell you? I thought it would be such fun to have you and the children here. He always spends Christmas Day with me, and I was planning to get a tree — "

"There is a misunderstanding."

I was dangerously near losing my temper. "I don't think so. What is there to misunderstand?"

"We have made our own arrangements. Daniel and I talked things over."

This, as I was to learn, was a favourite phrase, it was indeed a method of shutting me out. But I was too astonished and too angry to say anything more, only listened as the deep voice, rough now with temper, continued remorselessly to plough through me.

"He is coming home with me. I have spoken to my parents on the phone. You must have misunderstood. It is all fixed." Then she said, "We will look in on you when we come back."

I managed to remain polite. I could not have this developing into a shouting match, and that was plainly what it would become if it went on much longer. The hostility bristling from the phone was incomprehensible to me, and though when I got to know Vanda better, I understood a little of why she had to be so rude, I still find it strange. However, we ended with an exchange of conventional courtesies — happy Christmas, I look forward to meeting you — then the receiver clicked down, and I was left wondering through my bewilderment and fury why Daniel had picked himself such a graceless termagant.

I was to wonder a great deal more during the first year of their marriage, for marry they did, though I think it was very off and on for a long time, with Daniel arriving on my doorstep to say, "We're all washed up. It couldn't possibly work. Of course," he would add, "we still see each other, we're friends. She's a very nice girl. But I couldn't marry her. She quite understands. She's taken it very well." Then of course the quarrel was made up, it was all on again, and one day Daniel came unexpectedly, looking flushed and sheepish, saying when I offered him a coffee, "No. Wait. I think you'd better sit down. I've got something to tell you. I hope you will be pleased."

I said as calmly as I could, "You're married."

He burst out laughing, rather over-loud. "No! Do you think we wouldn't invite you? But we are getting married and we want you to come to the wedding."

I went of course to the wedding in Amersham. Vanda was dressed in a blue silk, and the children followed after her, clutching little bouquets. They were nice children, only Federico, whom they called Freddy, to show what a good Englishman he had become, went a little crazy with the excitement, and rushed round the church, shouting, "Boum, boum, boum!" all through the ceremony. Vanda's family were there, speaking nothing but Italian, which unfortunately I do not understand: we smiled at each other so determinedly that I felt as if my mouth were permanently stretched. There was father, mother, four sisters and one brother, and they were all dressed in black and sweating profusely. It was when I saw their round, peasant faces that I began to understand Vanda a little better. I don't know how Daniel communicated with them, but he looked very handsome in an elegant grey suit, and he was charming at the small reception that followed, which I had arranged in the local hotel. Vanda's mother and sisters cried all through the ceremony, but they cheered up after a drink, and her father became very gay on whisky and at one point pinched me.

My relationship with Vanda, after such a shattering beginning, could hardly get worse, but we had a very uneasy first six months. The first meeting was icy, and I looked at this big, handsome young woman who never seemed to smile, who asserted herself against me almost physically, who acted in a brash, sexy fashion as if to say, Keep off the grass, he's mine. I think the main trouble was that she could not make out exactly where I stood in relation to Daniel. She was not — she never will be — a girl who likes her own sex. As far as I know, she has no women friends: no one seems to come over from Italy to stay with her. To her I was an unknown quantity, I was not his mother, his lover, his auntie, his landlady or his friend, simply someone who was part of his family and therefore a potential rival. I could see her occasionally looking at me, less with hostility than bewilderment. However, though we will never entirely understand each other, we are now much more friendly, the children like me, which helps, and Daniel chooses to remain unaware of the faintest tension between us, which ironically helps too.

She is a strange girl. I don't know how old she is, but I fancy she is nearing forty. She has, I believe, no sense of humour, which is a pity, because she has a lovely smile that really does do what novels like to claim: it lights up her face. Nowadays she is no longer aggressive, indeed sometimes she is almost propitiatory, but I am still aware that she does not quite trust me. She speaks impeccable English, only occasionally falls into outmoded slang which comes oddly from so matronly-looking a girl. I remember that at one time she picked up the horrible phrase "yum-yum", and to hear her say in her deep voice of something I had given her to eat, "That was really yum-yum," was a shattering experience. I even begged her not to use it, and she gazed at me, startled, from the large cow-eyes. "Why not?" she said. "It is English." I could only say, "Well, actually, I think it's American, but it's the kind of phrase that children use." I never heard her use it again. She does listen to me. Sometimes I almost wish she wouldn't: she bullied me enough at the beginning, but that does not mean I have the right to bully her.

If I say that Daniel's marriage, which is working out extremely well, was a shock, I don't mean that it hurt me, simply that it signified another change at a time when everything I had held on to, was snatched from me. I see Daniel and Vanda regularly: sometimes I go up to Amersham, sometimes they come down to me. The children regard me as granny, and I am very good now at kissing hurts better, blowing noses and wiping milky mouths. I enjoy this very much. The shock of Steve's death was of course something quite different. I feel as if I will never quite recover from it, though in a way his memory is growing dim in my mind, his face is in shadow. Sometimes I wonder what would happen if, after a long parting, we suddenly met again the person we loved and anguished for: it is just possible that concentrated on the image in our memory we might brush against reality and pass it by.

But shocks, whatever their kind, take time to register. I was not aware of being in any way in shock when Timmy Hills walked in on me, I was working well, and I was very angry with my hairdresser.

I appreciate my own complete silliness. But a hairdresser to a woman is very much what a pub or club is to a man. It is not only the set and the bits and pieces that go with it, it is a lovely, sweet-smelling relaxation from the world, where for a brief hour one can absent onself, sit under the dryer, read magazines and forget one's problems. Even in moments of crisis — and for a time all moments were crises — I went regularly every week to a shop where I had been for over ten years. The girls changed. Jane, who originally owned it, got married, had a baby, found it all too much for her and departed. The next girl, Sheila, was equally pleasant and competent, and I still arrived every Friday at eleven o'clock, to be washed and rolled and combed and brushed, to sit under the dryer, reading the problem page in all the glossies that I could lay my hands on. I suppose it is because I run an advice column myself, but I am a compulsive reader of cries from the heart, and note professionally the different kind of advice that my colleagues give. Three-quarters of an hour later I would emerge, looking reasonably tidy and well-groomed, — "See you next week, thank you very much, have a nice weekend," — to return to my normal disorderly appearance next morning.

Then Sheila got married too. Hairdressers are usually pretty girls, though there was the sad pin-and-shampoo girl who came only at weekends, who had permanent adenoids and unhappy legs, who wore that irredeemably plain look that is far worse than ugliness. She was a poor girl, and I knew she would always be leaning against the wall at dances, she was

24

one for whom the phone would seldom ring. She did not even shampoo well, and she always dropped the pins she was supposed to be handing out. I wondered sometimes if she had ever written to me, Dear Elizabeth Ingram, I never seem to meet any boys, and I am so lonely. I don't know what happens to girls like that, they are after all normal human beings, and it seems cruel that they are deprived of satisfied love. Sheila was quite different, and we all saw the pictures of her wedding, we all bought her little gifts, and I used to give her recipes which I don't think she ever tried but which she religiously noted down. "I'm always so nervous," she said, "I want everything to be perfect for him." Then she became pregnant too, and after a while did my hair by a kind of remote control, with the baby kicking between us, until the time came when she too had to leave, and there were more little gifts and promises to bring the baby round, and goodbye, goodbye, see you next week, thank you very much, have a nice weekend.

Rita, who became the next manageress, was only seventeen, and fresh from her hairdresser's training course. She was far too young to cope, she kept us all waiting, I seldom came out under an hour and a half, she set hair rather badly, and her assistant was a pretty little girl who despised us all, and who spent most of her time doing her nails.

I still went back. I was used to it. My hair looked horrible, but then it so often does. Rita took on more and more customers so that all the old ones left, and the young woman whose name was Emma, grew more and more insolent, and tended to call me "madame", which made me feel as if I were running a brothel.

On that last Friday Rita was more autocratic than usual, left me under the dryer for nearly an hour, and paid no attention to my repeated requests to be taken out. In despair I turned to Emma who was sitting at the desk doing nothing but polishing her nails. "Perhaps," I said, "Emma could comb me out, for I have an appointment and I am already late."

From Emma's point of view this was plainly unpardonable. I suppose I smudged the red polish she was applying to her nails. She removed me from the dryer in a flaming temper, jerked my hair through the comb, set it abominably and, when I handed her some money, snapped, "Perhaps madame would get up while I find the change. My next lady is in a hurry, and I have already kept her waiting."

Madame was by no means pleased to have to stand while waiting for her change, but my next lady, a nervous-looking little old thing, was already standing behind me, there was no point in making a scene, so I did as I was told, and Emma kept me — and my lady — waiting five minutes while she rummaged in the till.

I left my usual tip, God knows why. One presumably tips for service and courtesy, but it does become an automatic action. It was only when I arrived home after the usual parting — see you next week, thank you very much, have a nice weekend — and combed out with considerable irritation my abominable hair that looked like an Afro-tangle, that I suddenly thought, What the hell.

What could possibly be more imbecile than travelling well out of my way — for I had now moved to my new flat — for a bad set, bad manners and an insolent young woman who plainly hated my guts? Then I knew that I must never go back, and I even went through the yellow pages and made an appointment for the next week with the first hairdresser on the right telephone exchange. All of this is of course trivial, yet not entirely, for I found myself unreasonably distressed, and the more unreasonable it seemed, the more upset I became.

I have already said that there are times when all normal supports seem suddenly to be removed. It is certainly absurd to call Steve a support, for he never supported me in his life, and I had not seen him for three years and now he was dead, yet in a way he had supported me by reason of his existence. He was someone to love, which we all need, someone to live my life by, someone who, for all he was sometimes cruel, often neglectful and always a bar between me and the day-to-day working life I was struggling to lead, was still a focal point. When he went he left me standing as it were on the edge of a cliff, with nothing to hold on to. And at that moment he was once more with me, like the time when the bell went so insistently, he was in the room beside me, and it made no difference that he had been a heap of ashes a long time ago. There was no Steve now, only his ghost, and there was no Daniel either, though Daniel was substantial — he is growing something of a paunch, on Vanda's good Italian cooking — and very much alive, with a practice that is beginning to flourish, and three lively kids to prevent him from brooding. Daniel is very much there, he rings me regularly, I still see a great deal of him, but he has moved back into his own world, which is no longer mine, and he has plenty to support now without my clinging on to him.

Other things — Friends become estranged or emigrate or move to the country. Shops that you have dealt with for years close down, your favourite bookshop vanishes, your doctor decides to go in for insurance, and the bank manager who was so friendly and who used to give me brandies when I went on holiday, leaves for a better and richer branch.

And now, confound it, I have to change my hairdresser. I think with positive sentimentality of that little shop with the cheap café next door, and the pet-shop at the corner where there is always a poor, clipped, frizzed little poodle sitting on the doorstep, presumably for advertisement. There was the old-fashioned ironmongery where one could buy things like flat-irons that modern shops no longer stock, and where purchases were wrapped up in newspaper, there was a quite awful second-hand clothes place with deplorable garments dangling in the window, and an Indian restaurant that I once went into, and never again, for it was so dirty that it frightened me.

Nothing, of course, to sentimentalise over, but I had loved that little shop with its six dryers, its two wash-basins and photos of highly coiffured ladies on the wall. There were never any magazines less than two months old, the coffee served was undrinkable, and the door sometimes stuck, but it was in its own way home and, as I came in, I used to leave my cares behind, even in the worst days when Steve had just gone and I was still dimly hoping that he might come back.

I found myself overcome with depression. I could not work. I had no wish to eat or drink. Emma, I suppose, would have been delighted, but then I did not know Emma at all, she was simply a pretty girl who was always doing her nails. And on due reflection I think she would not have been delighted at all, for I imagine she never even thought of me. She wore an engagement ring, she was probably just paying her way till she got married, she was bored with dull, plain old women and perhaps fresh from a quarrel with her boy-friend.

Yet I felt haunted, and despised myself for feeling so. I was thinking too much of Steve these days, and I could not imagine why. I am in the main one to cut my losses, I am no great brooder on the past, and not only was this love affair over but the lover was dead. It was absurd to think of him with such emotion. I should be grateful for some wonderful moments, ignore the bad times, and concentrate on the article I was supposed to be writing, which was going well, which was waiting for me at my typewriter.

One thing is certain, I shall never commit suicide. Once, in the wicked days when my world seemed to have ended, a friend, sincerely worried, begged me half in jest not to put my head in the gas oven. I had to point out that this would be impossible, however desperate I was. There is a pilot light in my oven that automatically heats the jets when turned on: if it goes out, the gas simply cuts off. It would be very frustrating to lie there, one would either roast or fall asleep.

I ran a hand through my catastrophic hair, and went over to the bookcase where I kept Steve's books. I picked up the one he had sent me, that very bad, dull book that I had lied about. And, as I held it in my hand, gazing down at the gaudy cover, wondering half angrily why he had written something so cheap, my door-bell went.

I nearly did not answer. I was in no mood for guests. I was not expecting anyone, and the laundry had already called. I could say now that I wish I had not answered it, but that would not be true: it was inevitable, it was something that had to happen, and Timmy Hills will never know how much he was to influence my future.

I first met Timmy — oh, it must be about ten years ago. I rather liked him at the time. He worked in the library where I once had a job. I haven't always run an advice column, and in those days my articles were not sufficient to keep me. For a while we were very friendly. He was always sauntering into my office where he used to sit on my desk with one leg swinging: he would regale me with scabrous stories about the rest of the staff, then we would go out to the local together, drink beer and discuss the world.

His main attraction for me was that the rest of the library was so dull. The Chief Librarian belonged to some esoteric sect — it was not Jehovah's Witnesses or the Brethren, but something similar. I have forgotten its name, but I know that it forbade almost everything. Members of the sect — and most of the staff were recruited from it — neither drank nor smoked, never danced, never went to the theatre, never even watched the television. The women did not make up their faces, and they all wore skirts decently below the knee, while

28

the men wore short back and sides, would rather die than be without a tie, and regarded me in the nicest possible way as the whore of Babylon, simply because I wore slacks and occasionally lipstick. No smoking was allowed, and I smoke like a chimney: as for my drinking habits they were all ex collegia and nobody need have known: everyone did know, and I have no doubt that I was branded as an alcoholic.

I said once to Timmy, "What do they do about the books they have to read?" For this after all was a general library, and some of the volumes that passed through our hands were of a kind that the Sect should have burnt on a bonfire.

"It's their only outlet, darling," said Timmy. "They can enjoy themselves and be shocked at the same time."

Certainly Timmy was as much an outsider as myself. He did not wear his hair long because he was almost bald, but he smoked in his office, kept a bottle in the bottom drawer, and made monstrous verbal passes at every woman in sight, young or old. He was so outrageous that in the end they came to accept him as a kind of resident devil whose smell of brimstone made them cosily aware of the nice, disinfected trumpets that awaited them on the other side.

I liked him because I could talk to him, but even then I found him rather strange. He could be kind and he could be extraordinarily heartless. If some unwedded girl in the library had found herself pregnant — difficult to link the Sect and sex, but stranger things have happened — Timmy would have taken up her cause with violent enthusiasm. It is true that he would have hinted that he was the father, but then he always boasted of his sexual prowess — "Timmy Priapus Hills, that's me," — indeed he talked about it so much that I always believed him to be impotent. Even his passes, which were almost non-stop, were mainly verbal, with secret hints as to the ineffable delights in store for females so honoured. As every female, from eighteen to eighty, was so honoured at least twice a day, this became extremely boring, only the other side of Timmy, the hatred of injustice, was endearing, so one learnt to ignore the dirty cracks, the winks and nods, the furtive pawing, and the fact that in Timmy's eyes to sit beside him at a lecture was sufficient to lose one's virginity. But Timmy, when serious, was so different a man that there seemed to be no resemblance. The pregnant girl, an office boy accused of stealing, someone fired without notice — all these brought

Timmy instantly up in arms, and I must say for him that if as a Don Juan he lacked prowess, as a fighter he was fine and bonny, with no holds barred, and so amusing with it that people did not realise until too late what had hit them.

He was married. I never met his wife. Nobody ever met his wife. At our rare office parties she never made an appearance. I cannot begin to imagine what she was like but, when he spoke of her, it was always with an odd, shy admiration, and I understood that she worked as public relations officer in some big department store. I think he loved her. I hope so. He sometimes gave the impression of loving only Timmy Hills.

I enjoyed working in the library, mainly because of the enormous stacks in the basement, from which I borrowed books by the hundred. I quite liked my companions, but the Sect stood between us so that conversation was restricted: it is depleting to be damned eternally because you spend an evening at the cinema. When I left, after two years, I still met Timmy from time to time, but he was a colossally vain man and one day I pricked his vanity and believed I would never see him again. Indeed, remembering that episode, I still cannot quite understand how he had the nerve to reappear on my doorstep: I can only think that he was determined to pay me out for insulting him — that is how he would have regarded it — and he must have been extraordinarily vindictive for he waited for three whole years until his chance came.

On that particular day I certainly thought I had seen the last of Timmy Hills.

He arrived in a strange, excited mood, the kind of mood that in a child promises tears within a brief while. He was almost babbling. Being by now nearly bald, he had combed what remained of his hair over the high-domed pate, and in moments of stress this straggly lock tended to stick upright like a frond so that he resembled a depraved and elderly baby: this effect was added to by his general appearance, for he was a big, rotund man with fleshy features, and a skin of extraordinary delicacy.

He almost danced into my room. I was not very pleased because I was busy: if you work at home, people seem to assume that you do not really work at all and can be disturbed at their convenience. He looked round instantly for the whisky, though it was only four in the afternoon, and said to me in his actorish voice, "Alone, my sweet? Why, I expected to find some dazzling man with you."

30

I saw no reason why he should expect anything of the kind and, when he went on to say how glam I looked, responded silently by pouring him out a Scotch. Indeed, I looked as glamorous — how I hate that word "glam" — as any middle-aged female looks when she is working, with no make-up on and not expecting or wanting visitors: as for dazzling men they may exist, but they seldom come my way these days except in the library novels I sometimes read. Timmy knew vaguely about Steve, indeed he once met him and behaved so impeccably throughout the meeting that I knew he was totting him up in his mind for future reference. All he knew now was that the affair had come to an end. I am as great a talker as Timmy when the mood takes me, but I am warier than I used to be, and something warned me not to be too confiding. The Timmys of this world do not care for competition and, though he would have oozed sympathy at the time, he might well have regarded my feelings for another man as a personal insult.

He sprawled in my best armchair, surveying the flat around him. This was my old flat, which he had visited several times: I was to move six months later. He must have been aware that he was not welcome, for I was fussing around at my typewriter, but he was a great believer in his own charm — admittedly considerable — and was plainly sure that in a little while he would have me eating out of his hand. He inquired about my lovelife, grinned when I replied shortly that it was non-existent, told me a few scurrilous stories about the library where he still worked, then suddenly to my dismay bounded across the room, flung himself on his knees beside me, and clasped me about with vast, pudgy hands.

He always flirted outrageously, but mainly in words, and this was something new. When it became obvious that this time he meant business, I grew furious. I released myself with some violence, and this and the look on my face provided a rebuff that even Timmy could not ignore, and in such matters he was hypersensitive, like all vain people. I suppose he had believed that if he did me the honour of making love to me, the only thing I could decently do was fall flat on my back with extended arms. As I shoved him off without dignity, and snapped, "Oh really, Timmy, what's the matter with you?" he moved away in an undignified backwards crawl, turning on me a look of such vicious fury that I grew frightened. I did not

31

think he was capable of rape, but at that moment he looked as if he were capable of murder.

He stumbled to his feet. He was a big man and not young. He smiled at me, and the smile was pure murder. "Very virginal today, aren't you, Elizabeth?" he said. He picked up his whisky and swallowed it in a gulp. "I gather your Yank's come back to you. At least it gives you something better to do than writing your slushy little articles. Still advising the lovelorn, I suppose. And how is he, the dear chap? Whoring around as usual?"

"He's married, Timmy," I said as calmly as I could. I found myself shaking and was afraid he saw it. I swung back — I was sitting on my typewriting chair — to my machine and tried not to look at him.

"So he is, darling. Surely that won't stop him."

I did not answer, and he went on, "Do tell me about your lovelorn, the poor souls. Pouring it all out on you like that — But I suppose it acts as a kind of masturbatory compensation."

This was just too much, even from Timmy, and I lost my temper. I managed not to shout, but then I am not really a shouter. I even managed not to burst into tears. I said I was busy, I had a deadline for my column, and I would be grateful if he went away.

He got up and moved towards the door. He remarked, "I always thought you were a bit les."

The only sensible thing was not to answer at all, for he was simply baiting me, but I was too upset to control myself, and I exclaimed, "Do I have to be a lesbian because I won't let you make love to me?"

"Oh no," he said. "Oh no, darling. That is just being a spinster. Of course you're a bit past it, aren't you? But I've noticed before, the way you look at other women. Why not? It must be quite amusing. What do you do? I've always wanted to know."

"Goodbye, Timmy," I said.

"Oh do tell me, darling. It's Timmy, pet, your very own Timmy. Do you — ?" And here he expounded on the theme with such indecency that I found myself flushing, and this delighted him so that he continued at greater length. He had a talent for obscenity. He would have done well in the seventeenth century.

I still managed not to answer, and then at last he too lost his temper, went a bright red and stormed out, crashing the door behind him.

I never for one moment expected to see him again, and when, this afternoon, three years later almost to the very day, he stood in the doorway, smiling, pale eyes bright and hard, waiting to be let in, I had the odd feeling that I was in some Priestley play, that I had been here before, gone back in time.

I had to tell him to come in. What else could I do? He gave me a little peck on the cheek, noticed, I am sure, that I looked a wreck, and let his gaze wander over my new flat with the inquisitive interest that was an essential part of him.

"Come up in the world, haven't you?" he said, and landed himself in the nearest chair, leaning back so that his paunch protruded, with his hands clasped round it.

"I'm glad you like it," I said, determined to do my best and not trusting him at all: how could he, after such a parting, dare to come to see me? Then I demanded involuntarily, "How did you find out where I was?"

This made him very happy. He beamed at me. I saw now that he had not worn well. I imagine he was thinking the same thing of me. The boyish, actorish manner was still there, but that delicate skin lined easily, the swathe of hair straggled thinly over his skull, and he had put on a great deal of weight. The smile was always on his lips, but the pale eyes were like ice, and I knew at once that he had never forgiven me for that afternoon, and wondered what broadside he had in mind for me. When it eventually came it was — and still is — incomprehensible to me, but at that moment he was simply concentrating on drinking my whisky, and telling me delightedly how he had discovered the new address. It was not really very difficult, and I think he just asked the new tenant who sometimes forwarded my letters, but from the way he talked it was some subtle piece of detection, the kind of thing that could only be performed by a genius like Timmy Hills.

"Well, I'm glad you're doing well, darling," he said. "How's the health? You're looking a trifle peaky if you don't mind me saying so."

Naturally I at once felt at death's door, especially as he somehow managed to convey that this was a gross understatement. And I was not feeling well, that was true, but I was damned if I was admitting it to Timmy. I replied bracingly that I felt fine, and hoped he felt the same: I tried for the sake

33

of good manners not to watch him as he poured himself out a second and enormous Scotch. But I had to feel that this was the most confounded cheek, and he must have noticed my expression for he suddenly looked concerned in a theatrical way and said in a tense voice, "You've not given up drinking, darling, have you?"

"No. By no means."

"Then why don't you join me? Let me get you a glass."

"Timmy," I said, "it's half-past three, and I'm very busy. If I start drinking in the middle of the afternoon, I shall get no work done for the rest of the day." And short of telling him to get out, I could hardly have given him a broader hint, but Timmy, when it suited him, could be as thick-skinned as an elephant, and he simply grinned and took another swig at his glass.

For a few seconds he did not speak. When he did, his voice had sunk a semitone, so that he sounded like an undertaker.

"It has been," he announced, "an extraordinary year."

I thought at first he must be talking politics. I was growing very bored with Timmy, not because I was uninterested in politics, but because he was sitting there uninvited, drinking all my Scotch, and showing no signs of going. Besides, I had in no way forgiven him for last time. I know now that Timmy had not forgiven me either, that he believed the grievance was entirely on his side, but I could only be amazed at the cheek of him, and wish passionately that he would drink up and go.

However, it seemed that he was talking about the library. He said, "You remember the Chief Librarian?"

"Well, of course — "

"He's dead, poor fellow."

I think I said, "Oh." After all I didn't know him personally, I had left a long time ago, and it is difficult to go into mourning for a complete stranger.

"Yes. It was so sudden. He went into hospital for a suspected appendix. It was cancer. He was dead within the week."

I said a little crossly, "Who is the Librarian now?"

Timmy gazed at me in reproach, as if to intimate that surely I could display a little more feeling. However, he gave me a name that meant nothing to me, and went on, "It really is as if the angel of death decided to roost over us." He paused, as if to give me a chance to assimilate this peculiar remark, then continued with a little wry smile, "The Sect must believe that

34

the second coming is at hand. Indeed, the only irreverent spirits left are myself and, if you will forgive me, Elizabeth, you."

I said in genuine bewilderment, "You really are talking the most awful nonsense, Timmy. What is all this? Who's dead now, and what's all this stuff about roosting angels and irreverent spirits? I don't understand a word of it."

He chose to ignore this. His eyes were glowing with malice. He said, "First the Librarian. Then — "

And out came the list, mostly of people I had forgotten or at the best hardly knew. It seemed they all had one thing in common: they were dead. Some of them were young. One I did remember, a nice boy who may or may not have belonged to the Sect, but who was always friendly and who, when I last saw him, was engaged to be married. I have forgotten what carried him off — something horrid, I know, like a brain tumour. And there was the woman in charge of the French section who had a heart attack, the accountant had been run over, and a little girl who made the tea and trotted around with files, had been drowned in a swimming bath.

There must have been half a dozen of them and, though it was true that I knew none of them personally, the cumulative effect was both grim and unpleasant, especially as Timmy's voice grew more and more unctuous, while the light, spiteful eyes raked me up and down.

He said, "Very sad, Steve's death."

And this time I did not even pretend to reply, only rose to my feet. I felt very shaky, and he must have seen this, for he said in a kind, inquiring voice, "You really don't look well at all, Elizabeth." Then, "They say he died in a ditch, poor fellow. He wasn't found till the morning — But of course you must have read about it in the papers."

"Timmy," I said, and thank God my voice was firm enough, "I don't know what all this necrophilic stuff is, or why you've come, but how Steve died is none of your bloody business. I can see you are enjoying yourself, and to me you're just like a ghoul or a vulture. Will you please go at once? Why you are regaling me with all this is something in your own mean little mind, and now you've done what you came to do, there is nothing left to say. Goodbye, Timmy, and please don't come back. I'd hate to have to shut the door in your face."

"I thought you'd be interested."

35

"Why should I?"

"Well, you worked in the library, darling. They are all people you have met. As a writer you should be interested in coincidences. It is after all unusual — "

"Goodbye."

"I must say this is pretty rude. I appreciate that you are a bit unbalanced by Steve's death, but — "

I felt the hysteria rising up in me. I said, fighting to control my voice, "If you don't go this instant, I'll ring for the porter and get him to throw you out."

At this he did get up. He was white and smiling and furious, yet plainly pleased with himself. "I do believe," he said, "you really are a little deranged. Have you seen a doctor?" But even Timmy did not want to be saddled with a woman in a fit of hysterics, for he did at last make his waddling way towards the door. He shook his head at me. He said, "The Sect possesses strange powers, you know. I think you should be more careful, darling. You've obviously let things prey on your mind. Perhaps you'd better try another kind of praying."

And with this he was gone. Like many fat men he was light on his feet. I heard him pattering across the hall, towards the lift. I think he was laughing.

Chapter 2

IT WAS FIVE MINUTES LATER THAT I MADE THE ALARMING discovery. Apparently I could no longer walk.

I heard the sound of the lift gates. I would probably never see Timmy again. He had come on his little mission, he had performed it, he had paid me back for rebuffing him, and now he would go away and forget all about it. He was after all an intelligent man, he could hardly derive real and permanent pleasure from frightening me. But frighten me he had. I am a coward, and this extraordinary tale of death, together with the strange remarks about the Sect made me shiver. I should of course have laughed. We should always be able to laugh. And there was not one laugh left in me: I can only say in extenuation that I was not feeling well, and it had been a beastly kind of day.

I do not honestly think that the Sect ever claimed any kind of magic powers. They were all, as I now look back on them, harmless, rather stupid people. They did not wish anyone harm, they simply knew that they were the chosen people and we, the outsiders, irredeemably damned. Christianity takes the oddest forms. They could view with dispassionate smiles the fact that I and Timmy and a million others were condemned to roast for ever in eternal flames, with themselves on the other side of the glass, drinking their heavenly Coca-Cola, wearing their decent, heavenly garments and doing — oh God, what would they be doing? — the heaven of such people always seems to be such (if I may be pardoned the word) an infernal bore. They had always accepted me. I went to the theatre, I watched television, I smoked, I drank, I spoke wicked words. As I was condemned from birth, there was no point in being angry with me. When I mentioned something I had seen on the box, they nodded, eyes calm and gentle, they said it must have been very interesting. And I knew, as they spoke, that they were seeing a devil jabbing me with his molten pitchfork. I told them occasionally, when I forgot, that I had been to the theatre. I lit a cigarette before them, dropped my lighter and said, Damn. It made no difference. To them I had only a short period of peace and happiness: after that I would suffer unspeakable torments for ever, there was nothing they could do about it, they were probably sorry for me. And to me, to be fair, they were equally strangers, with their dull hair-dos, their shining faces, their clothes that always buttoned up to the throat and came down to their wrists. I am sure they enjoyed their lives, fell in and out of love, laughed and cried like everyone else, and they must have performed the sexual act in the normal inelegant manner, when decently married. Perhaps occasionally in the privacy of their rooms they said, Damn. We got on very well, and from time to time they read my articles. It was absurd to assume that they would curse me, for cursing was surely forbidden — besides, it was unnecessary, I was cursed already.

I wish I could remember the name of the Sect. It was more extreme than most, though in our country with its history of Puritanism, such people have always prospered. I once stayed with a landlady who was a Plymouth sister: she held prayer meetings every evening. The thin, keening wails used to come through the wall. The only books she had around were copies of a Victorian periodical called *Sunday at Home*; I used to read these sometimes and remember vividly to this day a story called "Death in the Ballroom," where a girl danced a wicked waltz and found that her partner was Death. What really gave me the grues was my landlady's husband who was incapacitated by a stroke, and whom she washed and tended as if he were a doll. I saw him once. She opened the bedroom door for me to catch a glimpse of him. He lay there motionless, his face scrubbed and waxen, the sheets on which his white hands lay spotless, his eyes staring blindly up at the ceiling. She was quite proud of him, but sometimes she grew angry when he messed himself, and then I heard her scolding him in an ugly, growling voice. I suppose he did not understand. I hope not.

The Sect would surely not be so unkind. But I wished Timmy had not said what he did, I prayed that someone sane

38

and sensible like Daniel would suddenly ring me, or a friend arrive on my doorstep.

I decided to pour myself out a drink. I rose to my feet to get the whisky, and I fell down. I could not get up again. It was almost as if my legs had disappeared. At first I could not believe it. It took a couple of minutes before the full shock dawned on me. Then I was appalled and terrified and at the same time furious: this was obscene and humiliating. However, one thing was plain: I could not stay there sitting on the floor. By clinging on to the furniture I managed to heave myself up, and tottered towards the whisky bottle: never mind the hour or anything else, if this were not the moment for the stiffest drink imaginable I might as well turn teetotaller.

I remembered dimly that something like this had once happened to Steve. It didn't seem to have much point, and the memory was submerged in my own distress.

I drank about half a glass of neat Scotch then, still holding on to everything, dragged myself to the phone: the sweat was pouring down me and I believed I was going to die.

The ambulance took me to hospital. I think at first they thought I was drunk, which was understandable as the bottle and glass stood beside me, and they could smell the whisky I had slopped over me. However, the doctors, when they had examined me, stared down at me in bewilderment, assured me that there was nothing fundamentally wrong, that I would be up and about again in a couple of weeks at the most, then they all asked me the same question: Had I experienced a severe emotional shock lately?

I said weakly that no, I didn't think so. What else was there to say? When you work it out, life bristles with emotional shocks and I seem to experience them with the utmost regularity. I am not talking about Steve or Daniel or hairdressers, but simply the normal run of living. I answered their questions politely and calmly. Lying there in my hospital bed, I now hardly cared, I felt agreeably remote from everything. Yes, I was a widow, but my husband had died a long time ago. No, I was not embroiled in any personal relationship. (This was asked most discreetly, but the implication was plain.) And no, I had not yet started my menopause, no, I was not in financial difficulties, no, I had not had a bad fall or knocked myself or suffered any form of accident.

And so it went on, the doctors appeared to find me very

interesting, and little gaggles of medical students appeared at my bedside to gaze at me. Daniel came to see me, my friends brought me fruit and flowers, I read a great deal, I listened to music on my transistor, and I heard the life stories of my fellow patients. I did not worry any more about the Sect. I have no doubt that they would call this a judgment, but it was too inevitable for them to bear malice: if we had still been in contact I am sure they would have sent me flowers. It would be rather like sending flowers to a funeral, a dreadful waste but the thing to do.

Someone told me once that all the flowers left over after a burial are sent to the local hospital. I find this a little macabre, I hope they do not send the wreaths. I cannot feel that a wreath of immortelles over one's bedside artistically working out "R.I.P." would be an inducement to recovery.

I owe the fact that I at last tottered out on my own two feet, to one of the other patients in the ward. I grew very fond of most of my companions, but this ironically was the one I liked least. They were all very brave people. It was a ward for rheumatic and arthritic diseases, including some obscure, undiagnosed muscular complaints, of which I suppose I was one. Many of them were in constant pain, and some incurable. The one I am referring to was a female missionary operated on for a displaced disc. She was pleasant enough, with some knowledge of music, but she reminded me too much of the Sect for my liking, though she belonged to something else, some obscure and bigoted sideline of the Church of Scotland. She worked in Afghanistan, and I always pictured her standing in the middle of the Khyber Pass, which is the only part of Afghanistan that registers at all in my mind. She spoke sorrowfully and at great length of the terrible youth of today, of the lack of faith and of the permissive society. She inveighed bitterly against priests and clergymen who advocated greater leniency and understanding. The Sect was prepared to let us live in peace until we were flung into the flames: she wanted us flogged and manacled and hanged as well. She was a small woman with a soft voice: I have noticed before the marked violence that this can conceal. The tribesmen must have found her quite congenial. The only oddity in her was a startling love of lavatory humour, and I could never quite get over this. The very word "sex" was enough to bring the protesting colour into her cheeks, but she was always telling

40

me stories about wee-wees and widdling and pulling plugs. Sometimes she was giggling so much that she could hardly get the words out. I detest lavatory jokes, so it all became rather difficult, and one day I overheard her saying to a nurse that I was a nice wee thing, but what a pity I had so little sense of humour.

Apart from her there were innumerable people to distract my mind, and some of them, like old Mrs. Cohen, provided a theatre of their own. Mrs. Cohen, who must have been in her seventies, had had a foot amputated, and she used to skittle about the ward in a chair, propelling herself with her other leg. She was a naughty, rugged old girl. Her husband came dutifully to see her every day, and each time she quarrelled fiercely with him so that the poor old chap slunk out, looking ill and miserable. Then she would be overcome with conscience and propel her way to me, to get his number on the mobile ward phone. This I did, she would ring and apologise, and the next day it would all happen again.

Hospital life is never boring, and when we grew tired of life, there was always death. We all knew, of course, and in that strange, remote atmosphere we were all feverishly interested. The rail curtains would be drawn, and we would hear the sound of the body being wheeled out to the mortuary. Nobody ever mentioned it. In a few minutes the curtains would be drawn back again, and the nurses bustling about as if nothing had happened, as if we had never heard the commotion, the house physician running across the ward, the nurses dashing to and fro, the sounds of the dying.

I don't know what I imagined would happen to me. I fell into a calm, an apathy, an inertia. They made me try to walk every day, and I would totter a few steps. The therapist gave me exercises, and exhorted me in a hearty way to make an effort. Sometimes I wanted to kick her teeth in: unfortunately I did not do this, for it would have been most therapeutic. I thought and did very little. I did not think of the future. My office had given me sick leave, though sometimes they sent me the odd letter to deal with, thinking perhaps it would be good for me. It was obvious that I could not stay here indefinitely, but that was a problem I would face when it came. My friends were all very concerned, and Daniel sometimes became quite angry with me, but I paid him no attention. I paid attention to nobody and nothing.

41

And I suppose that might be the end of my story, had it not been for the lady missionary from Afghanistan. She did not help me intentionally. She assumed, as I could see, that I would never get better, assured me frequently that God knew best, and offered to pray with me. She was not offended when I refused, only gave me an understanding and forgiving smile, then cheered me up with another lavatory story.

"You should laugh more," she said. "God likes us to laugh."

I wondered if for her birthday — she was married to another missionary — her husband gave her an illuminated toilet roll.

She was almost well by now, and therefore more tiresome. I think on reflection that the tribesmen cannot have liked her very much, though it pleases me to think of her sitting surrounded by a circle of them, telling them wee-wee stories. The operation had been a painful one, and for a time she was quite human. But now she was up and about again, even helping the nurses, and she told me that in a few days she would be away, staying with her sister before returning to the Khyber Pass. She came to perch herself on the edge of my bed. She was a great one for perching on the edge of beds, and she was always accompanied by some little tract or leaflet which she pressed into my hand. "You don't have to read it, dear. I shall quite understand. But I think if you took a wee glance at it you might find it helpful."

She sat by me now. She was wearing a bright blue dressing-gown, well wrapped about her. She was really quite a nice-looking woman, and she seemed very perky as I told her.

"Oh yes," she said, "I'll be away in a couple of days, and I can't pretend I'm sorry to go, though it has been an interesting experience. One should always profit by experience, for it is sent by God. You should really regard yourself as fortunate, dear."

"Fortunate?" I was mildly surprised. The walking that morning had not been good at all, yet somehow I did not seem to care. However, I had been lying here for two months, and it seemed dimly to me in my inert state that "fortunate" was an odd word to use.

"Oh yes, dear." She was quite excited and leaned over me as she spoke. She had bad teeth. Perhaps the diet in Afghanistan was a poor one, and to do her credit, I could not see her wolfing down chicken and cream while the people starved.

"God has bestowed on you the wonderful gift of suffering. How lucky you are. I quite envy you. I can see you have the courage to endure it, and I am sure that in a little while God will speak to you in prayer. I pray for you every night, you know."

I said faintly, "Thank you." I was not liking this. I was aware for the first time of a stir of rebellion.

She said, looking away from me now, "These places are very good, you know. They look after you so well. Such dedicated girls — "

"What places? I don't know what you're talking about."

"You can't imagine you'll be staying here much longer?" She gazed at me in astonishment. "They need your bed, you know. After a time you have to go to one of those Homes. Incurables, they call them."

"What!" I was so outraged that I sat up smartly in bed, knocking over a glass that smashed to pieces on the floor.

She went very pink. She was an utterly tactless woman, but I think she was fundamentally kind. "Oh," she said, pressing a hand to her mouth, "Oh. Didn't you know? But of course I may be wrong. Only I assumed — "

I do not quite know what I felt. I was hardly seeing her at all. I was mainly aware of all the life that I had been denying swelling up in me so that I felt as if I would burst. I didn't even answer her. I was horrified, outraged, appalled. I leaned over the side of the bed, and called out in a resounding voice that must have sounded like a sergeant-major's, "Nurse!"

A nurse came running. I think she thought I had developed some new and deadly symptom. "Nurse," I said, "I want to go to the lavatory, and I don't want a bedpan. Will you please give me a hand?"

She was a nice girl, and she didn't argue as she might well have done. She must have been desperately busy, all nurses are, but she helped me out of the bed, and accompanied me on what seemed to be an endless walk, right across the ward to the bathrooms. She looked at me as I arrived, weak, breathless, giddy. She smiled in genuine delight, and at that moment I loved her more than I have ever loved anyone in my life.

"Good girl," she said, in the bracing way that nurses tend to adopt. "We'll have you out of here in no time."

Well, it took nearly another month, and another two after I came home. I said a weak and dizzy goodbye to all my friends.

Daniel had called for me in the car, and Vanda and the children were waiting at home with a meal already prepared. I still felt as if the ground beneath me were an earthquake, and I held on to everything available. My missionary lady had left some time before. She did not refer to the home for incurables again. I suspect that someone overheard and reported her, and that Sister gave her a telling-off. She was subdued and not particularly friendly. It must be very frustrating to mean to do good, when it is not good at all. She said rather coldly that she hoped I would feel better soon, and pressed one final leaflet into my hand. "I will always pray for you," she said, intimating that this in the circumstances was a vast favour. She added, "Of course, if you are ever in Afghanistan — "

I couldn't think of anywhere I was less likely to be, but I said that if I were, I would of course call on her. It sounded very strange — Hallo, here I am in the Khyber Pass, I'd love a cup of tea.

"You'll find our life very simple," she said, and her eyes moved sideways to the bottle of Scotch on my bedside table. She had never actually referred to it, but I knew she disapproved. "However," she added more cheerfully, "it will give you wonderful material for one of your little articles. Have you ever tried the *Mission News?* Such a good little paper. I know the editor, of course. I'm sure I could persuade him to give you a column or two."

I'm not meaning to sound conceited, and I am no high-power journalist, but apart from my regular page, I have published in all the national dailies and most of the magazines. I looked duly grateful and thanked her. Then she told me one more lavatory story, we said goodbye, and I watched her go, a trim little woman of about forty-five, who no doubt did an excellent job of work and who had dedicated her whole life to the tribesmen of the Khyber Pass.

When at last it was my turn, I said goodbye to Mrs. Cohen, who was due to leave next week so she would be able to quarrel with her husband full-time. I stopped at half-a-dozen of the beds, left a bottle of sherry with Sister, and at long last, crying as I always do in any emergency, stepped out into the outside world.

For the first time in three months. Three months —

"Well," said Daniel explosively, as he slotted me into the car and drove off, "this has been a fine carry-on, I must say.

44

What's it all about? It isn't like you at all."

"Psychosomatic," I said through my tears, for I was still crying. Then I said accusingly, "You've grown a beard."

He looked self-conscious. At least, I think he did, it was difficult to see through all the fungus. The beard was still in the embryo stage and, as he was a redhead, it was ginger-pale. I rather like the full messianic outfit, but Daniel was sprouting odd tufts here and there, and I did not find it dignified, especially as he has a firm and excellent chin that needs no camouflage.

"Vanda thinks it looks manly," he said. Then he braked outside my block of flats and, turning, put his hand on mine.

"What's the matter, Elizabeth?" he said. "You scared the pants off me. Something upset you badly, didn't it?" He paused, then he said in a muffled voice, "Was it me?"

"Oh no, of course not." And that was entirely true, though I suppose he contributed. I went on, "I don't quite know. It's as if everything piled up on me, and I just had to run away. There were all sorts of little things that in themselves don't matter, but I felt as if I'd come to a stage in my life where everything, everything, everything rose up to hit me, including a lot of things that happened ages ago. I'm sorry, Daniel. I'm being an awful bore. I shan't talk about it again. What I've got to do now is to get completely well again. I'm damned if I'm going to crawl around like a castrated millipede."

He blinked, both at my language, which he does not like, and this ridiculous simile which really meant nothing at all, but which somehow came to my unladylike lips. Then he burst out laughing, and we both felt much better. "I see you're pretty well cured," he said. Then he said more seriously, "I think you should take a holiday."

"Yes, I do too. And I know where I want to go."

"I bet it's France again," he said, smiling. Vanda and the children would be waiting in the flat, but perhaps he knew that when Vanda was there we could never really talk. He is not imperceptive, and he does put up with a cantankerous bitch like me. He knows well enough that I love France and, when I am feeling low and in need of comfort, nearly always go to Provence. We all have our special places, and Provence is mine. But not this time —

"No," I said. "I'm going to the Grand Canyon."

I suppose I might as well have said Afghanistan. I could see his point. I was barely able to crawl around, and here I was talking about a holiday in another continent.

He said at last, "You're crazy. You're completely nuts."

"Why? It's a well-known tourist attraction. I've always wanted to see it."

He said before he could stop himself, "It's that American friend of yours." Then he went bright red. Poor Daniel. We never mentioned Steve's name these days, and even now, as I had to notice, he designated him by his nationality. He muttered, "I'm sorry. I shouldn't have said that."

"But you're quite right. It is. In more ways than one. But anyway, apart from that, I've always wanted to do a series of articles on ghost-towns. And it was Steve's idea. I decided a long time ago to start with Arizona. The particular place I have in mind is Jericho City. It's about a hundred miles from the Canyon."

"This is your wild west complex," said Daniel, recovering himself.

"I suppose so. Partly, anyway. But also it's the most magnificent scenery in the world." Then I said, as he opened the door, preparing to help me out, "I've run into too many ghosts lately, Daniel. I don't know how it's happened, but I've got to lay them. And I have the feeling that if I walk into a town of ghosts I'll know how to set about it. Let's go in. I haven't seen my own home for three months. Oh Daniel love, let's go in."

And in we went, me crying away like a bloody fountain, Daniel more or less carrying me, and the porter greeting me like royalty, beaming all over his face. I had to think as I came up in the lift — it was only one floor but that shamefully was more than I could cope with — that perhaps I owed the Khyber Pass something. I think the mission must have been unprepossessing, and my missionary lady was not at all my cup of tea, what with her lavatory jokes and all, but in her own way she had brought me home, and my happiness for that moment was enough to break me asunder.

Vanda and the three children were waiting for me. The kids must have been well primed, for they were on their marks as Daniel opened the door with that peculiar key of mine that always takes me ages to work. As I hobbled in, supported as if I were a centenarian, they leapt towards me with a concerted, "Welcome home, Elizabeth, nice to see you back," pushed

46

into my arms an enormous bunch of flowers and held up their faces to be kissed.

I could hardly burst into tears as I was crying already, but this was really too much, and I had to be assisted to the nearest chair where a large glass was pushed into my hand, and everyone gathered around me, propping me up with cushions and almost crushing me, so that in the end I burst out laughing and, what with laughter and tears, was as near hysterics as I have ever been in my life.

Vanda greeted me cordially enough. She seemed to me to have changed a great deal, and the change was more marked each time I saw her. She no longer wore her silky hair long and straight, but piled it up on the top of her head. It suited her, gave her dignity, and she was a dignified girl with a big, beautiful body. I do not think either of us felt much warmth for the other, but by now it was not so much a matter of jealousy and emotion as simply a case of non-mixing chemicals. She had after all no reason to be jealous, and neither had I. She had Daniel, a good husband who might one day be very successful, a good home, not much money it was true, but she was by nature economical, and a fixed social position that would mean a lot to her. She looked older now but better-looking: she always dressed well, and she was the kind of person who would organise little dinners for Daniel and make the right impression.

The children I had always liked as I like most children, but I could see that they were difficult. Vanda has never struck me as a maternal person: she varies between letting them run completely wild, then suddenly screaming them down, often with a slap across the head. It was odd that someone so well organised could not organise her own family, but I imagine this was her peasant background, she liked having children, no doubt had them easily but had neither time nor patience to cosset them and train them. Mario was plainly a handful, Sophy seemed to me over-anxious, as for little Freddy, her favourite, he was adorable but riotously spoilt.

Daniel wore his fatherhood well. The children all loved him and would not leave him alone, fighting for his attention like a litter of puppies. Only occasionally did an exhausted look come across his face, for he was after all still pretty young, he was just starting in his profession, he had saddled himself with a full-grown family that was not his own. I believe Vanda has a little money of her own, but things must be tight all the same, and Daniel will never accept a penny from me.

Vanda had prepared an excellent meal, and it was pleasant and family-like as we all sat round the table, only I was very tired and when the nurse that Daniel had insisted on ordering, arrived, I was not sorry to say goodbye.

Daniel said, as Vanda took the children downstairs to wait in the car, "Will you be all right? I didn't get you a night-nurse, I thought you'd rather not. But this girl will be in every day until you feel stronger."

"I'm fine. Thank you for making my homecoming so lovely." Then, as he was going, I asked him the same question, I don't know why, I knew he would not like it, but somehow the words forced themselves out.

"Are you all right, Daniel?"

He looked down at me. I saw then, from my own exhaustion, that he was very tired indeed. He did not look happy, and the silly, straggling beard somehow made him look more boyish. He did not answer me. There was something wrong, obviously, but he was not going to tell me. He only said, "I wish I knew what was the matter with you. And why on earth do you want to write on ghost towns? They're dead and gone. I saw a picture of one once. It was nothing but a row of broken-down buildings, a hotel without a roof, a prison without walls, and a battered saloon bar with the doors blowing in the wind. It was all dry and dusty. There was nothing there, just a bit of wild stuff around, tumbleweed, that kind of thing. There were people there once, I know, your western heroes — and a fine lot they were, if I may say so, shoot you in the back as soon as look at you, drunken, beastly lot. What is there to write about? I don't think you're going there for an article at all. You've got some private reason of your own. If you hadn't been so damned ill," said Daniel in a gust of temper, "I'd shake you to find out what it is."

"You can't touch me," I said. "I'm too frail. I'm delicate."

He gave this a rather grim half-smile, then I said, "I don't know how you do it, Daniel, but if you'd set out to make me see a ghost town, you couldn't have done better. After your description, nothing could keep me away, not even my beastly legs. I'd go there tomorrow if I could, but even as it is, I bet I'm there within a couple of months."

He said once again, "You're plain nuts." Then, "But why?"

Daniel has never had much imagination, at least not of the kind that would drive him to a ghost town. He has instead a sensitivity without which a doctor would be useless. I think he will understand the strange defence mechanisms, self-deceptions and secret fears that obsess sick human beings, indeed obsess those who are not ostensibly sick at all. But he has an essential, realistic mind: if he ever climbs a mountain it will simply be to get to the top, it will not be any atavistic desire to do the bitch, to conquer an unexplored world. Daniel will make an excellent doctor, and I am sure he will never lose his compassion, but crazy women who suddenly for no valid reason decide to do something foolish are beyond his compre-hension.

However, he always has to know and, as I did not immediately answer his question, repeated it. "Why?"

"I truly don't know." I looked up at him from the bed where I was now lying. I could hear the nurse bustling about in the kitchen. She seemed to be a pleasant and efficient girl. I would far rather have been on my own, but it was true, I was too tired to cope, it was nice to have someone there to cook my meals and make the appropriate cup of tea. "It's true, Daniel. Oh, of course there's some reason. I know that. It is still something at the back of my mind and when you asked me if it were to do with Steve — "

I saw him instantly flinch. It is quite extraordinary how he cannot face up to the fact that his stepmother once had a lover. It is not as if I were his real mother. But I couldn't be bothered with this at the moment, so I ignored it and went on, " — I think you were right. This thing, and my legs too. I'll tell you about that some day. But it is a kind of compulsion. I can't fully explain it myself. Perhaps when I'm completely recovered I shall understand it better."

He exclaimed, almost in triumph, "It's that phoney astro-loger of yours. I bet she put it in your horoscope. Sometimes, Elizabeth, I think you're an awfully silly girl."

"Oh go away," I said. "Vanda will be wondering what has happened to you. And it is absolutely nothing to do with my horoscope, and I don't think she was phoney. At least she may have been, but she really believed in what she was doing."

"I think all astrologers should be banned," said Daniel, "and that goes for faith-healers, palmists and charlatans in general."

49

This gauntlet I did not take up. Daniel is Daniel, he is essentially practical, and he has always derided me for my occasional dabblings in the occult, though oddly enough in this matter Vanda is on my side, having an absolute passion for such things, from horoscopes to tea-cups. So I simply laughed and then, moving in his usual, violent, jerky manner, Daniel poured me out another drink, kissed me on both cheeks as Vanda has taught him to do, said, "I'll ring tomorrow," and was gone.

"Nurse will think she's got an alcoholic on her hands," I called after him, but I don't think he heard this, only the nurse did and grinned at me, poking her head round the door.

It was an odd episode, but of course she was not phoney at all, though possibly a little mad. No astrologer could be responsible for what Daniel believes to be my lunacy. However, I was interested enough to ask the nurse to hand me my folder, and I took out the horoscope and reread it. I saw with a faint shock that she prophesied my illness and spoke of travel. However, this did not mean much, we all fall ill, we all make journeys: I lay back, feeling like a cross between Beth March and Elizabeth Barrett, and thought about that strange day while the nurse washed up the lunch things and tidied the flat around me.

"Children!" she said, shaking her head, as she swept up the biscuit crumbs Sophy had scattered everywhere, retrieved Freddy's toys and stacked neatly the books that Mario had been reading.

"Have a drink," I said, then closed my eyes so that she would think I was asleep and not talk to me.

I went to see the astrologer out of pure curiosity. She had already done my horoscope for me at the instigation of a friend. I do not regard this as lunacy. It seems to me normal human curiosity. I am as interested in strangenesses as I am in ghosts, I am not sure if I believe in either but I can never resist a cautious dabbling. The horoscope, a long, intimate and detailed affair, seemed authentic enough, but then the sceptic in me insists on pointing out that certain things are true for all people and, if there were a few points that were almost disconcertingly accurate, it only made it more interesting. When the astrologer suggested that I might care to visit her, I accepted at once. After all, it committed me to nothing, it might give me an interesting article, and at its lowest level it meant a pleasant day in the country, for she lived in Surrey, in an isolated house that was a mile from the nearest village.

I drove down. It was a beautiful house with the loveliest garden I have ever seen, but it was too cold and remote for me. I am a town person, I could not hide myself away, I should wither and die. The astrologer was a pleasant, normal little woman, none of your trailing skirts, wild hair or beads, like another lady I visited a long time ago whose lucky colour was purple and who draped herself and everything around her with purple silk, hangings and ornaments. This one looked like an ordinary housewife, and her husband was a polite old man, plainly used to people arriving in his house. We had lunch, a rather stark affair of home-made bread, cheese and salad, with neither tea nor coffee, for these drinks, like alcohol, were not permitted. Afterwards we sat side by side on a low couch, and she waited for me to pour out my soul. It was strange, but I, who am normally so garrulous, could hardly think of one word to say, and I wished she would light a fire, for I was growing colder and colder, and I had left my coat in the car.

She talked a great deal herself, though I think my silence disturbed her. It disturbed me too, I felt I was being impolite, that I should at least find some small problem to lay before her. But all my problems were so big, and somehow I could not bear to unfold them before those kindly, practical eyes. I remember that she talked of meditation, and of Jesus who, she said, always appeared to her in a tweed suit. I see no reason why he should not, and a tweed suit is not nearly so absurd as the usual winceyette nightgown in which convention robes him, but it sounded a little strange, and I had to wonder if the halo were there as well. She spoke to me of clients in trouble, then asked me if I had any psychic powers. I think I must have replied to this rather awkwardly as the question embarrassed me, for to my surprise she burst into a great peal of laughter and said, "Oh you look quite shocked, sometimes you remind me of my mother."

The conversation never really recovered from this, and I left half an hour later. I remember noticing, when I went upstairs to the bathroom, that she was obviously a staunch Tory in politics. There were Conservative leaflets everywhere, even by the lavatory. I believe these psychic people usually are right-wing: indeed, the only other one I ever talked to with any degree of intimacy was violently anti-black, claiming that coloured people were virtually animals who would require innumerable stages of reincarnation to achieve human status. It has always seemed incomprehensible to me that people with extra-sensory beliefs should be so fascist in their workaday lives. However, the main thing that preoccupied me during my last few moments in this strange house was that I was shivering with cold, and I began in my common way to brood on stopping at a pub on the road home and restoring my circulation.

We said goodbye in a rather unhappy fashion. I felt that I had been rude, however unintentionally, and I suspect that she thought that in some way she had failed me, as I had not confided in her.

I stood for a moment in the doorway, looking at the garden then, wanting to say something warm and appreciative, said, "How lovely all this is. I've never seen so many flowers."

She turned to look full at me. She really was very ordinary in appearance, dressed in skirt and sweater and sensible shoes. Her eyes were smallish brown eyes, nothing remarkable, indeed there was nothing remarkable about her at all. She did not answer my remark, only said in her brisk quick voice, "You must make your search, of course, but I don't really think you'll find him. He's not there, you see. He never was."

I said in a whisper, "I beg your pardon?" I felt bitterly cold.

She said, "You do know your way, don't you? Follow the road until you come to the crossroads, then you take the right-hand fork and — "

I wanted to shout, What the hell are you talking about, what do you mean? But she just stood there, feet apart, very four-square, smiling at me, and her husband reappeared to say, "Do come again," and somehow I found myself in the car, waving, then driving off.

I never did come back. I never contacted her again.

I could not think what she meant, but it was obviously something deeply significant and, though I had no idea then of what lay ahead, it worried me badly. I stopped at my pub, in defiance of the driving code, and had a large drink. The words made no more sense after the drink than before, but the coldness vanished: it really was quite a warm evening. They made no sense to me now as I lay there with my eyes closed, but I knew somehow that they were important, and they remained in my mind even when I fell asleep.

It took me two months to recover and even then I was slow and unsteady, though I managed to go out. I was furious with my own incompetence. I was lonely too, not because my friends did not visit me or because there was not enough to do — I started work again at home almost immediately — but because I was enclosed in the strange isolation of dependance and gratitude, in a world that came to see me and which somehow retreated when I struggled to emerge into its fastness. I learnt in that time how to be alone, which, platitude or no, is something we all have to learn, for our own salvation. Not that I have ever been an aggressively gregarious person: I do not like parties, I feel no desire to dash out and see someone any more than I would watch the television simply because I have nothing better to do. I am never jolly, often morose, and there are times when I do not even answer the front door or the telephone. But it is infuriating not to be able to go out when you want to, and oh God, how weary I grew of being dependent on concern and kindness, even though without this I would not have survived. I had never before realised what a humiliating burden enforced gratitude can be, especially when other people are grateful for you. When I began to feel better and could go out again, I was made wretched by my friends being awash with gratitude every time anyone offered me a helping hand, it was a kind of sad progress, thank you, thank you, you are so kind, with myself as a recipient dummy, unable to say a word. I longed to push the kindly hands aside, and for a while refused to go out at all, because I could not endure having to lean on and to hold, to be hauled about as if I were a parcel, to hear people speaking of me in the third person. "You don't need to help her, you know, she's very independent," or, "Would she rather come round the side entrance where there aren't so many stairs?" One is thus reduced to a personal pronoun, an immobile thing that is mentally deficient.

Thank you, thank you. They call it being gracious. If ever I help a blind man across the road and he then swipes me over the face, I shall understand only too well.

Anyway, all that is now over. Daniel came to see me whenever he could, usually at weekends. Vanda did not accompany him: there were of course the children, as Daniel hastened to explain, I might find them rather tiring, and it was a bit of a procedure bringing them up by car, Sophy was sometimes sick. I was really rather pleased to see him on his own. It was like old times. He flirted outrageously with the nurse who was large and buxom and about fifty, he mended various bits and pieces in the flat, and we talked of all kinds of things, with not one mention of ghost towns.

He seldom referred to my illness. I sensed that it infuriated him because he could not understand it. Daniel in his time has put up with a good deal of my moods and vapours, but he refuses to admit that there are certain things that cannot be explained. Why a normally healthy woman, not so very old, who has seldom suffered from more than the usual run of colds and 'flus, should become paralysed without any obvious cause, was something he could not accept and, if he had known about Steve, he would have shouted me down. I sometimes saw him eyeing me sideways in a clinical fashion, and suspected he would love to have me on the operating table, open me up to find out how I ticked. Occasionally he slid in the odd question which he imagined was very subtle — how was my blood pressure, did I sleep well, had I been experimenting with any kind of drug.

I said with some irritation, "Are you accusing me of being an addict or something? You know perfectly well that I'm terrified of drugs, even the prescribed ones."

"Well," he said airily, "you know how you love trying new things. It's like going to that astrologer woman. I thought you might have been going in for a bit of transcendental meditation. Just for the hell of it, you know."

Then it struck him that the last sentence sounded very odd, and he laughed and began talking of the children, how Mario was a difficult, aggressive boy, the only one who seemed to miss his real father, and who at times was violently rude and disobedient, trying to make Daniel shout at him or beat him. I am quite sure that Daniel did neither; there were certain things he shut himself away from, because he did not want to know, but he had a delicate hand with people, especially the young, and he handled Mario with innate sensitivity and perception. Then there was Sophy who worried so about everything, it was a good thing she was going to school, and of course young Freddy who was a joy to them all, who seemed to have no complications.

He hardly mentioned Vanda except once when I asked him if there were going to be any more children, if for no other reason than that he could have one of his own.

54

He said with an over-loud laugh, "Don't you think we've got enough?"

"Oh, I don't know. Would one more make all that difference?"

Then he said quite coldly, "It would be a bit hard on Vanda. I don't think she wants any more at present. Perhaps later, when the practice looks up and we can afford some help."

I had the impression that all was not as it should be. Perhaps it was just a passing thing. I did not pursue the matter, and presently I told him that as I was so much better — the nurse had now left, and I was managing perfectly well on my own — I was thinking of making my journey.

He exclaimed in real anger, "Are you out of your mind?"

"No, I don't think so. Is it such a dreadful thing to do? I know it'll be a little difficult, but I'll swallow the Ingram pride and make use of all the airport amenities, chairs and taxis and so on."

"And what happens if you collapse again?"

"They'll have to fly me home, won't they? Oh Daniel, don't be so silly. I'm perfectly all right now. It was just one of those things. I don't suppose it will ever happen again."

"Just one of those things! You've been very ill, Elizabeth. You must realise that. I've been seriously worried about you."

"Oh, love! — Well, it's all over now. I admit it was odd and frightening. One day perhaps I'll understand what happened."

Daniel stood there, chewing his lower lip, a childish habit of his when angry or upset. The beard was better now, but still a trifle wispy. He wandered about my room, pushing the pots on the window-sill into line, straightening a row of books, picking up a cigarette end that had fallen to the floor. Then he growled into his shirt collar, "I'm sure — Do you mind if I ask you something very personal?"

"Not at all." But this was not true: I knew what he was going to ask, and I did mind, not because it was personal, but because Daniel disapproved, and I resented his disapproval, even for that moment thought of him as a young prig who should learn to mind his own business.

However, out it came, choked in disapproval, yet so shamefaced that I felt sorry for him, "That American of yours — It upset you very much, didn't it?"

"Well, of course. What do you expect? Incidentally, you

always call him American. He wasn't really, you know, he just lived there for a long time. Yes, it did upset me. After all," I said, resolved suddenly to blow all this cover-up to smithereens, "we lived together for two years, and I was terribly in love with him. In some ways I still am. I know I haven't seen him for three years now, but that doesn't make so much difference, and the way he died was horrible, even though I know that death in a ditch or death in a feather-bed is exactly the same thing. Why do you ask me this? You think it's something to do with my illness. Perhaps it is. I don't know."

"I just thought it might be," said Daniel to the window. He was standing with his back to me. I have no idea how he took this broadside. I had never put it into such blunt words before. But his voice was light and calm. "On the day when it happened, did you — did you reread his letters or something?"

"There weren't any letters. Writers never write letters."

He assimilated this. I knew somehow from the set of his shoulders that he longed to pursue the matter but did not quite dare. He only said, "It was his daft idea that you should visit this ghost town — what's it called? — "

"Jericho City. Yes."

"Well, it is daft." Then he dropped the subject of Steve, to my deep relief, and started once more to prove to me how impossible the whole idea was, how the journey would kill me, how at the Canyon the hotels were more like hostels with no luxury or comfort, and that it would be more sensible to take a little trip to the south of France, stay in some nice hotel and recuperate. "Next year," he said, "you could do this if you still wanted to."

But it was not next year, it was now, it had to be now, or I would never do it at all. It seemed to me — Daniel would regard this as nonsense, and perhaps it was — that I would never know Steve properly until I moved, if only for the briefest while, into his orbit. When things end in such catastrophe, it is as if the whole preceding episodes become set in time. You do not quite see them as they are: they retreat into the distance, become like a film still or pictures in a book. For my own sake I had to do this journey, and so I made my arrangements, booked my flight, and felt sick with fear and apprehension of what lay ahead of me.

Vanda came to say goodbye without the children. We got on excellently as we always did nowadays, only there was never much warmth between us, conversation was brittle and somehow contrived, nothing led on to anything else. I am sure she did not dislike me any more, and at times I felt a real affection for her, but to her I would always remain an unknown quantity and therefore potentially dangerous. She still could not understand what part I played in Daniel's life, but there I was, apparently nothing would remove me, and after all I was almost an old woman, and now lame into the bargain, there was nothing for her to worry about.

We had a cup of coffee, then I poured her out a drink. She was well-groomed as she always was, in a dress that she had made herself, though no one would have suspected it, her hair was sleekly piled up, and she wore scarcely any make-up on her smooth, olive face. There must be warmth there, for Daniel needed warmth as an old person a fire, there must be hidden tenderness, for he had married her, he had no need to marry her. But somehow we remained as remote to each other as holiday photographs of unknown people, and this seemed to me sad: to put it at its lowest level, we were lumbered with each other, we could never be entirely strangers.

I was beginning to wonder how long she proposed to stay and whether I should offer her dinner: the children would have to be put to bed by someone, and Daniel would be in his surgery. Then she exclaimed, her deep voice unusually animated, "I was so interested in your astrologer."

"Were you? I'll give you her address if you like. But Daniel won't approve, besides she does charge rather a lot."

She considered the matter, then shook her head. Whatever kind of wife she was for Daniel, one thing was certain: she would manage on almost nothing if necessary. She made her own clothes and the children's; cooked remarkable dishes with a piece of scrag-end, and walked miles out of her way to find fruit and vegetables that were a penny cheaper. She would never run Daniel up vast bills, or nag at him because he was too tired to take her out. She was, I think, entirely a peasant girl in most ways, and she had the virtues of this as well as the vices. I thought occasionally that she was capable of poisoning someone if she found it necessary — I always believe that poisoners are essentially humourless people, centred on their own emotions — but she would certainly make the poison up herself, and out of the cheapest household materials.

In this case she saw at once that to pay ten pounds for a horoscope was completely out of the question, only when I said, "I'll give you a horoscope for Christmas," she brightened up, even smiled: when she smiled she became beautiful, like a cinquecentist Italian madonna.

She said, "I am always interested in the supernatural. You did not know about my first husband, did you?"

I admitted that I did not, though she had mentioned him in that strange introductory conversation over the phone. However, that was something we had both long ago decided to forget; neither of us had ever referred to it again. I was both astonished and pleased. Vanda seldom confided in me; and now showed animated signs of being about to do so. I said, before she could change her mind, "I always wanted to ask you, — How did you meet him?"

"I was a waitress in a restaurant," said Vanda, as if this answered everything.

"Well, go on, love. You presumably waited on him."

I saw the great dark eyes go blank and inward, as if this were something she preferred not to remember. She did not mention the restaurant again. She only said, accepting another drink, "He was evil. He went in for black magic. I was so afraid of him — oh Elizabeth, I can't tell you. Even when I left him he pursued me. He still — " She broke off. She said, "For a long time now I put garlic on my window-sill."

"Vanda!" I almost laughed, thinking of a vampire-husband swooping up to the window, then I saw the fear in her eyes and shivered.

"Oh yes, Elizabeth, garlic is super-duper against evil spirits. Why do you smile?"

"Nothing, dear. Just such a funny way of putting it."

"Funny?" She wrinkled her brow at me, then went on, "And silver too. He tried so hard to get me back. He did such things to me — But I cannot tell you. I think if I had not met Daniel I would have gone mad, he tried to make me mad."

I saw that she was very disturbed and put my hand on hers. She was breathing quickly, and her face was very pale. It was frightening to see how afraid this prosaic young woman had become, and no one could deny the fear, she was trembling and sweating with it.

But she did not pursue the matter. Perhaps she regretted being so confiding. In a moment she was the old Vanda again, cool, composed, standing up and saying in her deep voice, "I must go. The children will be expecting me." She looked down at me as I sat there, for I was still easily tired and did not always get up to let my friends out. "I think," she said, "he still ill-wishes me."

And unexpectedly she crossed herself. I had forgotten that she was a Catholic. She could hardly be a devout one, for she was divorced and she had married an agnostic, but perhaps the religion still lay deep within her, perhaps, even with the garlic and the silver, it was the final security.

I said, "Don't think that, Vanda. I don't believe it's possible. No one can have so much power over another human being."

She said, "He makes me share in his pain. We are still so close. I cannot get away." Then, as I gazed at her stupefied, for I would never in a thousand years have expected such a remark from her, she exclaimed in a kind of agitated flurry, "But you must not say to Daniel what I have just said. He would not like it. He would be very angry."

Then I saw that the marriage would work out very well...Vanda was woman enough to want her man to be boss, and Daniel possibly knew how to manage her much better than I had realised. We kissed goodbye with real warmth, and I watched her walking down the corridor to the lift: she walked easily like one accustomed to carrying heavy loads, her hips swayed and her head was held high.

I brooded for a long time on her remarks. That Vanda of all people, practical, sensible, down-to-earth Vanda, should say such things — Her words frightened me a little. I wondered what Daniel knew of this. He must know something, for it was plain that this was an uneasy period for both of them. I told myself firmly that it was all nonsense, but one is easily possessed by lunacy, and that night I put a small cob of garlic on my window-sill. I knew it was nonsense, no black magician was pursuing me, and I derided myself for my idiocy, but there the garlic was, and there it remained until Daniel, some days later, saw it and remarked, "Why on earth have you left your garlic there?" and removed it to the kitchen where it belonged.

Fortunately he had no idea why I had done such a thing, and he spent the next few minutes in telling me what a wonderful cook Vanda was, how she too used garlic in almost everything so that sometimes in his morning surgery he had to suck deodorising tablets for fear of breathing fumes over his patients.

Then we fell to discussing my journey, and Vanda and garlic and evil were forgotten.

Chapter 3

I ARRIVED AT THE GRAND CANYON SOME THREE WEEKS LATER. The journey, severely supervised by Daniel who, once he had accepted my crazy decision, turned the whole of his practical nature on to the project, was much easier than I expected, though exhausting. I set off, stocked with tablets from his dispensary, in case I was overtired, in case I couldn't sleep, in case I lost my appetite, in case I developed stomach trouble. I knew I would be most unlikely to take any of them, but I could hardly refuse them, so I stuffed them all into my case. The customs official must have thought that I was an advanced hypochondriac. I also took with me a bottle of Scotch, which seemed to me far more useful and which I should certainly take. Everything was arranged for me, I was booked in at hotels, arrangements were made for transport, and I believe that if Daniel could have arranged for an accompanying doctor, he would certainly have done so. It was amusing, touching and a little embarrassing: when he drove me down to Heathrow, he made such a fuss that the officials were plainly uncertain whether I was abdicated royalty or so near death's door that he was anxious to be rid of me.

Death's door. It is now almost a platitudinous phrase, but what a good one. Perhaps in one sense I was standing there, even putting one foot inside, but not in the conventional sense, it was other people's deaths that concerned me.

I have now been at the El Saddle Hotel — what an odd name, I believe it is called after a mountain — for two hours and forty minutes. I have unpacked, hung up my clothes and, for the devil of it, arranged my little bottles of pills on the dressing-table. There are five of them. I am reminded of the

60

father of a friend of mine who took a different pill with every mouthful of food. At his daughter's wedding breakfast he produced bottle after bottle, even adding pills to the champagne, it was strange and a little macabre, for he obviously felt that without them he would instantly die. I suppose there was some kind of rota system. I do not touch any of the bottles but, it is true, I feel depressed, disorientated and desperately tired.

The hotel is an odd little place. As Daniel said, it is more like a hostel, though my room is comfortable, and the door at the end of my corridor leads straight on to the Canyon. There is no lounge, only a long foyer, with a shop at the side that sells local Indian goods; there is also a bar and a dining-room at the far end. There is a desk where one can book for coach trips or, as in my case, arrange for a private car, for tomorrow I am going to Jericho City, which is over a hundred miles away, and it would certainly kill me off if I tried to drive myself.

The guests seem to be mostly parties of foreign students. There is one very young couple, with a little girl who might be Vietnamese. She is about six and completely out of control: I itch in my interfering way to cart her off to bed, for she is wild with fatigue, rushes round the foyer, knocking into everybody and screaming with rage if restrained. The parents — have they adopted her? — are young Americans, and the little mother can hardly be a day over seventeen, and makes not the faintest attempt to control the child who is dressed in a ridiculous long silk affair that comes down to her ankles and trips her up. Otherwise there is nobody that interests me, but perhaps I am too tired to be interested, perhaps tomorrow I shall view them all with a different eye.

Steve would hate this place. Steve would by now be down the Canyon, gossiping with the Hopi Indians, or riding there on a mule, which, as the leaflet tells me, "should not be missed by able-bodied visitors". I feel remarkably unable-bodied, and it is only the memory of Daniel's gloomy prophecies about collapsing and being flown home, that makes me get up, rather unsteadily, to aim for the bar before dinner.

After food and a drink I shall feel fine.

I am going to feel fine.

It is all right for Steve, who contended that he liked living rough, who would be pitching his tent somewhere or other, after having no doubt shot his moose and grilled it. He always claimed to despise luxury, made fun of my flat as a bourgeois little pied-à-terre, and stated at frequent intervals that women are such feeble creatures, they were all right in their own way, but give him the company of men, back to nature, stark reality, and so on.

In actual fact he was a great luxury-lover, dressed well, liked good food, and on the rare occasions when I dined with him at his flat, prepared the meal with an almost spinsterish precision, serving everything on little mats, with the right complement of cutlery neatly laid out on folded serviettes. As for the company of women, the feeble creatures, he could not do without it, as I and innumerable other females knew to our cost. There were of course times when he preferred masculine company, but I don't think there were many evenings when he slept alone.

I am thinking too much of Steve, far too much. I keep on seeing him here, perhaps with that film actor he mentioned, Paul Ducane. It is true that if it were not for Steve, I would not be here at all, I would never even have heard of Jericho City, but all the same Steve is dead, I doubt if he ever set foot in the El Saddle Hotel, except possibly for a drink, and this is my holiday, I am going to enjoy myself without Steve leaning over my shoulder to make fun of me.

It has been quite a journey. I think I am quite tough, I am proud of myself. I flew to Los Angeles, to stay two days there with an old friend, then flew to the Canyon via Las Vegas, which I detested as one of the rudest airports and the greediest, with its clusters of fruit-machines everywhere, the constant rattle of money and the unmistakable Mafia atmosphere that pervades it. But I enjoyed the little flight to the Canyon, with the air hostesses all dressed in bright yellow, and as we flew low before landing, looked down unbelievingly at its amazing contours, rainbow-coloured in the setting sun.

Dear God, this sounds like a bloody travel film. This is not after all a guide-book. If you want to see the Grand Canyon, go there, it is the most beautiful and extraordinary place I have ever seen, but there are dozens of picture books, all the photos of it are pure fantasy and, if I really tried to depict it in words, I would become a kind of verbal paintbox, for indeed it defies description. We will leave the Canyon, and here I am in the El Saddle bar, still in my travelling slacks, for here, thank God, no one attempts to dress for dinner.

I did not stand by the bar, for I still cannot stand for more than a few minutes. This helped me a great deal on my journey, for airports are used to sickly travellers and very helpful. I hope I am not becoming one of those people who trade on this kind of thing, but it is lovely to crash all queues, and to be allowed to board the plane before anyone else, with kindly hostesses rushing to supply you with drinks before you faint away. However, this time I ordered my drink then made my way towards one of the little tables in the corner. It was almost pitch dark in the strange way of American bars — perhaps they think that drinkers do not want to be seen — and I stumbled, might have fallen, had someone not put a hand under my arm and removed the glass from me.

A sweet and gentle female voice said, "Do let me help you. It's so dark, isn't it? Here's the chair."

I said, rather crossly, with the forbidding spectre of Daniel at my elbow, "I'm fine, thanks," and saw without pleasure that my new companion had sat herself down in front of me.

This was ungrateful of me, but I was so tired and in no mood for conversation: however, there was nothing to be done about it, so now that my eyes were growing used to the candlelight — perhaps the darkness is simply economy — smiled at her, offered to buy her a drink and looked at her to see what she was.

She explained almost immediately. That sweet voice would jar badly on my nerves after a time, especially as she never stopped talking, but she seemed a nice little woman, and the sweetness and friendliness were obviously part of her profession. She accepted the drink with enthusiasm. She told me at once who she was, waited briefly for me to do the same then, as I said nothing, continued to prattle about herself.

"What a pity," she said, "you weren't here two days ago. It has been so exciting. You would have loved it. Of course you're English like me, and it would have been quite an experience for you. I am a cosmetician, you know. I work for a film company." She added quickly, "I also do private work, of course. It's quite inexpensive, so if you would like me to give you a facial, I would be delighted. It is too dark here for me to see you very clearly, but most of us let our skin go, don't we, and I do think a facial and make-up is so refreshing. Morale-restoring. Don't you think so?"

I do not bother much about make-up, apart from a little lipstick and something on my eyes if I am going out. It is no virtue on my part, simply laziness and the fact that I dislike the feel of a lot of stuff on my skin. Steve didn't like it, Harry would not so much as have noticed, and Daniel tends to disapprove in a rather priggish way of girls who titivate themselves, saying that they make their eyelids look like rotten meat, and he couldn't kiss a scarlet gash of a mouth. I found this rather silly, and pointed out that he was simply old-fashioned: nobody wears bright-red lipstick these days, and in any case he probably wouldn't recognise make-up when he saw it. If he went out with a girl who wore none, he would think she looked pale and plain. However, none of this applies to me, I just don't like it for myself, and the thought of enduring a facial and a make-up nearly made me jump to my feet and leave the bar.

I said, "I'm afraid I don't really have the time. There always seems to be so many other things to do."

I can see now that this stupid remark to Eve — for that was her name, do call me Eve, may I use your first name, it's so much less formal, isn't it? — was rather like someone saying to me that there was no time for reading. I could feel her stiffen, but she spoke pleasantly enough. She said, "It doesn't take long, you know. I make up every morning, I have to after all, and how long do you think it takes me?"

"Oh, I've no idea."

"Seven minutes! Of course I am accustomed to it, but you would be in a very little while. Why not come to my room after dinner for a drink, and then I can show you the kind of stuff I have with me. I always carry it around, though the film people have all gone by now."

"Were they making a film here then?" I asked, interested for the first time.

"Oh, they always are. Jericho City, you know. You'll have seen it in dozens of films. It's what they call a ghost town. It's one of the best preserved, so I understand, and of course it's marvellous for Westerns. Such a pity the film is finished. Most of the actors are gone now, but Paul — Paul Ducane — is still here, he has his ranch not far away, and after making a film he always goes there to recuperate. You know Paul, of course?"

Well, of course. I did indeed. I didn't say that I thought he must be dead by now. I was oddly excited. He had, after all, been a friend of Steve's.

Eve was still talking. "He's such a nice fellow. Hits the

64

bottle, of course, but then so manyy of them do. It's almost an occupational disease, isn't it? If he ever drops in here for a drink, I'll introduce you. He does so love meeting his fans, especially someone like you."

"What do you mean, someone like me?" I asked, surprised. I was thinking that really — never mind Steve — it would be better not to meet Paul Ducane at all. It would destroy for me all the glamour I had once attributed to him. Even his greatest admirers never pretended that he was intelligent, and I could imagine that his conversation would be a monologue about himself, with an occasional arrow aimed at the terrible Reds. I preferred to remember him as the handsome hero saving the town from the bad men, not as a possibly drunken bore, offering me a signed photograph.

"Well, you're an artist, aren't you?" said Eve, adding quite archly, "Now don't deny it. I can always tell."

"But I do deny it! I'm not an artist at all." And I found myself unreasonably irritated, for after all the appellation is not exactly an insult, but then I was very tired, and Eve was not really the companion I needed.

"Now don't be so modest," she said. She was a predictable woman, I could almost have said it for her. As I did not answer — I'm not really modest at all, having a fair opinion of my own capabilities — she continued, "You're a writer. I sensed it at once. It's the way you talk. It's unmistakable."

As I had said almost nothing, this was astute of her. But I could not help being intrigued, though God knows, my column hardly entitles me to so grand a title. I laughed, offered her another drink and said, "Well, in a way you're right, but not perhaps quite as you mean it."

"I knew it." She was delighted with herself. "What is it? Poetry? Novels? Biography, perhaps."

"No. I'm just a journalist. Not even a celebrated one. Just a run-of-the-mill journalist."

She gave a little cry of excitement. She was a girl who would always give little cries of excitement, probably because she worked with film people. She exclaimed, "Oh, isn't that splendid? You are here to do an article on Paul. You'll find him very co-operative. Unlike some of them, he is always so polite to the press."

It seemed a shame to disillusion her, and I nearly left it at that, only it struck me that I might find myself saddled —

appropriate word — with an eager Paul Ducane, committed to do an article that nobody wanted and nobody would print. I said, a little deprecatingly, that I was not here to do an article on anyone, I had been ill, this was a holiday, and I wanted to take a look at Jericho City.

I think she was disappointed, but she rallied at once. She asked me earnestly if I were feeling better, perhaps I would like an introduction to Paul all the same, and I must let her do me a facial, it would do me such a lot of good and she wouldn't charge anything for it. We were by this time walking towards the dining-room through the well-lit foyer, and I saw that she was examining my face closely.

She said consideringly, "You have let your skin go, haven't you?"

"Probably."

"But then of course you've been ill. I've the very thing for you. It's a new cream, just out. And the eyes — You've lovely eyes, my dear, you ought to make the most of them. A little violet eye-shadow first, then a grey-blue. A light lipstick only, I think — And we'll have to tone those lines down, of course. I could make you look ten years younger." She gave a little girlish laugh. "Now you can't say no, you just can't. I'm quite an expert, you know." And here she told me whom she had made up, rolling off a stream of famous names, with biographical details thrown in. "She's a good mum, but she does drink rather a lot, quite difficult sometimes to cover up those bloodshot eyes. And then there was — you'll remember her — lovely body but a bit nympho, they don't care much for her on the set. As for — "

It seemed almost rude to refuse her, so I half agreed that later on, perhaps tomorrow, perhaps the day after, I would let her make me up. And after dinner in my own room I sat in front of the mirror and contemplated myself as a ghost visiting a ghost town, for it seemed to me that Eve's experienced hands would remove not only the lines but everything else that was me, so that I would be left as a characterless mask, like one of those ageing film stars who look as waxen as an effigy in Madame Tussaud's. I did not tell Eve this, but this had happened to me once before. One of these travelling cosmeticians was wished on me by a friend, and I submitted to her ministrations, which took over an hour, after which I was compelled to buy various pots of creams and lotions which I knew I should never use. The process was soothing, the result was horrible. I felt like a corpse from the American way of death who had been through the hands of an experienced mortician. Smooth, tinted skin, heavy-lidded eyes, mouth elegantly shaped, and no lines at all — I wanted those lines. They were my lines. I had worked for those lines, they were part of me, they revealed my character however bad it might be. I made faces at myself, stretching my skin so that the colouring cracked, then I washed the whole thing off. I never told the cosmetician, though she plagued me for some time afterwards with phone calls and little letters, suggesting that I might want something for a party, that I might be meeting an important publisher, that she would be prepared to come early in the morning to beautify me. She hoped I would recommend her to all my friends, and if some of them were young mums — that, I remember, was her phrase — she had special reduced rates of five pounds, which included a free lipstick and a sample bottle of perfume. It would have been no good telling her that young mums have better things to do with five pounds than making up their faces, for like all people of her kind she could not visualise poverty or privation: like Eve she dealt with stage and film people, and she had no conception of common folk who simply washed their faces and pulled a comb through their hair.

I am sorry, Eve, but the answer is no. I am an ordinary, middle-aged woman who has been ill, and I look like an ordinary middle-aged woman who has been ill. My only claim to any kind of looks is the structure of my bones, the mobility of my features and what brain there is behind them. I feel hemmed in by ghosts, I must at least retain my own reality. I am forty-eight, at the moment I look older, I have no wish to look ten years younger because I am not ten years younger, and I would never look it, you know, I would simply look like a painted doll of forty-eight. It is never possible to disguise your age, you can only blur it.

I don't sleep much that night. I take a look at the Canyon before going to bed. It is bitterly cold. The snow lies on the rocks. It looks unreal in the moonlight, and I think of the Indians who live there, and the strange birds and snakes and plants. It is so beautiful that it is frightening, it makes me shiver. There is a man on the balcony taking photos by moonlight. We stand at different ends of the enclosure, we do not speak to each other, even to say good night. He takes so many photos that I feel he does not see the Canyon at all. When he has used up all his film, he goes back silently into the hotel, and I follow him almost immediately.

I drink some Scotch and put my dressing-gown on the bed because I feel so cold. I take a look at Gideon's Bible, then am compelled to experiment with a strange mechanism at my bedside that promises me soothing sleep if I feed it a quarter. I do so, and it sets my bed shaking and quivering so that I can only clutch on to the sides and pray that it will stop. If this is supposed to be soporific, surely an earthquake would do just as well.

When it has stopped — and never again — I read Gideon's Bible for a while and this does make me sleepy. The hotel is dead quiet. It is the kind of place where everyone goes to bed early, there is after all nothing else to do, and we all want to be up at some ungodly hour to see the Canyon at dawn. Tomorrow no doubt the young guests will all be riding on mules and exploring. It must have been entertaining when the film people were there, but they have all left now, the Western has been made, and now we have simply the routine parties who seem to come largely from Japan. They must feel at home here. The shop is stocked with their goods. I took a look round it when I arrived, with a dim idea of buying presents for Vanda's children. There was a disgraceful woollen donkey with "Grand Canyon" written across it: I picked it up and discovered hidden under its tail the notice: Made in Japan. But some of the Indian stuff was very attractive, though extortionately expensive, serve us right for so misusing them.

I did not see Eve before I left. Perhaps the make-up takes rather longer than she admits, or perhaps she likes to lie late in the morning. It must be exhausting having to be permanently beautiful and cheerful, there is something to be said after all for being a loverless woman of forty-eight. I was thankful to miss her, and foresaw a great deal of dodging. I had a quick breakfast, and my car called for me at eight o'clock.

And now I am in Jericho City.

"It's the most beautiful place in the world," Steve said. He was talking of Arizona, not Jericho City. "I'm going back there one day. I don't know why I stay in this bloody country. It shuts me in, I feel cramped. But I guess you wouldn't know what I'm talking about. You're too English. You just don't

68

know what open spaces mean. If one talks of open spaces to you, you think of Regent's Park."

You never went back, Steve. Why didn't you go back? I don't know how you could bear to stay away.

We didn't reach Jericho City until nearly two. My driver was a pleasant boy, dressed like someone out of a Western, Stetson, boots, dude shirt and all. It seems to be the nationel costume. All the young men here are dressed the same. They are all very handsome. It was a beautiful day, hot and dry, and I could feel my skin growing parched as the dusty wind blew in through the window. Eve would be running after me with some moisturising cream and, as I touched my cheeks, I felt for the first time that I would not have refused. We drove through canyons, forests, river-banks, mountains and scrub-land, through bright, garish little towns, each with its own airstrip, each bursting with neon signs. Monstrous cacti grew by the roadside, there were vivid flowers and strange trees, sometimes it was barren, sometimes it flamed with life. We had lunch in a roadside café, then at last came up the hill to the City.

I asked my driver to leave me there for an hour.

Most of the town is as it was — a place for bored cowboys itching to spend their money, with its bars and brothels and sleazy dives: for a brief while it became a rich mining town that dwindled and dwindled as the mines began to close. But the film people who had been here, had left their traces. A scarlet-painted "House of Joy" — which I cannot believe the matrons of Jericho would have tolerated for a minute — stands there, and some irreverent person, perhaps a bored extra, has chalked across its wall: Reservations Only. The prison has plainly been restored with plywood, the sheriff's office newly painted, and the hotel, burnt and gutted by some dreadful fire, provided with a new, bright façade so that the heroine could stay there. The old houses wiith their verandahs have been flimsily restored, the shops are stocked with period goods, and the saddlesmith has obviously been put into some kind of working order.

There were not many people about. I crossed the road, stepped up the high step on to the wooden-slatted sidewalk, resisted the temptation to tether an imaginary horse to the post provided, and stopped in front of the saloon bar.

It was exactly as Daniel had described it. It too had been

renovated, but perhaps the film had involved some violent brawl, for the paint was half off, and the doors flapped in the breeze. It looked disreputable and startlingly real, and I stood there for several moments before, glancing furtively over my shoulder, I pushed the doors open and came inside.

This obviously had been a film set. No bar could have lasted for such a long time. It was entirely strange, it was stepping back into the past, and for the first time I felt well again, my exhaustion dropped from me: this was what I had come to see, what Steve had compelled me to see, this had meaning for me, for all it was bogus, recreated.

There was the bar counter with the rows of bottles at the back. There were the small tables for the poker players who took the cowboys' money off them and, as I stood there, the bar began to fill with people: the stony-faced men, the smooth professional gamblers, the silly boys who hoped to earn themselves a few extra dollars. The girls would be there too — not the pretty little scrubbers of modern films, but hard, vulgar, raddled whores who would certainly not be decked out in dainty off-the-shoulder dresses, sequins and feathers. The stairs at the side led up to their bedrooms. The film fight must have taken place there, for the banister was broken. There was even a honky-tonk piano, and this was too much for me. I sat down on the stool and began to play with one finger, "Home, home on the range." It was not really a very suitable song, but it was the only one I could remember: besides, I no longer play the piano and could not have attempted anything more ambitious.

By this time I was out of myself, so enchanted with it all that I no longer cared. I began to sing the song, my voice being on the same level as my piano-playing, and when the remark cut across me, I was so appalled that I blushed scarlet and simply sat there, not daring to turn round.

"That's mighty fine, doll," said the voice in a slow, deep drawl that was somehow, even through my confusion, familiar, "but I wouldn't mind something with a little more zazz."

I swung round. I couldn't after all sit there, looking like an idiot. Besides, I had to see who it was had the temerity to address me as "doll" which is really singularly unsuitable. And the "mighty fine", for God's sake! —

I recognised him of course. The last of the cowboys, or so they had called him. I had after all sat through *The Great*

Divide, Arizona Flame, The Lonely Ranger and *Bonanza at Moose City*. Paul Ducane was sitting at the table at the far end of the bar, beneath the broken banister. He was dressed for the part, as if he had come straight from the set. Perhaps he never wore anything else. There it all was, the shirt, the breeches, the flaps that all cowboys wear, the big hat lying on the table before him, and — oh no, too much — the holster with a gun that looked as if it were loaded.

He rose to his feet, slapping his hat on his head, and came towards me. He doffed his hat with a little bow, then put it on again. It was entirely strange, unreal. Once, a long time ago, I went to Prague, and there I saw the "Magic Lantern" show where people walk out of a film and tumble on to the stage. Paul Ducane was doing precisely that. This was the hero who took all the Apaches on single-handed; this was the good, simple country-boy who foiled the bad men, the lonely cowboy who rode away into the sunset. I saw at that moment that that was all he could do. He had acted in cowboy films for all his life, he had never attempted anything else, and now it was his reality, he was the cowboy hero, it was no longer an act because he believed in it himself.

At first glance he was as handsome as I remembered him then, as the doors flapped open and a shaft of sunlight came in, I saw that he had not worn so well, that he was indeed in his sixties, perhaps older. This was what Eve would make of me. His face was smooth — lifted? After all, it is done to men too — the dark hair had receded over a fine forehead but was still glossy and untinged by grey. The beautiful bones would always be there: neither age nor dissipation nor indeed death could touch them. But the eyes were smudged, there were heavy veins on his cheeks, and I did not need the sight of the bottle on the table nor the echo of Eve's remark, to see that he drank heavily, had drunk heavily for a long time. His body was fine and spare, corseted perhaps, but with the belly flat as a board, and he moved lithely like a younger man. Only there was no expression on his face, as there seldom was when he acted: his love scenes, unless carefully controlled and subtly photographed were as emotionally moving as a still-life. For all his many marriages it was impossible to visualise that face filled with tenderness or passion: he would frankly ride a horse better than a woman, and possibly feel more emotion in the process. Some men prefer animals to people. I am sure that

71

Paul Ducane was one of them: people after all expect personal consideration, and a horse is content to be fed and groomed, with the occasional pat or lump of sugar thrown in.

He came up to me so close that he brushed against me. We must have presented the oddest sight: small, middle-aged woman swinging round on the piano stool, and tall cowboy with his hand instinctively feeling for his gun.

He said, "You a reporter, doll?"

"No, Mr. Ducane, I am not."

Reporters and commies — I suppose these filled his life. He looked as if he did not believe me. He put a hand in his pocket. "I guess you'd like a signed photo," he said.

Now really, there was nothing I wanted less, though this exactly fulfilled my prophecy. I am long past the stage of signed photos, though I collected autographs when a child, mostly of the "by hook and by crook I'll be the last in the book" variety, and later sold the few good ones because I was broke. However, I could not decently refuse, so I thanked him rather awkwardly, and he at once produced a sheaf of photos, and leant on the piano to display them to me as if they were a deck of cards.

I looked at them over his hand. He had good hands, long and elegant. He flipped over the photos, his face intent. Now that he was so near me I could smell the whisky on his breath, and I could see too, a little to my dismay, that he wore make-up, very subtly applied but perceptibly there. This presumably was Eve. There was a faint shadow on the eyelids that was not natural, and I swear that a foundation cream covered up some of the lines that a fresh young cowboy should not know. I was embarrassed: this was something that I should not see. I concentrated on the photos. There was Paul Ducane, gazing out across the hills, Paul, hands swinging at his side waiting for the enemy, Paul on horseback, one hand patting his steed's neck. There was never anyone with him. He was always alone. I would have liked to see what his present wife looked like, or his children — he was reputed to have dozens. But even here he could not bear competition.

He said at last in the deep voice that would be recognisable anywhere, "I like this one. I'll give you this, doll. Wait. I'll sign it for you."

I took it while he rummaged for a pen. I looked down at Paul on horseback, hat tilted back on his head, hands lying slackly on the reins. The magnificent profile gazed out across the plains. He might have been looking out for his enemy, or simply have been gazing peacefully across his homeland. But I think he was looking out for Russians in snow-boots to appear over the hills, and his next remark, coming out of the blue, confirmed this.

"You're staying at the El Saddle, ain't you?"

"Yes," I said, surprised, for I could not believe that where I stayed was of the least interest to Paul Ducane.

"You look out for that Commy couple."

I got up from the ridiculous piano stool, feeling rather cross. This was destroying the illusion. I said, "I don't know what you're talking about. I only came yesterday. I've no idea who is in the hotel."

To my surprise he smiled. When he smiled you could understand why he was a star. It was nothing to do with looks or talent. Paul Ducane certainly had the one, and I doubt if he had the other, but when he smiled he was glorious, and you could forgive him all the Indians that lay dead at his heels, the appallingly stiff dialogue and the wooden love-scenes. He said simply, "Care for a drink, doll?"

I don't know what got into me, I am not normally so rude — indeed I am supposed to be rather timid, or so Daniel tells me. But I really could not stand this form of address any longer. It was so ridiculous. It was the kind of thing that might have been said to some little floozie in a bar, or one of the saloon girls when encouraging patrons to spend their money. I said very stiffly, "I doubt if reality goes quite so far. Those bottles all look empty. But please, Mr. Ducane — "

"Paul! You Britishers are all so damn formal."

I don't like being called a Britisher either. What is the matter with me today? I've become so prickly. However, I tried to ignore this — if I wasn't careful he would soon be commenting on my cute little British accent — and simply said, "Please do me a favour."

"Anything." But he looked astonished, as well he might.

"Do stop calling me doll. I hate it. I — I know you don't mean to be rude or anything, but it gets on my nerves. I'm too old."

He burst out laughing. He didn't actually say, Doggone, but it was a near thing. I believe he simply had to speak as if he were in one of his own films. He said, "Well, if that don't beat

73

everything," — and that was straight out of the studio too. He went on laughing, and the laughter was so infectious that I recovered my temper and smiled at him.

"I don't mean no harm," he said. "I'm just a country boy. What's your name, — ma'am?"

Well, I suppose it was preferable to doll, in fact I quite liked it. I said, "Elizabeth."

"That's a real nice name. I guess they called you that after your Queen."

I really could not see my decently left-wing parents doing anything of the kind, and the lady and I were born about the same time, but I could not keep on disputing with Paul Ducane who was so plainly out to be friendly, so I said, yes, they probably did. Then I thanked him for the photo, which had, "Your Friend, Paul Ducane," scrawled flamboyantly across it. Perhaps Mario would like it. Or perhaps I would keep it, put it on my mantelpiece, it was after all something of a curiosity. I tucked it away in my handbag, and he strolled over to where he had been sitting, and came back with a half-full bottle.

"This one ain't empty," he said, took off the top which was a little drinking cup, filled it to the brim and handed it to me.

We sat there drinking in silence, me back on my piano stool and Paul Ducane lounging against the bar, as he must have lounged innumerable times. He had pushed his hat to the back of his head: I remembered the gesture in a dozen films. Once again I was almost torn with the reality of this unreality: it was like having a fever where everything is sharpened to the point of pain, where one feels as if one no longer belongs to the normal, living world. Here we were, in a ghost town that had died many years ago, in a saloon bar that had been reconstructed for a film: a sick woman who was better now yet still disorientated, and a film star past his prime, who still dressed as if he were acting a part, who looked and talked like a romantic cowboy and who, if removed from his setting, would, I could not help feeling, shrivel up like the characters in *Lost Horizon.*

Then unexpectedly he did not speak like a cowboy at all, he spoke like one of McCarthy's aides, and indeed, I remembered that he had once shopped a great many of his fellow actors, no doubt for the noblest of reasons.

"You got to look out for those Commies," he said again.

74

"What Commies? I don't know any Commies." And this was by no means true, for the views of some of my friends would have brought that gun level with their heads. I was up at college at a time when most of the intellectual young belonged to the Party: some of them had died in Spain, some fighting against Nazism, but there were many left who believed that fascism was still the real enemy and who stormed out to have their heads broken by Mosley's bully-boys. I grew a little angry, for Paul Ducane was destroying my fantasy, he was speaking now like an ordinary, stupid man. If he had to warn me against anything, it should have been against the Apaches, but Commies — such a revolting word — had no place in this fabricated past.

"I saw 'em. I don't miss much. Why'd they have to adopt a Commy kid? There are plenty good American kids need adopting. It's infiltration. Anybody could see that. Have another drink, ma'am."

I automatically held out my little silver cup. It seemed to me that I was going to need it. Then I realised what he was talking about, though it seemed so absurd as to be inconceivable. I remembered the very young couple with the little oriental girl who was so out of control. I had thought at the time that she must be Vietnamese, with her neat, pretty little face and those slanting black eyes. Oh God almighty, how utterly absurd — I wanted to answer him, but experienced the strange weakness that comes upon one when talking to an alien being. Paul's ideas, if one could call them that, were so completely opposed to my own that I was lost, I simply did not know what to say. I remember how once a friend of mine, whom I had known for several years, suddenly burst into a long diatribe on the racial problem. I had never heard him talk like that before. I was aware of course that there were vast differences of opinion between us, but I believed that we had tacitly agreed to shelve them: there were after all a great many other things to discuss, and on most topics we entirely agreed. I don't know quite what got into him to say such things, knowing so well my own views, but it broke our friendship. "I could never tolerate a multi-racial society," he said, bringing this out without sequence or logic, for I think at the time we had been discussing food. He said, "They should never have come over here in the first place. I don't wish them any harm, but after all their standards are not ours, they breed like rabbits and in a little while we shall be over-run." He added, "It makes me hot under the collar simply to think of them," then, "Do you understand what I mean?"

Yes, I understood. I understand English. I do not know what I answered. If he had jumped up and smacked my face, I don't think I could have been more shocked. I think that for a while I simply looked at him, wondering if I were really hearing him, if perhaps I had been suddenly afflicted with delusions.

I felt a little the same now, though only for a moment, for the circumstances were entirely different. Paul Ducane was no friend of mine, and I was already aware that his political views were extreme. Only he had broken my dream, and this made me angry. For those few minutes I had been away in the apocryphal West, surrounded by gallant Virginians, chivalrous Gary Coopers and cowboys who lived by a boy-scout code of honour. I knew it was absurd, but it had been a delightful escape, and here was this idiot voicing his impossible views on a perfectly harmless young couple who had decided to adopt a Vietnamese orphan, and the best of luck to them.

I now realised one thing, however, and that was how he knew so much about the El Saddle Hotel and my arrival there. It was plain that Eve, everybody's rattle, while gently massaging the lines away with hormone cream and doing her best with those bloodshot eyes — what can one do about bloodshot eyes, perhaps a light red on the eyelids to distract attention? — had gossiped and prattled: he had certainly heard that I was a reporter and that no doubt was the reason why I had found him propping up a bogus saloon bar.

I said coldly, "I think you're talking the most awful nonsense."

I half expected him to stalk out, for this is no way in which to address celebrated film stars, but he did nothing of the kind, only laughed again, and this time the laughter did not seem to me infectious at all, it was simply inane and irritating.

He said, "Quite the little firebrand, aren't you, ma'am?"

Then I knew that this was another well-worn shot: the temperamental little woman from the city who spoke her mind and who held silly views on matters of which she knew nothing. By the middle of the film she would be kidnapped by the nice, kind, simple Indians she had been defending, and the hero would come to her rescue and swing her over his saddlebow.

I had no intention of putting up with this, I was not going to be swung over Paul's saddle, and I did not consider that my views were half as silly as his. I slammed my little cup down on the bar counter, which instantly cracked: it was after all only plywood and not made to endure such treatment. Half of it collapsed on the floor, and I nearly went with it, only managed to clutch on to the piano just in time. I saw that Paul Ducane, though still laughing, looked disconcerted, and I rounded on him with more energy than I had shown for some time.

"I've seen them," I said. "What's all this balls about infiltration?"

He blinked at this. Western ladies do not use such language, neither, I suppose, do ladies full-stop, but I wanted to shock him, and the coarse word seemed applicable.

I went on, "The kid is six or less, both parents seem to me in their teens, and I would make a guess that they were shocked by the Vietnam war and decided to do something about it by adopting one of the orphans. They probably are as communist as you. They are just humane people. Why do you say such things? I thought you were an intelligent man."

"Now listen here, doll," he said, apparently forgetting his vow not to call me by this absurd name. He came close to me. His face was furrowed, his voice deep and grave. I think by this time he was pretty shot but as, I suppose, he was this most of the time, it in no way affected his speech except to make it heavier. "I know what I'm talking about," he said, "and there's no call to swear at me. A nice lady like you shouldn't say such things."

He waited, presumably for my apology, but this time I was fighting-mad; I managed with an effort to remain silent.

He went on, "I know there's a Commie conspiracy here to take over this country. I could name you names, but I reckon it wouldn't be wise. For you. They'd gun you down as soon as look at you, these people. This kid you're talking of — I daresay six seems young to you, but it's not to them, and in any case these yellow folk are smaller than we are, and always look kind of young. It wouldn't surprise me at all to learn that she's at least twelve or thirteen."

It was plain that either I charged into a useless battle, or simply let it ride over me. I contrived in some way to do the last. He was still talking, but I pushed the words away from me, and presently there was a pause, then his voice said again, "Have another drink, ma'am."

"No thanks. I must be going. My driver will be wondering what has happened to me." I looked at him, now back at his table as if he were planning to stay there for the day. Perhaps he would take a brief break in the House of Joy, or wander off for a chat with the sheriff, to discuss the hanging due next day. I believe he would have done all of these things. The talk on Commies had brought him briefly back to the present day, but I could see now that he was away again, riding the plains, shooting down Indians, rescuing pretty, foolish girls. He raised his head to look at me. I don't think he saw me at all or, if he did, I was somehow in the guise of Calamity Jane, not as she really was, a tough, butch old trollop, but as Jean Arthur or some elegant Hollywood star playing the role. I had a wild urge to call him partner, to say something like, A man gotta do what a man gotta do, or, I guess we've got some growing-up to do, let's go and gun down some Indians. I think if I had, he would have leapt to his feet and prepared instantly to accompany me.

I wonder what sort of life his wife has, his wives had. None of his marriages lasted, and one could hardly be surprised. Does the present incumbent have to make him hominy grits, whatever that is, prepare endless jugs of coffee, ride into the sunset with him every night? Or can it be that reality occasionally breaks through? There must surely be moments when he sees himself as a has-been, whose audiences such as they are, must now all be of nostalgic middle-age, an old man who makes up his face, who has outlived his world, whose only entertainment is Commie-bashing —

And because this was frightening me, because I was on the verge of weeping for this poor old show-off who was as much cardboard as his sets, I said what I did not intend to say, and it came out loudly and defiantly so that he turned towards me with a jerk.

"Do you remember Steve Olsen?"

He answered slowly in a blurred voice. The drink was beginning to tell at last. Perhaps it was dangerous to remain sober. "Old Steve?" he said. "Why, ma'am, Steve and I were buddies a long time ago. Old Steve — Those were the days. I wonder now what happened to him."

"He's dead, Paul."

78

"Old Steve — " (Oh for God's sake, stop saying, Old Steve, you make me want to scream) "Well, doll, we all have to go, sooner or later. I ain't had no news of him for a long, long time."

"Did you really know him?"

"Of course I knew him. We used to ride out together. I always wondered what happened to him. How did he die, ma'am, if I'm not taking a liberty in asking you?"

"In a ditch."

His face flickered. At that moment he looked very old. He did not answer this. It was not the kind of reality he could endure. He said suddenly, "I'll tell you one thing about old Steve, doll. He was a kinda clever man, you could call him an intellectual. Not that I like intellectuals, but I guess some of them are okay. He wrote books. I never read them myself because I'm not a reading man, but I know he wrote them, once he showed one to me. I don't know what it was about, but he wrote it, he said so. And I'll tell you something else, doll. He came here once with me, and we sat where I'm sitting now, and we drank good Scotch, and we kinda pretended it was a hundred years ago. We had a shooting match. If you look at the wall above the bar, you'll see where the bullets went. I was a better shot than him. I was quicker on the draw. And now he's crossed the great divide, old Steve."

Then he smiled at me, it was a death's head smile, and I was by now backing towards the door, I was very tired, I felt a little weak: when I got back to the hotel I would take one of Daniel's pills. But I could not help looking at the wall. There was nothing to be seen. I daresay some film company had plastered it up a long time ago. I was glad. I could not bear it. Two silly men shooting at a wall, for God's sake — The deep, slow voice was still talking.

"I'll tell you something more, doll. The next picture I make, I'll give you a free ticket for the first night, then afterwards I'll take you out for a drink. You just leave me your address. I'd like to do it. I think you're a swell person. You're kinda clever too, it's been a real pleasure talking to you."

I thanked him. I did not leave him my address, but he did not even notice. I think he had already forgotten. I knew I would never go to that film. It would hurt me to see him riding out, playing the gallant cowboy: I should always see him as a painted old man, sitting in a phoney saloon, nodding his head over his whisky-dreams.

I came out into the afternoon sun of Jericho City, where my driver was reading his paper, waiting for me, and I looked round me because I would never see it again; any further research on ghost towns would be done in the British Museum Reading Room, there were ghosts there too, but not like this.

People, real live people, still live in Jericho City. I don't suppose they trouble themselves with ghosts. The guide book informs me that there are nearly three hundred inhabitants. The original copper shop is flanked by Larry's TV Shop; the original post office, fire station and hotel nudge against Scotty's Rock Shop and Paul and Jerry's Bar. I see now that the House of Joy is a restaurant, so the remark about "Reservations Only" is not as witty as I imagined. The real madams and their cribs lived off Main Street, and the buildings are nothing but ruins, like the madams themselves.

I climbed a little feebly into the car. The driver put down his newspaper. "I thought the Indians had got you," he said.

"I'm sorry I was so long. I didn't mean to stay. Paul Ducane was there, and we got talking so that I forgot about the time."

"Oh him — " The driver started up his car, and we swung round by the old Spanish church, which is built on dynamite boxes. Jericho City is all one way, so we had to go right round, passing the saloon bar again. I wondered if Paul Ducane were still there. I think he must have been. There was an enormous Pontiac parked round the corner, and the number was PD 1. It should have been a horse, I am amazed it was not a horse, but perhaps even romantic cowboys have to march a little with the times, and the saddle would be hard on his poor old bones.

"Do you know Paul Ducane?" I asked.

"Oh, everybody here knows him," said the driver. He grinned at me. He must have been in his middle twenties. He was a good-looking boy with a fresh face and bright blue eyes. He would never go to one of Paul's movies. Skin-flicks would be more in his line, with a nice girl next to him to cuddle. "He's nuts," he said.

"He's an old man."

"He's still nuts. Going around, calling everyone stranger,

80

and toting that gun of his, like the old movies. Makes me tired. He ought to go back to his ranch and retire. Can't think what anyone saw in him."

"He was very well-known once." I don't know why but somehow I had to defend Paul. "I loved him when I was a kid. That'd be a bit before your time, of course."

"I guess so." He was not interested. He said with sudden enthusiasm, "Do you like the Osmonds?"

"Well, they — they're all right."

"Okay with you if I turn the radio on?"

"Of course." And in a way I was relieved, for it saved me the bother of talking, I was very tired, and I wanted to think, I wanted to be alone.

Steve of course had talked of introducing me to Paul Ducane, in the way people do when they are quite sure the occasion will never arise. He was always doing that. In my time I have been offered vague introductions to well-known cricketers, prizefighters, Australian artists and American comedians. I suppose Steve really knew them. It hardly mattered, I certainly never met them. But he obviously was a friend of Paul's, they must have made an odd couple, especially as Steve's politics were very left indeed. Yet it was natural that they should meet; Paul had a ranch not far from Flagstaff, and both of them would count as local celebrities. Probably Paul in his younger days was not such a bore, he would certainly be a staunch drinking companion, and Steve might find it entertaining to consort with a cowboy who still came from the golden west. I wondered what on earth they talked about, when they were not shooting holes in saloon bar walls, but then Steve could talk with anyone when he chose, and I have no doubt they held forth interminably on women, drink and Paul's career, all of which would suit Steve very well, be jotted down in the tablets of his mind for some future book.

It was growing dark. The driver was content with his music, and did not talk to me, except to point out one or two things that he thought might interest me: an Indian museum, a canyon with some strange history. The lights came on in the small towns — we passed Flagstaff, I had to notice, I wondered if I should stop then decided not to — illuminating with neon signs the "niteclubs", "eateries" and an extraordinary number of advertisements for cocktails. It was growing very cold, and the driver, seeing me shiver, switched on the heater. "It's not spring," he said, "and the Canyon's covered with snow."

But it was not entirely the cold that made me shiver. I think it was Flagstaff that revived the memory I had all this time been pushing back into my mind, that had momentarily emerged when I fell ill, and been instantly shoved back again. It was almost as if Steve had been ill-wishing me, but that, I am sure, he would never do: he could be abominable and cruel, but it was himself he was savaging, I don't think he wanted to destroy me.

Now the memory came out clear. How could I even have pretended to forget? There was a great deal I had forgotten, chosen deliberately to do so, but this seemed to have some fearful personal application, a kind of telepathy that frightened me. I felt almost as if I were being terrorised, and this made me angry so that I compelled myself to look at that abominable memory fair and square. Steve was dead, I had no fancy for the hand stretched out from the grave, I wished him frankly to keep his ghostly self to himself.

He called me in the middle of the night. We never lived together in the general sense of the phrase. Sometimes he stayed the night with me, sometimes I with him, but live with me he would not: he had his own spare, empty little flat, with nothing to make it personal, only its table and chairs, its locked cupboards where he kept his papers, and his drink. I suppose he thought that if I lived there I would at once add feminine personal touches, and perhaps he was right: women usually do this even if they occupy a place for the shortest time.

He rang me about three in the morning. His voice was high with hysteria. "For Jesus' sake, come round. I'm dying."

"But Steve, have you rung the doctor?"

"I tell you, I'm dying!"

"All right, darling, all right. I'll be round as quickly as I can. Don't you want me to bring a doctor with me? I mean — "

He swore at me so savagely that I thought he was not so near death after all. The strength in that voice was the strength of the living. Besides, he was something of a hypochondriac: like many strong people who are proud of their bodies he went to pieces when he fell ill. Steve with 'flu was on his deathbed, Steve with toothache suffered the agonies of the damned, and once when he broke a finger, one would have believed him a paraplegic for life.

When I was ill, it was of course quite different: he had no time for female vapours and refused to come near me.

But despite all this I was very frightened. I stumbled into slacks and sweater, then ran to the garage where I kept my car. I did have a key for his flat, and he had mine. It was one of his few concessions. I drove over like a lunatic, paying no attention to traffic lights or sharp turnings: fortunately it was the middle of the night and the roads were almost empty. I tore up the stairs and into his bedroom. I was shaking all over as I opened the door, terrified of what I was going to find.

The room stank of sweat and fear and whisky. Whatever this was, it was dreadfully real in Steve's mind. Steve lay on the bed, his arms flung out as if crucified. His face was ashen white. He was turning his head from side to side. He gasped in a shrieking whisper, "I can't move. I'm paralysed. I think I'm dying."

I came and sat beside him, taking his hands in mine. They were clammy-cold. I said as calmly as I could, "Steve, I'm going to ring the doctor now. I am sure you're not really paralysed, and you're certainly not going to die, but something has to be done, and I am not really competent to help. Give me his number, please, or tell me where I can find it, and I'll get on to him at once."

I could hear my own calm, reassuring voice. I was appalled and terrified by the sight of him, but there was no point in panicking, it would only make things worse. I could feel the tremors of anguish and fear running through him, and all the time he kept on turning his head from one side to the other until in despair I put a hand on his forehead, which seemed to calm him. I could see that he had been drinking. I could only pray that this was some form of D.T.s. Steve was a heavy and constant drinker, but he was not an alcoholic, he had never to my knowledge had any symptoms beyond a violent hangover, though drink made him aggressive and liable to provoke a fight. I tried to get up, to reach the phone, but he hung on to me. The strength of his grip once again made me sure it was not as serious as he imagined. I found myself thinking with a strange detachment that,when he recovered, he would find it hard to forgive me for being a witness of his weakness. I said, "Let me go, Steve, please. Steve — "

He shouted, "For Jesus fucking Christ's sake, don't you see I'm dying?"

83

At last I managed to drag my hand away. I realised that I did know the doctor's name: I had had to ring him up once before for some minor ailment. I looked him up in the directory and dialled his number.

The doctor was not best pleased at being rung at four in the morning, but my frantic voice must have convinced him of the emergency, for he arrived within twenty minutes. He was an old friend of Steve's, had no doubt seen him through a great many crises, and I left him there, going into the sitting-room, shivering now with reaction, sick with apprehension as to what I was going to hear.

The doctor must have noticed my expression. He said at once, quite crossly, "All nerves. Nothing wrong with him at all."

"But there must be something. He — "

"Well, I daresay there is something. Mostly whisky. He's on his feet again. I think," said the doctor, looking at me carefully, "you'd better go in to him. He's had a fright. He needs someone to say there-there to him. You look as if you could do with something like that, yourself. Do you want me to prescribe for you?"

"No, thank you. Is he really all right?"

"As right as he'll ever be." He paused, then he said, "You shouldn't take him too seriously, you know. I know it's difficult for you, but do try not to worry too much about him. He's all right. You bother about yourself for a change."

I didn't know what all this meant, and I really didn't care. I went in to find Steve looking quite restored, pouring himself out a glass of Scotch. His colour was back, and there was nothing wrong with the movement of his legs. He looked at me sourly with a shade of embarrassment, then said suddenly, "I thought I couldn't get away. I thought I was bloody stuck there. Oh Christ, not to be able to get away — "

And that was all he said about it. I stayed the night with him. I think I was more shocked and upset than he was, I could not stop shaking. He never referred to the matter again.

Now, driving back towards the Canyon, I still could not begin to understand why I should be overcome with the same kind of paralysis. I could only feel that somehow Steve was latching on to me, and it was absurd, unreasonable: we had once been bound but now he was dead, it was all over, I wanted to be free from him.

By the time we arrived back at the El Saddle Hotel I was exhausted. I settled up with my driver, who offered to take me anywhere I wanted during my stay, thanked him for being so helpful and went into the lobby where I was by no means pleased to find Eve waiting for me.

"Now," she said in her bright little voice, "you are going to have a drink with me and then you can tell me all about it."

I am a weak character. There were two things I passionately wanted to do, on reaching my own room. I wanted to take a shower and have a quiet drink all by myself. I was weak with tiredness, my legs were giving beneath me, and though I knew this was inevitable after so long a day, it was alarming enough to make me crave for privacy. But I lacked the strength to say no. Steve, to whom I had never said no, used to make fun of this, though if I had denied him he would never have forgiven me. So, wretchedly and crossly, I said yes, and there I was back in that dark little bar, with Eve sitting opposite me.

At least it was too dark for her to see how bad my skin was: I am sure that the Arizona air had dried it to the texture of an autumn leaf.

"Now you must begin at the very beginning," she said. I imagine that in her profession an unquenchable vitality was essential. I had not realised before how extinguishing such vitality could be. I wondered if she were married. She was quite good-looking. She went on, "Paul really fell for you. My, you know how to charm when you want to, don't you? Isn't he the nicest possible fellow? I somehow knew you two would get on. Drink up, Elizabeth, and I'll get you another. It's all on me this evening. Then tomorrow morning I'll do you a lovely facial, the Arizona air is so drying, and it will do you lots of good."

I said, "You and Paul seem to be on a hot line."

This was unkind of me, I know, but it took her aback a little, and I felt that she was considering me carefully before replying. Then she said in her usual cheery way, "Well, I guess he does ring me quite a lot. There's not much happens here, you know, and I think he misses all the gaiety of Hollywood."

From what I had seen of Hollywood, during my brief stay in Los Angeles, the gaiety consisted of footprints in the pavement and a couple of broken-down film studios that looked like their own sets, but I did not trouble to argue. This in its odd way was reviving me, and I was beginning to feel better.

"After all," said Eve, rallying still further, "it's always news when a celebrated reporter meets a famous film-star in Jericho City."

This was now sounding like a game of consequences, but I laughed, saying, "You do exaggerate, don't you? I'm not a reporter at all, much less a celebrated one, and Paul Ducane is not really famous any longer."

"Now that is simply not true," said Eve quite snappily. Perhaps she felt this was some reflection on her powers of make-up. I don't think she had any special feeling for Paul. I am not sure if she had any special feeling for anyone, seeing us all as violet eyelids, blotted out lines and shiny lips. She said, "Paul is a very dear friend of mine. I think he is a very special kind of person. I know his films are a wee bit old-fashioned now, but there are a lot of people, Elizabeth, who would still rather see a nice, romantic adventure story with everything ending happily than all this dreadful sex stuff we have nowadays. Paul simply won't go to see these modern films. He says the people who make them are mentally diseased. I think myself he's quite right. I'm sure you agree with me."

This was a gauntlet I refused to pick up. I am not sure if I like either corn or porn, but Eve's description was enough to shoot anyone into the nearest skin-flick. I simply said, "We met in the saloon bar. I had no idea he would be there. We had a rather odd kind of conversation."

"Odd?" repeated Eve, wrinkling up her forehead at me. "Now why was it odd, Elizabeth?"

She was one of those people who use your name on every possible occasion. But it was not this that made me hesitate before replying. I found that I did not really want to talk about what had happened, at least not to Eve, for I did not see how she could understand. It was not that she was stupid or imperceptive, it was simply that it had all been so strange that I did not fully understand it myself. But I always have to put things into words so I answered her, almost against my will. "It was unreal," I said. "It had no reality at all. We sat there in a film-set saloon bar that hasn't been used for more than half a century, and it was all blown up to be real, with counter and tables, bottles and chairs, even the piano. And Paul was dressed like his own heroes, gun and all, he talked to me as if he were acting in a film, it was like being enclosed on a screen. I didn't like it very much. I can't imagine why he rang you up to tell you about it."

86

Eve did not reply at once. I think she probably thought I was drunk or a little mad. She certainly did not understand one word I said. Then she said in the reassuring voice she must have used to countless temperamental actors, "Oh, it's just his way, you know. He is really the nicest man. But I suppose he's acted in Westerns for so long that he just feels at home in those clothes. After all, half the young men here dress in the same way. It doesn't mean anything. And I know he enjoyed talking to you. He said you were such an intellectual girl, it was a real pleasure meeting you. You must meet him again, perhaps here. He likes to look in for a drink occasionally."

I said I should enjoy that, then, "Will you forgive me, Eve? I really am very tired, so I think I'll just get myself something to eat and go to bed. I have to get up very early tomorrow. There's a coach tour round the Canyon, and it starts at eight o'clock."

"Then I'll do your facial at seven," she said. She really was the most indefatigable lady. The idea of a facial at seven in the morning would deter most people, it certainly deterred me, but Eve apparently took it in her stride. I believe film stars sometimes start work at five o'clock, so she probably was used to it. I had a sudden vision of myself on the coach tour, all painted and bedizened, it was rather horrifying. But it was obvious that this had to be stopped, so I gathered together my courage and said as gently as I could, "Look, Eve, you're very kind, I know my skin is in rather a bad way and I'm sure a facial would do it good, but — "

"It would make all the difference. You'll see!"

"Yes, I know. But please, I don't mean to be rude, but I — I just couldn't take it."

Now she was offended. I heard her voice go stiff and cold. "What do you mean? I don't understand you, Elizabeth."

I said a little desperately, for we were somehow on different wave-lengths, "I think I'm a very lazy kind of person. It's not that I don't like to look nice or that I don't bother about anything, but I like to wear comfortable clothes like sweaters and slacks, and I never really think of making up much unless I'm going out or having visitors, and even then it's really so little that you wouldn't call it make-up at all. I know you'd improve me enormously, but I think I'd rather look just as I am, lines and blemishes and all. I wouldn't feel myself with a lot of stuff on my face. It would worry me."

She said more coldly than ever, "I only wanted to help."

Then I suddenly saw my way out. I rose to my feet. I let myself stagger a little and held on to the back of my chair. "You see," I said, praying that God would forgive me, for I do not like pleading ill-health, "I really have been quite ill, and it's left me so exhausted that a day like today, when I've been driving around since morning, just knocks me out. I'm so nervous now that I simply couldn't stay still for something like a facial. When I get better again, I'll need it of course to restore me, but at the moment I just couldn't take it. I'm sure you'll understand. I'm not used to being ill, and this has really left me a bit sorry for myself."

At once, forgetting her hurt feelings, she was all sympathy. She really was a very nice, kind-hearted person. It was just her ill-luck to run into a thrawn bitch like me. "Oh you poor thing! she exclaimed, catching hold of my arm and nearly knocking me down in the process. "I'm so thoughtless, I should have realised you were still feeling a bit groggy. Do let me help you into the dining-room. I'm so sorry but I can't sit with you this evening, I'm expecting a client, but of course I'll be there to help you back to your room."

I assured her with heartfelt gratitude that I could get back to my room on my own, but she insisted all the same on escorting me to the dining-room ahead of the queue. What she said to the waiter, I do not know, but he eyed me apprehensively all through the meal, as if expecting me to die in the middle of it.

She said, as she prepared to go back into the lobby, "I really don't want to worry you, Elizabeth, but do you know, I really feel in my bones that the facial would do you a world of good. I know you think it's just silly old me, but I am rather good at my job, even though it's me as says it, and if you could just relax, you'd be surprised how much better you'd feel. However," she added hastily as she saw me open my mouth, "I mustn't pester you now, my poor dear, and when you feel better, just tell me, and I'll fit you in somehow, however busy I am. The fish looks nice, I had some for lunch. Or perhaps the fried chicken. That's very American, you know, and they do it nicely here. Try the Roquefort dressing on your salad. You'll feel so much better after a meal. You do look so tired. I'm quite ashamed of myself, I really am a naughty girl."

And here she gave herself a little slap on the wrist as punishment.

By this time I was so battered that I was not sure if she were about to apply Roquefort dressing to my face, or press a fish on it. Her final remarks convinced me that I was dying. However, on the principle that nothing mattered any more, I ordered myself fried chicken and soup to start with. Eve waved me a jolly goodbye, assured me she would be back, and I saw with relief that there was another exit to the dining-room that would lead me straight into my own corridor. I would be lucky to get away with my face intact, but I was resolved to do a vast amount of dodging during my last three days here: if my travellers' cheques permitted, I would drive into Old Tucson to indulge in some Paul Ducane-free nostalgia, and that would bring me back too late for anything but bed.

I didn't see Eve again that evening. I imagine she must have been relieved: she was not there after all to saddle herself with an invalid, and an ungrateful one at that who had the temerity to prefer her own unfashionable face. I enjoyed my meal, felt a great deal better, decided I would not die yet after all, and slipped out by the side exit to go to my room, where I wrote some postcards for Daniel and my friends, and read myself quietly to sleep with a thriller I had bought in the shop.

On my way I was nearly knocked down by a small child who was skittling up and down the corridor. My balance was still insecure. I looked into the face of the little girl from Vietnam. It really was the prettiest face imaginable, the child was definitely not older than six, and if she was a Communist spy, I was my own grandmother. She was more sensibly dressed this time in denims and tee-shirt, but I could not help thinking once more that she should have been in bed. However, this view was plainly not shared by her adoptive mother, who glared at me as if I had no business to be in the little girl's way: she gathered the child protectively to her, as if to save her from me. The child clung to her, and both turned accusing faces on me, the little round clotted-cream face and the young American face, not much more than a child, herself. As a couple of Commie conspirators they did not strike me as very convincing, but I suppose Paul Ducane would call that their diabolical subtlety: no one could possibly suspect them of anything.

I said to the little girl, "What is your name?" I am not after all a kid-basher, I was upset by the combined mistrust. But the child only buried her face in the protecting waist, and the young mother said nothing at all, so I stroked the little girl's shiny black hair, said goodnight, and went into my room.

It struck me as I closed the door that perhaps they regarded me as the spy. Let Paul Ducane sort that one out, and the best of luck to him.

I stayed another three days in the Canyon before the last lap of my journey, which was to stay with friends in New York. I did not see Paul Ducane again and I managed to avoid my facial. It was all very pleasant, I felt quite well again, I did not think particularly of Steve. I took the coach tour and two more drives. I had a farewell drink with Eve the last night, and she looked rather despairingly at my tanned face, but did not mention the matter of a facial again. My plane, after all, went at a quarter to nine in the morning, and even someone as zealous as Eve had to see there would not be much time.

Only she said, as I walked back to my room, "I'll leave you my telephone number in New York and, if you give me yours, I can contact you when I'm in London. We run a nice little line," she said, optimistic to the last, "in perfumes and cosmetics that I'm sure you would love for Christmas presents. I think in any case I may be coming over to London for a few months, so we can meet there."

I wrote down her telephone number and later threw it into the wastepaper basket. I had no doubt whatsoever that she hung on to mine. This has aroused all my native obstinacy. It is almost a kind of rape, and I will not have that facial, I will not, even if she turns up on my doorstep with all her beastly eye-shadow and graded lipsticks.

As for my stay in New York, that is nothing to do with this story, and when my three weeks' holiday was over, I arrived back safely at Heathrow, to be met by Daniel, and the atmosphere of a general election which I had forgotten all about.

Chapter 4

DANIEL WAS WAITING FOR ME AS I CAME OUT OF THE CUSTOMS, loaded down with duty-free perfume, duty-free drink and a tangle of presents for the children. I was at least walking on my own two feet, though still with a tendency to hold on to whatever was available, and I could see from his face that my face, even if unmade-up, was back to normal, for his look of apprehension was replaced by one of acute relief. The beard was now in full splendour, red and glowing, complete with sideburns, and he had grown his hair longer too so that it was as if he were enveloped in a hirsute halo.

He saw me looking at him, scowled then laughed. "Vanda likes it," he said. "I think myself it's rather distinguished."

I only said, "Are you all right, Daniel?"

He said, "I should surely be asking you that: Are you all right, Elizabeth? You look much better. I gather the holiday's done you good. I hope you had no recurrence of the trouble. You seem to be moving reasonably well. How are the legs? I've no doubt you overtired yourself."

"You make me feel like a corpse on the dissecting slab. Oh, I'm fine but I'm glad to be home. It was a strange holiday. I saw my ghost town and it was full of ghosts. Did the children get my cards? The cowboy one was for Mario."

"I don't know what else you'd expect in a ghost town," said Daniel who was not really listening and looking out for his car. "They're devils here," he said. "They'd slap a ticket on you for taking time to breathe. What the hell have you got in this case? It weighs a ton."

"Whisky for you," I said, "and perfume for Vanda, so don't be ungrateful."

"From the feel of it you've bought a whole distillery." Daniel had found his car, and hoisted my case into the boot. We set off for home. The entry from most airports is always unattractive, but I found myself so delighted to be back that I stared out of the window at what must be the most unappealing view in all London, in a kind of patriotic fervour.

"I hope you are voting Conservative," said Daniel.

"What are you talking about? You know my politics perfectly well, and in any case — "

"It seems to have escaped your attention that there is an election next week."

"Oh God, is there?" And I saw that three weeks can provide a most extraordinary gap in one's life. It was such a small sliver of time yet it seemed like a year to me: things like elections, which would normally interest me very much, were so remote that I could not really assimilate them. However, I could not let this pass, so I said as I have said many times before, "You're not still all Tory, are you?"

"What else could I be?" asked Daniel. He is indeed a staunch Conservative, but fundamentally is not interested in politics at all. I suppose it suits his conventional nature, but it never fails to surprise me. It seems so incongruous that a woman of my age should be firmly Labour while Daniel, young and intelligent, wears his blue riband with the best: he is a firm believer in the National Health but presumably his sympathies lie with the type of patient he never sees.

I sighed and left it. There is no more point in discussing politics than religion. I suspect, however, that most people, if challenged, would find it hard to explain why they vote as they do: it is a kind of inbred principle that is often in complete opposition to one's upbringing — working-class vote Tory and the nobility Labour. But there is no point in saying so: it merely provokes a row after which we all vote precisely as we have done before. So I jabbed him gently with my elbow as a mark of mute reproach, then asked how the children were.

There were difficulties. It was chiefly Mario, who had now been requested to leave his school. They don't expel them these days, but it comes to the same thing. "It'll be all right," said Daniel, looking so much the father that it hurt me a little: he has accepted his responsibilities as he always will, with complete absorption. "He is at a difficult age. The other two are too young to take it all in. He is the only one who misses his father, for all the bastard was so unkind to him. He still looks on me as the interloper. We have had some nice little talks, and I don't think he's quite as hostile as he was. At least he no longer tries to poison me."

"What!"

"Well," said Daniel in his most clinical voice, as he steered neatly between two bad drivers determined to shove him off the road, "he did go through a phase of dropping things into my food. It was all very unsubtle, we knew he was doing it. Even if we hadn't actually seen him tipping the washing powder into my soup, we would have known something was up from his guilty expression."

"Good gracious!"

"He's stopped that, I'm glad to say. Of course it's not quite right yet. Sometimes he won't speak to me at all, and sometimes he's deliberately rude just to provoke me. But on the whole we don't get on too badly. It's a pity about the school, but I think it was largely their fault. He's not a child you can bully around. We've found him another school. I hope he'll stay there. Vanda gets very upset about it all, but then she's so sensitive."

I suddenly remembered that I had once visualised Vanda as a potential poisoner, but this was no moment to say so. I glanced at the calm, bearded face beside me, and thought that on the whole Mario was a very lucky little boy.

Daniel said, "But you haven't told me anything about your holiday. It was obviously a success. What was it really like?"

"I suppose it could be called a study in unreality."

"What on earth does that mean?"

A Liberal Party car passed us at this moment, and we both turned our heads in astonishment. It was like an ice-cream van: every few minutes it let off a fanfare of music, after which a booming voice could be heard announcing that he was the Liberal candidate. I half expected a horde of children to come pouring out of the surrounding houses, clutching their pennies in their hands. It seemed an odd kind of introduction to a potential member of parliament.

I said, waving at the car, "That!"

"Oh, that," said Daniel without interest. I don't think he even recognises the existence of the Liberal Party. "They haven't a chance," he said. "It'll probably be your beastly lot. I don't know what you're talking about anyway. What was so unreal?"

93

I knew he wouldn't really understand, and I did not think he would be interested, but I like putting things into words, it is after all my profession, so I answered, "Oh, a woman who specialises in new faces. She's a Hollywood cosmetician, and she followed me around trying to persuade me to use violet eye-shadow and have my lines removed. I had quite a fight to get away from her. She offered to do me a facial at seven in the morning."

"I hope," said Daniel severely, "you didn't listen to her."

"Do I look as if I did? The same old lines are there for all to see."

"It's appalling for the skin. I can't think why women are so stupid."

"Is it any worse than growing a beard?"

He looked sideways at me. I could see the glint of his teeth through the fur. "I see you really are better. She doesn't sound unreal to me, just nuts. Anything else?"

"Oh yes, a scare about communist spies. There was a little Vietnamese child in the hotel. It seemed that she might be a subtle case of diabolical infiltration. And of course Paul Ducane — "

This did interest Daniel. He stopped at the traffic lights. We were almost home. "Paul Ducane?" he repeated. "Good God, he must be about eighty. I remember going to see him when I was a kid. It was a Western — I don't think he ever did anything but Westerns. Wait a bit and I'll remember the title. 'Arizona something or other' — "

"*Arizona Flame.* And you do exaggerate, Daniel. He's nothing like eighty. He'd shoot you if he heard you."

"Well, he must be pretty past it. The last of the cowboys — I thought he was super when I saw him. He'd bore me to death now. How on earth did you come to meet him?"

I told him about Jericho City and the saloon bar, I even recounted something of our strange conversation. "He gave me a signed photo," I said.

We were home now, and Daniel drew up in front of my block of flats. There was fortunately a space. He turned towards me. He was smiling. "I'll take that off you," he said. "Mario would love it. He's just the right age for that sort of nonsense. I would have wanted it myself when I was young."

I glanced at this old man of thirty-three. I wish he wouldn't always talk as if his youth were so far away, yet in a sense he is

94

right, he no longer has the time to be young, what with his work, his wife and three children, one of whom is a problem boy. But I only said as I got out of the car, "Of course he shall have it. I'll look for it when we get in. It's probably somewhere at the bottom of my case, but even if I can't dig it out now, I'll post it on to him. Do you think he'll have the least idea who Paul Ducane is? I can't exactly see him a riot in Italy, even in his prime. His love scenes were always terrible."

"Oh, he'll never have heard of him. But it'll be quite enough to know that he was once a famous film-star. It will cheer him up. Sometimes," said Daniel, heaving out my case, "he worries me quite a lot. I know it's tough on a kid of his age to switch fathers in mid-stream, but he does take life so seriously. And daddy Salvatore was a horror from all accounts. I think Vanda is still frightened of him. She has laid in supplies for you, by the way. You won't starve on your first evening. She's made you one of her casseroles, ossi bucci, I think. You only have to heat it up, and there's some salad and fruit as well."

It was wonderful to be home again, the central heating was switched on, and it all felt cosy. I collapsed into an armchair while Daniel made some coffee. He remarked a few minutes later as we were drinking it, "Vanda's really very fond of you." He said this with some surprise. I was a little surprised too. "She's sent you a little homecoming gift. It's a funny sort of thing to give you, and I told her I didn't think it was quite your line — "

"Oh Daniel, really!"

"What's wrong with that? It's true, isn't it? You never wear this kind of thing. Here it is, anyway. I think it's something of her own. She seemed very keen on your having it. I got the impression it's something you've already talked about. But she went all secretive on me, so I didn't push it."

I opened the little parcel. It was prettily wrapped up. Vanda always did this kind of thing with elegance. It was a little silver charm bracelet. Daniel was perfectly right, though I would never have admitted it to him. It was not at all the kind of thing I wore, It was never intended for a middle-aged woman. Young girls wore these charm bracelets and added to them as the years went by. I could have given something like that to Sophy. For a moment I could not imagine why Vanda had chosen to give me this, but I at once fastened it on my wrist — where, I must admit, it looked rather incongruous — and said enthusiastically that it was charming, I would ring Vanda up later that evening.

Only as I said this the dim memory of our last conversation came back to my mind, and I suddenly shivered, so perceptibly that Daniel noticed and came instantly to my side. He may not be perceptive in some things, but he is a doctor, and this to him was a symptom that must at once be analysed and, if possible, alleviated.

"You're overtired," he said. "I knew the journey would be too much for you. It's all that time lag and things. We'll have the fire on as well for a little while, and I'm going to pour you out a drink. You didn't have any recurrence of the symptoms, did you? I never know if I can believe you. Those tablets I gave you — I bet you never touched them."

"I'm fine, I'm fine. Don't fuss me, darling. Yes, I am tired, and as you say, there's the time lag: I believe it knocks over tough businessmen. I'll go to bed early and be as right as rain in the morning. Isn't that a stupid phrase? Right as rain! It must mean something."

Daniel did not answer this little outburst. He gave me the kind of look that I suspect he gave Mario when he caught the little boy pouring Daz into his soup. He did as he said, put on the fire — I am not used to central heating, and I do like something to look at, I know it's psychological but that's the way it is — and poured us both out drinks. I noticed that he had bought me a bottle of whisky. This was naughty of him because he could not possibly afford it, but it was considerate of him all the same. Anyway I had a bottle for him in my case, and I suggested he opened it to take this out, as well as the presents for Vanda and the children.

He still wore the expression that I knew only too well. He had something to discuss with me and, being Daniel, he was not going until he had got it off his chest. I think he makes a good husband, but he must be quite difficult too. He is always right, he is not over-tolerant of feminine vapours, and he certainly has this marked tendency to speak his mind. It was Vanda who had once liked to talk things over: by now, I suspect, she must occasionally be weary of a husband who resolutely does the same.

They have both changed a great deal. I can see in Daniel now the man he is going to be. He does not greatly resemble his father, who was a far gentler person. Perhaps he is like the mother I have never known. Certainly the romance has been knocked out of him, which may be a good thing. It has never been knocked out of me, and sometimes I think this is a pity. This is no world for the romantic sentimentalist. The romance has gone from Vanda too. Sometimes when I think of the aggressively hostile, sexy young woman who came to my house to assert herself, to say, He is mine, he is nothing to do with you any more, keep off the grass, a tall and arrogant girl who brushed me aside and defied me with every look of her dark eyes, I find it hard to equate her with Vanda as she is now, polite, a little nervous of Daniel, a little nervous of me too, anxious to help as much as she can, always in agreement. And sending me a silver charm bracelet —

Garlic is very good against evil spirits. And silver too.

"Why do you keep on shivering?" demanded Daniel. He took my wrist in his hand and grumbled audibly because he had selected the one with the charm bracelet. "I can't think why women wear these things," he said, then, having pushed the obstruction aside, proceeded to take my pulse, his eyes on his watch as he did so.

I asked, "Do you believe in evil spirits?"

"That seems normal enough to me — What? Of course I don't. Unless you mean bad whisky." Daniel laughed as he said this. He really has very little sense of humour. Then he said abruptly, "Don't be so silly. These things are all in the mind."

But people are never so imperceptive as one fondly imagines, and Daniel in his own way knows me very well. He sat opposite me, his drink in his hand, and I could see that he was about to speak his mind once again, only this time he looked nervous, which was ominous, indicated this was something serious.

I said, "I don't think you can quite dismiss it like that. And I don't really mean evil spirits; that is quite the wrong way of putting it. There's a primitive people in New Guinea, I've forgotten their name, who believe that in the forest there is a world of spirits that mirrors the world of men. That's more the kind of thing I'm talking about. I don't think there's anything evil about them. I don't believe in witches and vampires, though I'd rather die.than sleep in a haunted room." I saw his lips begin to twitch. I said crossly, "Well, would you?"

"Of course I would," said Daniel.

And of course he would too, and sleep as soundly as a log. If a headless ghost appeared and laid a clammy hand upon his brow, Daniel would simply push it away, turn over and go to sleep again. I on the other hand would be dead from fear after the first half hour. But there was no point in pursuing this, only I could not leave it quite alone so I said, "I do feel a bit haunted. I don't know why. Perhaps it was that ghost town. It was very strange, not so much because it was a ghost town but because it had been re-created. I don't think I liked that very much. That was what made it so unreal, not the ghosts of the miners and the cowboys, but the phoney people strutting around it."

Daniel was chewing his lower lip. He was plainly not interested in Jericho City. Then he said, flushing up a little in that easy way of his, "Elizabeth, I hope you don't mind, I don't mean to be rude, but could I ask you about — about Steve?"

Then, as a little astonished I prepared to answer him, he went on quickly, "I think I've been bloody silly. It's like treating you as if you weren't a human being. Do you mind me talking like this?"

"No, of course not. In fact I'm delighted. If I don't mention him to you, it's because I'm frightened of embarrassing you. After all, I'm old enough to be your mother — "

"Not quite!"

"Well, maybe I'm one of the precocious ones. More or less, anyway. I do know how it is. When one is young, the idea that older people — how shall I put it? — enjoy themselves, isn't done. It's rather indecent."

"I'm not as bad as all that surely," mumbled Daniel. He was by now a fiery red.

"No. You're not bad at all. It's only natural. When you're twenty, anyone of thirty is past it. It's only when you get to about forty that things begin to level out. Oh darling, I'm not making fun of you. What do you want to ask? I'll do my best to answer you, only you must realise that the inhibitions are not entirely one-sided. The young mayn't like hearing about such things but the old don't always like talking about them. That's all. It's very simple."

Daniel said after a long pause, "What was he like? Would I have liked him? I only met him a few times, and then it was just for half an hour or so. He was a tall, gangly sort of chap, with an American accent. That's all I remember."

I did not for one moment believe that Daniel really wanted to hear about Steve, at least not in that way. If nothing else, there was, as I had just said, an enormous age gap. Nowadays it is all less important than it was when I was young, but after all when I was a girl — in such a connotation I always want to pronounce it "gal" — it was just after the war, we had not fully awakened to the new freedom, permsoc. and all, and the generations kept to themselves, each disapproving of the other or making fun of it. Now, when old men of eighty marry teenage girls and even raise a family, we do not mind so much, or pretend we do not. Old women take young lovers, and we accept it, especially if they are well-known people. It always helps to be a well-known person: you can get away with murder and sometimes do. But a conventional young man like Daniel prefers even now to think of older people as a race apart, and this sudden interest in Steve was nothing what-soever to do with being bloody silly: it was simply that he still was determined to find out what had been the matter with me, and that intuition — which is nothing to do with intelligence or emotion — told him that it had its root in Steve.

Well, I wanted to know too, and of course it was something to do with Steve. So I decided to play along. I answered him as he wanted, only I could not entirely like it: I was digging down into the dust and God knows what I would disinter.

"I met him at a party," I said. "In my world we tend to meet people at parties. It is never a good idea. The men you meet, once they discover you're unattached, either think of you as a good lay and make the kind of vulgar pass they would never dare to do in other circumstances, or else they assume you're past it and go to bed with a good book. It's rather like visitors in other people's houses who are meticulously tidy in their own but who, when they come to you, stub their cigarettes out on your Sheraton table and grind broken glass into the carpet."

I looked up for a moment after this tasteless outburst, then instantly away. Poor Daniel! He has never really known how vulgar I can be. He was getting a great deal more than he had asked for. The beard was a useful camouflage, but it could not hide his disturbance, and his colour was still high. But now I had started I could not stop. I had never really talked much of Steve to anyone. When we are young we talk interminably, and sometimes when we are older too, but in this case I always knew deep within me that it could not last, and what I had to hold on to was so slight, so frail, that I dared not dissipate its strength. To confide in a friend, however near or dear, would be to set out in cold, blunt words something that hardly existed, yet which was immeasurably important to me: far from helping me it would destroy the little that remained of my own self-confidence.

I said, "I don't mean to recount our personal progress. It wouldn't interest you, and I think I don't even want to discuss it. Affairs of this kind have a dreadful similarity. Almost all of them could be described as classic cases. You've only to read the novels in which young women write about their first traumatic love-affair. They are all the same. To the female involved it is something unique — the first meeting, the ecstasy, the first quarrel, then the gradual diminuendo and the ugliness of the final parting. It's like the standard magazine plot: boy meets girl, girl loses boy, girl finds boy again. Only of course it isn't, it's boy meets girl, girl loses boy, period. So we'll leave all that. It doesn't matter any more. Only I too think it was different, I suppose we all do. The ugliness was there, my God and how, the pain, the waste of emotion, but there was something else, I swear there was; there was through everything a curious kind of bond that even his death in a ditch left intact."

Daniel, huddled there under the barrage, woke up suddenly at this, and I saw the clinical eye fixed upon me. Middle-aged women who speak in this preposterous way of psychic bonds beyond death possibly need certifying, but when these women are struck down with an inexplicable paralysis, it becomes medically interesting.

"Well," I said, "we met at a party, and in a way we parted at a party. Parted at a party! It sounds like a comic gag. There weren't many parties in between unless you call drinking a party. Steve drank a great deal, he made me drink too. If I sometimes seem to fall on the bottle like a baby, that is why. But he was not just a drunk. He wrote books. He wrote one enormously good book and, if you think that's patronising, just consider how many people do. Most of us who write, write a great many mediocre books. A few of them are slightly better than the rest, and that is the best that can be said. Steve's one great book really was great. It was magnificent. He never again wrote anything that came near to it."

"Why not?" said Daniel. It was the first thing he had said.

"I don't know." I could hear the disbelief in my own voice. "Truly I don't. It was about the Normandy landings. He was there of course. It was completely real, so real that, as you read it, you could hear the infernal row of war, the bangs and crashes and shouts and cries, the desperate footsteps, the silence of death. I think all the people in that book are now dead. They were Steve's friends. I suppose in war friendship must be intense because it's likely to be so brief. If you are going to die together, you must know each other. It was a wonderful and unbearable book. He will be remembered by it. At least I hope so. The life of a book is so transitory that one can never be sure. I can think of so many books that meant a great deal to me, and no one has heard of them now. I remember being furious — There was a woman in my youth, you'll never have heard of her, so I won't bother you with the name, who wrote historical novels. At least, they were a kind of fictionalised biography, but they were superbly done, and superbly documented too. I·loved and admired them. They had an extraordinary humanity. It was almost as if she lived in the period she described, and knew the characters as friends. She died last year. She must have been a very old woman. She had an obituary of two lines. It said that Miss So-and-So, a writer of romantic historical fiction, died yesterday. It was horrid. It wasn't true. I was so angry that I nearly wrote an abusive letter, but it wouldn't have done any good, even if they'd printed it. Perhaps in a few years' time Steve will be forgotten too."

"I've never read the book," said Daniel.

"Then you ought to. I'll lend it you, if you swear black and blind that you'll return it."

"I always return books," said Daniel rather smugly.

People usually say that. They don't. Daniel doesn't, either. He must have at least a score of my books in Amersham, but of course it doesn't really matter, and I have far too many books anyway. But this book mattered, and I hesitated, only it meant something to me that Daniel should read it, I believed he would like it, it was the kind of thing that interested him. I got up and went over to the big bookcase at the back of my bed. I knew Daniel was watching me, was noting that I knew exactly where the book was. I took it out. It still had its jacket. I opened it. Steve had inscribed it, which was unusual in him:

he never dedicated his books to anyone, and he disliked writing in them. When people wrote to him, asking for his autograph, he never answered. I said once that I thought this was arrogant and discourteous, and he simply answered, Why should I, what good will it do them? But he had consented to write in this, and he did so in a curiously formal way. He wrote, 'Written under protest to one of my dearest friends.' Then he signed it. The signature was almost illegible. He had a wild, almost illiterate handwriting. He was anything but illiterate, but an office boy would have managed better.

I handed the book to Daniel, who immediately looked at the fly-leaf. Then he said, "I really will return it."

"You'd better!"

"What else did he do? I mean, did he have a job or anything?"

"Not really. He was a full-time professional writer. He did a certain amount of journalism, and he broadcast on one of the American radio stations."

"What sort of career did he have before the war?"

"Well, he was pretty young, you know. He was only eighteen when the war broke out. He was at school in England." And I mentioned a well-known public school where Steve had been unspeakably wretched: I could not imagine anyone who would hate a public school more. "His parents were in the diplomatic service. He lived for a while in London. I once went to have a look at the house. It was just a very ordinary suburban kind of place. He joined up here the moment the war came. He was a prisoner-of-war in one of the more notorious camps. I think he was pretty badly beaten up there. He never had any respect for authority, German or otherwise. He escaped. One day I'll tell you the story if it interests you. After the war he went up to Oxford. They did that kind of thing with ex-servicemen, though of course they were usually older than the rest of the students. He was at Balliol. He got a double-first. He was, when he surfaced over the drink, a very brilliant man, though he wasted his talents terribly." Then I said, "He lived for a time in Arizona, in a place called Flagstaff. I saw it. It's not much. He spoke with a western accent, though sometimes I think he put it on mainly to annoy people. He liked annoying people."

"Do you know," said Daniel, "you are telling me this backwards?"

102

"Am I? Yes, I suppose I am. It's natural enough. A person whose background is not known to you personally, tends to recede as he grows younger. It would be the same with me. You only know me from the time I married your father."

"What else? There must be more than that," said Daniel, ignoring this.

"Well, of course, but I don't think it would interest you. You hardly want to know what he was like as a lover, do you?"

I saw the colour seep up again, and was sorry: there was no reason to upset Daniel because I was upset myself. I said quickly, "He was always fighting. He was a dreadful fighter, especially when drunk. There were a great many women too — "

Daniel exclaimed angrily, "Why on earth, Elizabeth, couldn't you fall for someone more civilised? I mean, you're a civilised sort of person. You don't fight people — "

"I'm only five foot, love, and rather unsteady on the pins. How could I?"

"You don't get drunk — "

"No. Not really."

"Well then?"

"Oh it's nothing to do with it. Nothing at all. Women far more civilised than me fall for maniacs and ruffians. It's the way we're made."

"Well, I don't understand it," said Daniel, then, "I suppose I'd better be on my way. Vanda will be wondering what's happened to me. You didn't tell me about his wives. You said once he was married. What became of them? They must have had a pretty lousy time."

He was gathering up what he tended to call his loot: the things I had brought back with me. There was quite a pile, not only the drink and perfume, but a number of things for the children. It is always pleasant buying gifts for children, and I tend to go a little mad so that the result looks like Christmas and birthdays combined.

I said, "I really know nothing about the second wife. I never met her. The first, I gather, was a neurotic girl with an obsession about his being unfaithful, who made his life a misery and refused to have children. He loved children."

"Did the second wife have any?"

"Yes."

Yes. I saw Daniel looking at me, but I could not say any more. To me this was becoming almost indecent, I would not

103

go on with this preposterous monologue. I began to talk of Vanda and the children, hoped I would see them soon, they must all come down one weekend. And so on. And so forth —

Daniel said as he kissed me goodbye, "You're tired. I should never have made you talk like this, after a long journey too. I'm a selfish bastard. Will you be all right?"

"Of course I'll be all right, idiot. Thank you for meeting me, and thank you for laying in supplies. I'll ring Vanda tomorrow morning to thank her. You're very sweet to me, the pair of you."

"You eat your casserole like a good girl, and go to bed early."

"I'll do that. Goodbye, Daniel, and thank you again."

"I'll ring you later in the week."

"Okay, love."

And he was gone in his usual violent hurry, and I was left, to think of all the things I had not told him.

The second wife. Joanna was her name. That incredible scene in the pub. There were a great many scenes in pubs. Until I met Steve I do not think I set foot in a pub more than once or twice a year, and then it was always to meet an editor or my agent. Pubs were Steve's favourite rendezvous, and during the two years we knew each other I think I spent more time waiting, oh God, waiting, waiting, waiting, with the one glass in front of me, fury and desolation within me, and people around looking at me — or so it seemed — with derisive amusement. Why didn't I walk out? Ask any woman that. There is no sane answer. Then there was the party. The second meeting. And the third and the fourth — Daniel would not believe a word of it, if he did he would begin to think I was mad, but then, despite what he had just said, he really thinks of me as a kind of mother, a little perhaps as a friend, but chiefly as a middle-aged woman too old to be so emotionally involved.

One thing I am resolved on, and that is that in my next reincarnation I shall not wait at all. The phone may ring, the postman knock, the pub table may be empty — but I shall not be there. Indeed, this has had such a profound effect on me that I am permanently nervous at all meetings, and invariably turn up for an appointment half an hour too early, and catch the train before the one for which I have a ticket.

Next day the ghosts receded. I slept well, I felt less tired, and

104

I began to pick up my ordinary life again. The election thudded around me, but I could not summon up the slightest interest. Loudspeakers bellowed in the street, two people called on me, a variety of literature poured through my letter-box into the wastepaper basket; normally this kind of thing fascinates me, but now it held as much reality for me as Jericho City. I did not even type my duty envelopes, though I will say in my own favour that it would have been rather late. I used to enjoy those envelopes, though I knew well enough that nobody would read the contents. It was like taking the lid off a district and peering down, with perfect justification, into the private lives beneath. I did this once for my own district, and for some time afterwards, whenever I was out shopping, used to think with a kind of wry delight how horrified people would be to learn what I knew about them. I knew who lived with whom, how many people were illicitly in one flat, I discovered that groups of people, old, foreign, professional, tended to live near each other. It made a very dull job almost exciting. But this year I did not even trouble to contact my committee rooms: I would record my vote and that would be that.

I thought a great deal about ghost towns, and decided that next week I would go to the British Museum Reading Room to start my research.

I discovered, purely by chance, that a Paul Ducane movie was playing at the local flea-pit, so I went to see it. It was very dull indeed. I gazed at a much younger Paul doing all the routine things, riding, shooting, drinking, fighting and, at the very end, bestowing a decent kiss upon a young woman who was so nebulous that I now have no memory of her at all. I hadn't realised what a wooden actor Paul Ducane had been. There was no expression on that handsome face, and he moved like an elegant robot. Only the voice jarred me, for that had not changed, it was the voice of the old man in a phoney bar, talking of communists and calling me doll. What would Daniel have said to that? There was as much reality in that film as in an old postcard, and it was clear that reality for Paul Ducane was in that mock-up saloon, it was there that he played the real hero, was the real hero, Stetson, dude shirt, boots, gun and all.

I wonder again as I wondered then, what kind of life his wife must lead. And his children — Does he ever come to life for his children, or does he simply look on them as minute cowboys with himself as the foreman? It must be terrible to live and sleep with a ghost, spend your nights in ghostly copulation, received the ghostly kisses, pour out the morning coffee for a cardboard figure sitting opposite you. Then as I think this, a coldness comes upon me, almost as if I had done the same.

This of course is entirely absurd, and I realise that I am not yet fully recovered from my illness, though I get around reasonably well, do my work, and am no longer so tired. Life begins to trundle on in its normal way. Once I even met Timmy Hills in the High Street. I do not know whether he saw me or not. We both, after that one flicker of a glance, looked the other way. I crossed the road and went down a side turning: this was not where I wanted to go, but the thought of that voice and smile chilled and horrified me. I daresay he saw me and decided there was nothing left to say. He had done his little bit of mischief, why God only knows, he had been snubbed for his pains and I could only hope he would never have the satisfaction of knowing how much he had harmed me.

I set off for the British Museum the next Monday. I took a taxi. I still cannot walk far, and I don't like getting on buses which never nowadays make the faintest attempt to wait. I am obviously becoming a hypochondriac, I should compel myself to take a bus — and as I make these worthwhile resolutions, I hail a taxi which, after my holiday, I cannot really afford.

As a study in unreality the British Museum Reading Room takes some beating. I have gone there for years now, and find it entirely changeless: the same people still hem me in, I am sure they sleep at night in the stacks, dust themselves down in the morning and take up their regular place, sustained, I suppose, by a snack lunch in the canteen so that they never leave the premises.

There is the strange, ageless little woman with mad eyes who, summer and winter, always wears drill shorts, socks and a dun-coloured sweater. She has her hair bobbed in the way we wore it at school, taken back with a slide at one side. Once, when I had been working there for several weeks, I thought it would be a courtesy to acknowledge her presence, so I wished her good morning. She gave me such a look that I never dared speak to her again. It was a glare of manic fury. She did not answer. I felt her eyes boring through me as I returned to my

106

desk. There is the dapper, neat little old man ceaselessly researching, there are the earnest oriental students who must queue up for they always have the best seats, and there are the eccentrics who talk to themselves, wear peculiar clothes and make wild gestures. And there are always a couple of furtive types who, so I imagine, are absorbed in some esoteric pornography, for they never look at you and slide away if you seem to be looking at them.

One of the librarians told me once that some of these regulars can be very naughty. When the mad fit takes them they write rude words in precious books. If they are suspect characters their books are always carefully examined when returned. If there, are four-letter words in the margin, the miscreants are banned from the Reading Room for some specified period, the most dreadful punishment imaginable. When at last the culprit is allowed to return, he is well-behaved for a long while: when he breaks out again the punishment is repeated.

I see as I come in that the lady in her shorts is there, also the dapper gentleman. Most of the desks are taken, but I find one at the end, a long way from the desks and catalogues, which is a nuisance, for it means I shall have to cart my books back almost the length of the room. However, I select my books, which takes me over an hour, then return to my desk.

In the old days I would probably have gone out into Great Russell Street and wandered about the bookshops. The Reading Room takes anything up to three hours to produce the books required. But I am still too exhausted to climb up and down the steps again, nor do I feel like wandering about the Museum itself. The shelves that run round the room are always interesting, so I stroll over to look at them, thinking I might reread some of the eighteenth-century law reports or start looking up people in the who's whos.

My eye is caught by the university calendars.

One is compelled to wonder from time to time if anything happens by chance. I could say, if I were whimsical enough, that Steve was behind me, propelling me towards this particular shelf. But then I see no reason for him to do so, for what I was to discover was in no way to his credit. On the other hand I must think, I will always think, that what was to happen originated in him, and the reason for that, indeed the whole business, is so far beyond me that there is no point in discussing it.

Whatever the reason, a sudden urge came upon me to take out the Oxford Calendar for the year 1949, when Steve was up at Balliol, to see his name there among the first-year students, and then three years later to see the record of his degree.

It was very childish. It was not the kind of thing a staid, middle-aged woman ought to be doing. It would have been fine for a young girl in the passion of her first love-affair, when anything to do with the beloved has glamour, even the mending and washing of his socks. I do not know what Daniel would have thought of such lunacy. However, I was quite excited at the prospect and, with the two university calendars under my arm, returned to my desk.

There was a solemn Japanese student on my left, and a ramshackle girl with unwashed long hair on my right. I had already noted that the boy was studying medicine and that the girl was interested in ancient maps. Neither looked capable of indulging in such childish behaviour as mine.

There was still no sign of the books I had ordered, so I prepared to amuse myself with the calendars. I turned to the end of the first volume to find the correct page: all the students' names were listed. I looked for OLSEN, Stephen David George. His parents apparently preferred the staid, orthodox names. I could not see it. I thought I must have missed it, so I started on all the O's and went methodically through them, even making sure with my forefinger that I was missing nothing out.

It was not there. There was Stanley Oldworthy, James Thomas Olford and Arthur Olpratt. There was no Stephen David George Olsen. There was no Olsen of any kind.

It was in its own way a great shock, and my illness had left me over-susceptible to shocks. I felt almost dizzy with it: for a second I had to hold on to my desk. Then I saw that I was being ridiculous. Even university calendars make mistakes. The proof-reading of such a book must be as complicated as that of a telephone directory, the name had been left out and would of course be in the college list.

I found Balliol College at last. I am easily sidetracked, and I suspect that something within me held me back. I looked down various other lists, made a mental note of some of the more extraordinary names, in case one day I should actually write the novel I always threatened to produce — and it was some five minutes later that I came to Balliol and the History section. Steve read history. I must admit that this always seemed to me a little odd, for it was not a subject he showed much interest in, and once when I asked him for some information to help me with an article, made vague promises that he did not keep.

I looked down the list of First Year history students. There was no mention of Steve. Then, when I had gone through the list three times, a fierce determination possessed me. I went through the list of every school, English, Languages, Mathematics, Electronics, Law, and everything else. There was one Olsen there, among the Natural History students — I cannot think of anything more unlikely for Steve — but his names were Charles Edward James, and I could only think that, despite the unlikely surname, he was a member of the Jacobite Society. Apart from that there was no Olsen, no Steve, there never had been a Stephen Olsen at Balliol in 1949, nor — for I checked this also — in 1948 or 1950.

I looked through 1952 for the History degrees. I knew it was absurd, but I thought I might as well. There is a bloodhound streak in my character, and I do not like being made a fool of. There was of course no record of Steve there either. It did not take me long. There were six Firsts among the History students, and none of them was Steve, nor was he among the Seconds, Thirds, Passes or anywhere at all.

Steve had not been up at Oxford.

I forgot about the ghost towns. In a way this was a ghost town. I went out of the Reading Room, out of the Museum, and into a little restaurant in a side street, where I ordered myself a lunch I did not want. I have no idea what I ate. The only alternative would have been to drink, and somehow I wanted to face this dead-sober. The librarian, when he came at last with the books I would never see, must have thought me crazy, but then they are used to crazy people, I doubt he would have thought much about it. The Reading Room is the kind of place where readers and students wander to and fro, as if books were the only thing that could moor them down. There was now simply a free desk, and it would immediately be reoccupied.

In view of what was to come I had every reason to be distressed, but when I arrived home I was a little irritated by myself, for after all this was nothing so terrible, it simply meant that Steve had lied to me. It is not pleasant to be lied to

109

by people you love, but it happens, we all lie a great deal of the time, sometimes out of politeness, mostly out of fear, and it means very little, it should mean very little.

Yet this was a monstrous kind of lie in that it was so extraordinarily unnecessary. I am well aware that like many professional people of my kind I am something of an intellectual snob. I try not to be in principle, I despise such things, but of course I instinctively assume that people read, enjoy the things I enjoy, hold reasonably humanitarian views, like discussing things in detail. I don't know. I don't at least put on any kind of act, nor do I expect other people to do so. I always considered, will always consider, that Steve had a much finer brain than myself: I have a discursive mind that leaps from subject to subject, seldom dealing with anything in depth, I would have done splendidly in the eleven plus, while Steve, far deeper, far more solid, would probably have failed, if only because he would have read into the problems something that was not really there. It certainly mattered nothing to me if he were up at a university or not. And I would never have expected him to have gone to an English university: it would have been simpler and safer for him to have said that he was up at Harvard or Yale: if he had said that, I would never have known, indeed it would never have entered my head to question it.

He talked a great deal about Oxford. He always said he was happier there than he had ever been in his life.

I was up at Oxford myself. Oh yes, that is perfectly true. You can if you wish check on me in the university calendar, and there you will find Elizabeth Ingram, English Literature, a rather poor second. I was in no way an exemplary pupil. I did not work very hard, but I enjoyed myself, I did not actually bring disgrace on the family, and I learnt how to learn, how to read, how to obtain information, I learnt too how extraordinary is the range of English literature and the English language.

I was up at Lady Margaret Hall, which we called L.M.H., and the year was 1945: I came down in 1948. It was very different then from what it is now. We did not invite our boy-friends in at weekends to sleep with us and share our breakfast, we were hemmed in by innumerable regulations to protect our virginity, and we were really very young compared to modern standards. In the end of course we behaved exactly

110

as everyone behaves now: virginities were lost like umbrellas, and vicars' daughters, away for the first time in their lives from papa and home, took after the first staggered gasp to a great many things that the vicarage would not have wanted to know. If the boy-friends did not come officially to breakfast, we visited them unofficially after supper, and we sneaked in over garden walls and crept back to our rooms: I think we had more fun than the permsoc. realises, because it is always more exciting to do something that is forbidden. If apples had grown free in Eden, Eve would never have looked at them. But we were young in our own way. It was all so new and strange, from drinking sherry to punting on the Isis, working in the Bodleian to coffee in the Kardomah. There was the English tutor we all fell in love with, there were some horrible exams, and there was the permanent pleasure of sitting up in the small hours, discussing everything in the world and beyond.

I was very happy there, and did not do so badly after all: it was not that I didn't enjoy working, it was simply that there was so much else to do.

Steve said, "1949 — So we missed each other by just one year."

Oh Steve, I wish you hadn't said that, I wish I didn't remember it.

We missed each other by just one year.

This was at the beginning. I think Steve really loved me at the beginning. For one thing we were so bound to each other, by a strange kind of E.S.P. that frightened me a little and which he refused to admit. Later, though the bond remained, the love became on both sides a kind of reluctant obsession, but at the beginning, for the briefest period, we were friends as well as lovers, and we could hold this kind of conversation.

He said this to me one happy day, one really happy day, when he called for me unexpectedly in his ramshackle Citroen — not the elegant kind that looks like a fish, but the tanklike taxi sort that bulldozes its way along.

I was not expecting him. The bond did not always work that way. Once or twice it worked very strangely indeed, but at that moment I was not thinking of him particularly. I suppose in a way he was always in my mind, but I was busy on an article that was already late — I did not do my column those days, I only started it in the second year of our acquaintance — I was typing away, and when the bell rang I did not think it was Steve at all.

111

He came in, looking very pleased with himself, said he was going to take me out, we would drive out to the country, there was a nice pub he knew, and afterwards we might perhaps call on some friends of his.

There always was a nice pub he knew, but at that moment I would not have cared if it had been a milk-bar. So I slammed on the cover of my typewriter, the article would be even later, and in a little while we were driving in the direction of Sussex.

It was a nice day. It was a good day. We talked. We drank at the nice pub he knew, then we drank again at another nice pub he knew, and ended up at a third nice pub where we had lunch. It was fitting that our last two desperate meetings should also be in pubs, but then that was Steve's milieu: it was not mine, but it was inevitable that we should end as we had begun.

I do not remember how we came to talk of Oxford. I have never, until recently, liked to go back in time, and it was after all a great many years ago for both of us. But in that bright afternoon of our love the name came up, and it was an extraordinary delight to me to know that Steve had been there just after myself.

We missed each other by just one year.

He certainly knew Oxford. Of that there can be no dispute. He spoke of it, with the utmost affection, and if he knew more pubs than I did and less of the other attractions, that was simply his way. He even knew the tutors — How could he know them? He must have lived there, had friends there, perhaps attended some seminar. But he talked knowledgeably of this and that, and the only slightly jarring note came when he spoke of a barmaid who worked at some country pub outside the town. I knew the village if not the pub, but then barmaids do not interest me, I look on things from a different angle.

Do you know, even then I was not quite sure about that barmaid, for all that Steve went on and on about her throughout the entire lunch.

I remember her very well. She was a simple, gentle, amenable girl with large breasts. He referred to the breasts several times. I personally dislike this mammalian cult, these film stars with extraordinary measurements, and I sometimes suspect that men who harp so on this particular female embellishment, were probably weaned too early, and developed over-maternal anxiety symptoms as a result. There was, I remember, a minor star whose only real claim to fame was her chest measurement, and who was infuriated once in Australia when someone in the audience cried, "Show us your tits, love," instead of asking her to sing. I think she had no right to complain, apart from the small fact that she could not sing. If one relies on a vulgar gimmick, one is not entitled to resent being regarded as a freak. Such women always remind me of a prize cow I once saw at a cattle show, whose udders were virtually trailing on the ground. I am not suggesting that Steve's barmaid was a freak, but this coupled with her sweet, accommodating nature, made me look down with some reserve into my beer. These simple, earthy country girls usually have their sole existence in a certain kind of novel: back to nature and into bed they represent to my mind the kind of thing that may be attractive on paper but which in real life would be a dead bore. And Steve was only too easily bored. Besides, these days barmaids have to be tough to survive, a sweet country girl would be unlikely to choose such a profession. They are less likely to say in a burring country accent, "Come to bed, m'dear, and tell me all your troubles," than simply, "Half a pint of bitter, love?" and leave it at that.

I grew very tired of this barmaid, but I was too happy to protest, and after all she was well in the past. By now, if she ever existed, she would probably be married, and, as simple girls of this kind rarely trouble about contraception, she would certainly have a roomful of kids. I did not at the moment really doubt her existence, I simply thought that Steve was exaggerating, his memories sugared with the passing of time.

"I used to go over every evening," said Steve reflectively. "She was a darling girl. I don't know what I would have done without her. I'm leaving her something in my will." He looked at me, smiled and laid his hand on mine. "We're all too sophisticated now, Elizabeth. Not many people are simple and loving any more. I'll never forget her. Do you know, you would have liked her."

I knew I would do nothing of the kind, I should want to tear her eyes out, but then I am neither gentle nor amenable, and my bust is normal. Then we stopped talking about that bloody barmaid, and Steve reminisced about Balliol, his work and his tutors. Et ego in Arcadia vixi, and that was what it sounded like. He did not mention any other girls. I am certain there were plenty, for he was constitutionally incapable of living without women, and the barmaid would never have sufficed him, apart from the fact that she would only be available outside licencing hours. But he did not talk about them; indeed his memories of Oxford were curiously rhapsodic, as if it were something out of time. It certainly must have been strange after the Normandy beaches, to sink into the quiet cloistered calm of a university town. There must have been a great many like him, quiet, savage men who had been through the war, who carried their memories like medals and found it hard to adapt themselves to a world of bright young boys who had no conception of their experiences.

"What were you like up at college?" Steve asked suddenly, as we drove away from the pub into the country. I wanted to find a farm that sold fresh non-battery eggs. "I want to see the hens scrabbling," I said, "Hens in the plural. If there's only one hen, I shall feel she's just there to create an impression, while they sell battery eggs in boxes."

What were you like up at college?

I doubt if I would have interested Steve. I am not sure if he would have interested me. I was very young, almost as simple as his barmaid, but in no way so amenable. I think Steve, with his direct approach that was likely to end in bed the very first meeting, would have shocked me. I had no sexual experience whatsoever beyond the casual hug and kiss, I was very earnest in my views, knew no bad language, much less used it, indeed I was very much mummy's little girl, and a confounded prig into the bargain, with absolute standards of right and wrong. I cannot begin to imagine what would have happened if at that juncture I had met Steve. After my first year, of course, I shook down a little, began to recognise the fact that other people held different views from my own and were not on that account necessarily to be condemned. I made a great many friends, lost my home shackles and also some of my proprieties, worked rather less and lived rather more. But we seldom move entirely outside our own circle, and I still remained protected. I would have had no defences against a battered wolf like Steve, still half-sunk in the war, moving rangily from his lair, with only an innate compassion to mitigate his lack of scruples.

"I was very young," I said.

"Would I have liked you?"

"I don't know. I don't think so. I have never been pretty."

"I don't like pretty girls."

"I think you would have frightened me."

"You talk such balls. Why the hell should I have frightened you?"

And so on and so on, and at the time it seemed unimportant, it was light, trivial talk, it meant nothing, and I don't know why I have dredged it up from my memory. It was only when we were coming home that he remarked, "1949 — So we missed each other by just one year."

I remember being stupidly upset by this. I did not see myself as I then was, only somehow visualised the girl Elizabeth as I am now, vaguely younger and much more attractive. I saw us walking down the High together, meeting occasionally at lectures, having coffee in the Kardomah, driving off into the country. I would so gladly, as I am now, have climbed my college walls for Steve, crept back in the morning, broken all the absurd chaperone rules — how modern students would laugh — and probably failed all my exams. We both grew quite romantic over this charming picture, laughed at ourselves, then grew romantic again. There were not so many romantic moments after all: to think of this still gives me a little glow.

But we did not miss each other by a year. We did not miss each other at all because Steve was never there.

What was he doing during those three years? Why did he have to create this fantasy? Why did he have to lie? It would have made no difference to me. It would have made no difference to me if he had been in Sing-Sing. Perhaps he was. I was beginning to see now that I did not know him at all, and already there was growing in my mind the picture of some long, dark tunnel in which I had already set my foot, with Steve somehow at the end of it, a ghost of a man, lost, lying, no longer real.

Then I saw that all this was getting me nowhere, and decided to forget the whole matter as much as was humanly possible. It was after all none of my business — not that that on its own would have stopped me, for I am an inveterate minder of other people's business, and extremely inquisitive. But I was becoming afraid. I did not like that long, dark tunnel. Suppose other things were lies too. The war at least was not a lie, because a newspaper had commissioned the book: if Steve had not been on the beaches, he would never have been asked to write it. And I was certain he had been a prisoner-of-war, and the things he had told me about his unhappy childhood had the personal ring of truth. About his first wife I was not so sure, but that was a matter of masculine equivocation rather than fantasy: knowing Steve as I did, I could well believe him to be an impossible husband, despite his protestations.

But there was that extraordinary business about the cancer — I had forgotten that. I had chosen to forget it. And the conversation in the pub —

I think that at this point I really would have pushed the whole matter out of my mind, had it not been for Leni and Daniel. The two turned up almost at the same time — not together fortunately for they did not get on — and, though I did not realise it at the time, between them compelled me to go on, despite my doubts and fears.

Chapter 5

Leni is Austrian and considerably older than I am, though she never admits to her age. She is an oddity rather than a friend. We have known each other a little unwillingly for a great many years, we have nothing in common, yet she comes to see me at regular intervals, rings me admonishingly from time to time — "I don't seem to have heard from you for months," — and disapproves of me in a slightly quizzical fashion.

I met her after Harry's death, when I took up temporary work to prevent myself going out of my melancholy mind. She is small, very plump, with a high, brittle voice, and she lacks both the graces and a sense of humour, though she laughs more than anyone I know. She is one of those who will always say, "I do not like that coat," or, "Those slacks are too young for you." She follows such remarks with peals of laughter. Perhaps she thinks the mirth mitigates the rudeness. She is very cultured in a Middle-European way, which means that she wholeheartedly despises my journalism. There is a strange, violent kind of Middle-European culture that is the most snobbish thing I know. It is utterly uncompromising. If Leni arrives when I am listening to Radio Two as a background to my cooking, she will not only exclaim, "Oh turn that off, surely you can put on Radio Three or something," but she will actually turn it off herself and put on a Bach record. I like the Bach record, it is after all my own record, but when I am peeling potatoes and dashing about the kitchen, I don't listen seriously to anything, I find the Muzak company. Not so Leni. For Leni it is Bach or nothing. She never reads popular fiction, only that acclaimed by the critics, and to talk of a professional writer is for her a contradiction in terms. Needless to say, she wholeheartedly despises my work. I am a journalist, I write for women's magazines — how low can you get? — and as a final mark of damnation I earn money. If I starved in a garret, I suppose Leni would respect me. She would still turn up for dinner and expect to be given a nourishing meal, but at least I would be an artist, for a true artist always starves.

I once lost my temper with her. Indeed, I am always losing my temper with her, but it makes no difference, she pays not the least attention and I doubt if she even notices. However, this time I actually shouted. It was when she made the remark about the professional writer being a contradiction in terms. "What do you imagine," I exclaimed, thumping on a cushion in my rage, "that we're supposed to do? Must we starve? Do you think Shakespeare starved? I daresay he turned out a few potboilers in his time, especially with all those babies arriving." And I longed to add, If I were so artistic you wouldn't be eating such a nice dinner, but managed with a superhuman effort to restrain myself. And Leni, devouring a porterhouse steak, baked jacket potatoes and broccoli, newly in season, gave one of her high trilling laughs and cried out, "Oh, so you think you're Shakespeare now, do you?"

I said more calmly, "No, Leni, I do not think I am Shakespeare, but I do not see that it is sinful for an artist to earn money. After all, if he starves to death, he produces no more art."

"Oh, so now you're the great artist," mocked Leni, helping herself to another potato, then draining down her apple-juice. She does not drink. She says she suffers from her liver. I am not at all surprised. Once she came to a party of mine and took a sip of wine. "Oh, I'm quite tipsy," she told everyone. Afterwards she went round saying that I had been so rude to her, I hadn't introduced her to all the interesting people there.

What, apart from love and friendship, compels one to go on seeing people? I never really liked Leni from the beginning, though I only got my temporary job (as an interviewer in an employment agency) because she had an accident. Some workman dropped a hammer and hit her on the head. It was faintly comic, because the Lenis of this world tend to suffer in a comic manner, but it was very serious too, and she did not come back to work for nearly six months. However, she was soon well enough to come and supervise me, which she did until she nearly drove me out of my mind. She would totter in with a huge bandage round her head, looking very pale, and insist on sitting through my interviews with clients, her face puckered up with intense disapproval. She would barely wait until the girl was gone before crying out in a high, shrewish voice, "Now really, Mrs. Waterman — " (we were not yet on Christian name terms, we were certainly not on Christian terms) — "it was rather silly of you to say what you did about the employer. Suppose it gets back to him. He'll probably never come to us again. I think a little sense would have shown you — And really, that girl was not suitable for the job. Such a common accent, and all that make-up. Employers don't like it, you know. I wouldn't like it, myself."

I looked at that pallid, unmade-up face. Eve would have thrown her hands up in despair. I said nothing, only one day, when this had happened a dozen times, I suddenly exploded. I was after all nervous and desperately unhappy, I didn't think I was too bad at my job, and I was certainly too old to be supervised in such a fashion. I did not actually tell her to bugger off, and I don't suppose she would have understood me if I had done so, but I said flatly that either I managed my interviews my own way or I left that very moment. I did not propose in future to see my clients with Leni monitoring in the background, she could take her choice.

She was quite meek about it. I had no more trouble in the office, indeed I quite enjoyed it, and one day, if I am not regarded as too old, might even go back. But it was almost as if being told off took Leni's fancy, for after that she was always on the phone to me. It seems to me now, looking back, that we saw far too much of each other. Sometimes in the despair of boredom I took her to the theatre, struggling to find something cultural that would not shock her: another contradiction in terms. We saw *The Taming of the Shrew* together, where as a gimmick the men all wore enormous codpieces. "What a funny costume," she said. Once I took her out to supper, in a small Italian restaurant I liked: it was a simple, homely place with good, well-cooked peasant food, and there was a guitarist who played sad Italian songs. I remember Leni gazing incredulously at the proprietor, when he came round to see if all were well, and remarking, "I've never in my life been in such a place."

I don't suppose she meant anything derogatory by this, but it did sound as if the restaurant were a brothel of the most perverted kind: the proprietor was quite offended, and I never ate my pasta there again.

Leni met Steve once. It was the purest accident. I seldom introduced him to my friends, chiefly because I wanted him to myself. In any case I am not a great believer in introducing friends to friends, it so seldom works. One displays different facets of one's character to A, B and C: if A, B and C are there together, things become confused. And it was plain from the very beginning that Steve and Leni would never get on.

She knew there was somebody. She was always trying to find out who it was. "Oh," she would say if I ran to answer the phone, "that must be some gentleman, you're in such a hurry." She tried to coax it out of me. "It's always so much better," she said, "to share things, don't you think?" I didn't think this at all, I never mentioned his name to her and managed to stave her off, but one disastrous evening, when I thought Steve was on a job abroad, he turned up after we had finished our dinner.

It was our usual sort of evening. Leni ate a large meal, told me that I looked very tired, and what had I done to my hair — "I never have to do a thing to mine, it's natural," — then burst into a long, lyrical description of some book she had just read, by a Polish refugee. "Now that," she said, "is real art. I've never been so moved. What he suffered — And so wonderfully written. Of course I don't think it's really your kind of book," — and at this moment Steve walked in, using the key I had given him.

It was quite disastrous, and my only consolation is that I am sure Leni never knew how disastrous it was.

There could not possibly be a more incompatible couple, Leni, small, dumpy with that unmistakable spinster-aura, dressed as usual in a cosy, hand-knitted sweater, which was always baby-pink or baby-blue, a tweed skirt and nice sensible shoes and stockings, and Steve, over six foot, a little drunk, striding in as if he owned the place, which of course in a way he did. His light grey eyes roamed over this girlish little woman of fifty, whose eyes brightened at the sight of him, who greeted him with her customary, brittle, high-pitched laugh.

She knew at once that this must be my gentleman. She greeted him effusively, all the time looking sideways at me to see how I was reacting. Steve treated her with perfect courtesy, but I knew that the laughter was welling up inside him, and I knew too that in his own way he was amusing himself with her, though this fortunately was something she would never realise.

She refused to go. Usually she never stayed much longer than half past nine — "I have to get my beauty sleep, you know, I work, I don't just sit at home answering letters," — but this evening she sat there on the sofa, her knees wide apart, making bright, chatty conversation, with Steve listening to her as if she were royalty, assenting courteously from time to time, agreeing with all her more absurd profundities, and leaping to his feet whenever she dropped her handkerchief, wanted another cup of coffee or expressed a desire to see the news.

I was growing terrified that it was Steve who might go, for he was easily bored, and the novelty of this little rattle must be wearing thin, especially as she chose to discuss the election in her own omniscient way, shaking her head at the horrors of a socialist government. "We need a strong man in charge," she told him, "and after all these working-class types don't really have the proper background, do they?"

"I do so agree with you," said Steve, who had once worked on the old *Daily Worker*, and really, this was too much for me: I got up and poured myself out a large drink.

The bright little eyes swivelled round to me. "You know, Elizabeth," said Leni in her most whimsical manner, "you shouldn't drink so much. I realise of course it's an escape, but it is so bad for you. I don't drink at all," she said, turning back to Steve, "it just does nothing for me. But of course I lead a very full life."

"You're perfectly right," Steve said gravely. "I'm always telling her she overdoes it. At this rate she'll be an alcoholic in two or three years' time."

This from Steve was wonderful, but fortunately it was now half-past ten, and even Leni could not sit it out any longer. Steve went downstairs to get her a taxi, and she remarked to me as she tied a scarf round her head, "You needn't be jealous of me, you know. I never set out to attract my friends' friends."

When Steve returned to say the taxi was waiting, she offered him a lift, and I could have crowned her. But he politely refused, and I can only hope that, as she trotted gaily down the stairs, she heard him exclaim, "Christ, where the hell did you dig that from?"

After that I decided that my friendship with Leni — if it

could so be called — was over. I neither wrote nor rang and, when she rang herself, pretended it was a wrong number. But the Lenis of this world are not so easily discarded. A card arrived from her, one of those correspondence cards with a spray of flowers in the corner. She wrote, "It really seems to me quite extraordinary that two people who have so much in common should never see each other, especially as I am always ringing, though the phone never seems to answer. I think the least you can do is to contact me and invite me round. I'm sure it's just thoughtlessness on your part and I am not really offended, but I expect to hear from you by return."

I could not think of anything more calculated to break a friendship on the spot, especially as it might have occurred to Leni that she too had a flat, and had never once extended an invitation to me since our first introduction when she did actually ask me to tea, though this was only to instruct me in my duties. It was a cosy, fusty little flat, with heavy German furniture and a great many family photos. There was a piano, and Leni played to me. She played rather well. We ate shop cake and drank tea. I remember that I brought her some flowers, which seemed to astonish her considerably. But I was never invited again, and in the meantime Leni had eaten a great deal of steak and chicken at my expense. She did not like foreign food. It always had to be something English and plain. It is surprising how expensive plain English food can be.

However, there is something about sheer bloody cheek that carries the day, and after all the unhappy episode had occurred a long time ago. Besides, my conscience twinged me, for though Leni seemed to have the hide of a rhinoceros, she was in some ways very vulnerable, and I imagine that the brash behaviour and over-frequent laughs concealed a pretty vast inferiority complex.

Besides, I felt so bedevilled these days that I thought she might prove a distraction. I rang her that evening.

She gave a great shriek, and burst into that terrible laughter. I don't like laughter very much. I do not care for people who roar and scream, and one of the ugliest sounds in the world is the concerted, organised mirth of an invited audience at a smutty television show. However, Leni has always been a laugher, and now she was convulsed. For a minute she could not get one word out. Then she gasped, "Oh my, how I'm honoured — To be rung by the celebrated authoress! Oh, it's too much, it really is."

It really was, and I nearly put the receiver down. However, I managed to say in a suppressed fashion that I had been ill — "Oh, why didn't you tell me? What was the matter? Did you have to go to a nursing home?" — and knew at once that she visualised me being removed with screaming delirium tremens. I said it was nothing much, I was quite recovered, and I had been on holiday, and would she care to look in for a cup of coffee.

I did not feel I could endure her for the whole evening, but she said instantly, "Does that mean I'm invited to dinner?"

No, I said, I was sorry, but I was very behind with my writing, I couldn't really spare the time, but I would love to see her, perhaps she could look in after work.

She turned up on the dot of five, looking exactly as she had looked three years ago. She wore a pink sweater, this being one of her little-girl days, the same tweed suit, and she had a little pork-pie hat on the back of her head.

She shook her finger at me as she came in. I saw from the swift motions of her head that she was taking in the new flat. "You are a naughty girl," she said. "I thought you were really cutting me out of your life. Now tell me all about it. I see you've moved." And to my astonishment she closed her eyes and said in a quivering voice, "Oh, that lovely old flat."

"I think this one's a great deal nicer."

She gave me a reproachful look, then said briskly, "What has been the matter? Are you better now? You look a bit cheap, I must say."

"Oh, it was nothing much. A nervous thing, really. I think I was a bit overtired."

I realised too late that this was confirming her in her diagnosis, but she merely gave me one of her quizzical smiles, her head a little on one side, then frowned as I deliberately poured myself out a drink. "You really shouldn't," she said, sipping her own coffee, "It's so bad for you."

"I think it's very good for me. Well, Leni, how are you, and what's your news?"

But to my annoyance she did not respond as she usually did, with a flow of gossip about the employment agency, the difficult employers and those dreadful modern girls who took a job on Monday and walked out on Tuesday. She said, "I read about your gentleman."

"Yes, I expect you did. Do have a biscuit."

"So sad. I liked him, you know. We got on at once, somehow. You must have been very upset."

"Oh, it's a long time ago," I said. I detested my own casual tone, as if it did not matter, as if I no longer cared — but I could not bear to confide in this little person who, as it seemed to me in my egotism, would not understand one word of it.

One underestimates people. It is true, I think, that Leni has never fallen in love, though of course I do not know: there may have been some desperate passion hidden away under that pink-sweatered bosom. But she is not stupid, only for the most part unaware, and she has a curious, almost malicious perception of what one does not want her to see, rather like a child who listens and observes while pretending to be doing something else. She remarked, nibbling at her biscuit, "I thought he was a little peculiar."

I said savagely, for all this was getting under my guard, "I expect he was just a little drunk."

"Oh, was he? Did he drink too?"

Too! — "Like a fish."

Forgive me, Steve. I have no wish to insult you now that you are dead. I never wished to hurt you when you were alive. But this horrid little creature is trying to entrap me in emotion, I cannot bear it, I don't want her to know. I want her to think that it never really mattered and that now I have forgotten all about you.

Leni simply said, "Oh?" and frowned, trying to assimilate this new, fascinating information.

I said, rather desperately, "Do let me make you some fresh coffee. This looks quite cold." I added, "You're sure you wouldn't like a drink yourself now that we're talking so much about it."

"You know perfectly well I don't drink," said Leni quite crossly, and her face twisted with disapproval as she watched me light a cigarette. "I don't smoke either. I see no reason to shorten my life more than necessary."

I was beginning to see considerable reason, I could have shortened it that very moment. People who neither drink nor smoke are entirely sensible: both are unpleasant habits and smoking is certainly a lethal one. This does not, however, give them an excuse to be so superior. But I made no comment, then Leni remarked suddenly, "It's funny, but he just didn't seem to be quite here."

"What on earth do you mean?"

Then she broke into one of her little giggles. "Oh how fierce you look, Elizabeth. I don't know what I meant, really. It's just that I felt he wasn't with me. He didn't seem quite real. I'm odd that way. I have these intuitions. Sometimes I think I'm quite psychic." Then she told me a long story about a clairvoyant who told her she had extraordinary powers, and after that, much to my astonishment, offered to read my hand.

I refused this. I felt I could not bear Leni looking into my future. Only, because this was hitting me on the raw, because this was in its own odd way following my own thoughts, I spoke to her as I should not have done. One should never confide in the Lenis of this world, for they store it all up like hamsters, and at some future date spit it out against you. I said, "I think we are none of us quite real. Only sometimes the barriers go down, and then we don't know what we'll see. It's like that M.R. James ghost story. I don't know if you've read it, 'Is there anybody there, Count Magnus?' And the first bolt falls. It's dangerous to go on. Look what happened to the poor chap in the story."

But Leni, if for one moment she had been on my wavelength, was now a light-year away. She said, "I never read ghost stories. I think they're silly. You do look awfully tired, Elizabeth. I suppose you've not quite got over your — your illness." The pause was pointed. Then at last she began to talk about the office, no doubt because she felt it was bad for me to brood. I heard about the new interviewer, the employers with prejudices, and a really rather dreadful girl who changed jobs like underwear, only, "I don't suppose she does change it, she really smelt, Elizabeth, I mean, I don't want to be nasty, but we all noticed it — "

At this point I glanced furtively at my watch, and saw that it was nearly seven, but Leni still showed not the faintest sign of going.

I knew well enough what was happening. Leni earns a good salary, but she will never miss out on the chance of a free meal. As far as food goes, she is one of nature's scroungers. Everyone in the office was aware of this. If she had been a pub addict she would have been the kind who always slides out without paying her round. In the office we always celebrated birthdays by bringing a cake: Leni gobbled up the free cake but it was as if she had never been born, for not once in her seven years there — so I was informed — did she bring so much as a crumb.

She knew perfectly well that I always ate around seven. I suppose she thought that hunger would drive me into asking her to stay. I was equally resolved not to ask her on any account whatsoever. She sat there, always talking, her eyes moving hopefully over me, and by now I hardly troubled to answer, determined that even if she stayed till midnight I would not offer her so much as a slice of bread.

At a quarter past eight she left. She was furious with me. Her face was red with anger. She could hardly bring herself to say goodbye. I saw then that I had at last achieved it: the beautiful friendship was over. There would be no more jolly little chats on the phone, no more cards with flowers painted in the corner. She snapped as she pulled the pork-pie hat fiercely on, "I hope I can get a taxi. I really feel too tired to take the tube."

"There are always plenty of taxis in Baker Street. Would you like me to ring for one?"

"Certainly not. I simply wouldn't have the time to wait for it. I have after all a dinner to make, and I can't sit up till all hours like you do." She did not give me the ritual peck on the cheek: if she had done so she would probably have taken a mouthful out of me. She looked at the bottle of Scotch beside me. She said, "You really should stop drinking."

This was just too much. I said, "You really should mind your own business, Leni."

"Well!" Her voice shrilled up. She stalked towards the door, her face flaming. She turned round towards me as she opened it. She said in a little thin voice, "I suppose I should be sorry for you. They say people like you can't help it. But it's plain to me it's just six of one and half a dozen of the other. Goodbye!" And with this she slammed the door behind her.

I do not quite know what she meant. I went rather shakily into the kitchen to make that long-delayed dinner. By this time my appetite was gone, and it was quite true, I had drunk too much whisky on an empty stomach. I suppose she was referring to me and Steve drinking our lives away, each in our own corner, a bottle on our knees. But I did not waste time in thinking of Leni. I will never see her again, which is just as well. She will almost certainly be saying a great many nasty things about me, but she does not know my friends, there is

126

nothing there to hurt me. In future she will have to get her free meals elsewhere.

I managed to make myself a proper meal. It was one of the things that Daniel insisted on. "I don't know," he said with obvious irritation, "what's really the matter with you, but one thing is certain, you're completely overtired. You simply must eat properly, none of that confounded bread and scrape you women go in for when you live on your own."

Daniel is out-of-date. Women don't go in for bread and scrape now, it is more likely to be grapefruit, lettuce leaves and anorexia nervosa. Most of us, as far as I can make out, are on diets. I prepared meat and vegetables, felt my appetite return at the good cooking smells; I took my meal through on the trolley so that I could sit by the fire and watch the television.

But I did not switch the set on, though there was a thriller on that I thought I might like. I thought uneasily of Leni's strange remark. What did she say? *He didn't seem quite real.* And this from Leni, of all people! It was almost as if the remark had been forced out of her, as if she hardly knew what she was saying. It was like Count Magnus. *Is there anybody there?* Steve, I do not want to know, I am afraid of knowing. You are there. You will always be there. If there is any sense left in me, I must leave those bolts intact. One has fallen. I wish to God it had not. I tell you, I do not want to know. I don't care if you were up at Oxford or not. I don't know why you had to lie about it, because it does not matter, it never mattered, but I prefer to think this was just an aberration, that you never lied to me about anything else. I do not propose to investigate any more. I hope the remaining bolts are firmly fixed.

When I had finished my dinner, I put on Vanda's silver charm bracelet.

I think I might have kept my resolve. I don't know. But things were taken out of my hands. It was as if I were not to be let off so easily.

Daniel rang me about ten o'clock. I knew at once from his voice that something was very wrong. I had never heard him quite so distraught. All the calm doctor-manner had deserted him; he sounded like a badly frightened boy.

I said, "Daniel, what's the matter? What's happened?"

"I've got to see you."

"All right, love. Any time."

"I can't come tonight. I wish to God I could. But Sophy —

Would tomorrow be okay? I can't give an exact time, but I could probably arrange for a baby-sitter. About seven. Would that be all right?"

"Of course. Is Sophy ill?"

There was a long pause. Daniel did not answer this. He said, "Vanda's left me."

"What!"

"She's gone back to that ghastly first husband of hers."

"Oh Daniel, no!"

"She's taken the two children. She's left Sophy with me. I don't know what to do," said Daniel.

I was so appalled that for a second I could not say anything.

He said, "Elizabeth, what the hell am I to do?"

Obviously I must pull myself together. I said with a confidence that I did not feel, "Well, there are a lot of things to do. For one thing, I imagine Vanda will be back any day now. But the first thing is for us to talk things over. I'll expect you tomorrow. Would you like to bring Sophy with you? Perhaps she could stay here for a little — "

I did not really want Sophy here. I did not feel strong enough to cope with a nervous, disturbed little girl. But I would have done anything to remove some of the strain and unhappiness from Daniel's voice, so I repeated, "Let her stay here. I'd love to have her."

However, he said, "No, that wouldn't work. I'll explain when I see you. Goodbye, Elizabeth. It's all quite bloody, isn't it?"

It seemed to me, as he rang off, not so much bloody as incomprehensible. I could not see Vanda behaving in such a fashion. If I am beginning to grow quite fond of her, that is perhaps through force of circumstances. She is after all Daniel's wife, she is legally married to him and divorced from that first mad husband. I am lumbered with her as she is with me: we must both try to make the best of it, and I have believed that we are doing precisely that. I have even felt that we are at last becoming friends. There has always been something about her that is unsympathetic, but one thing I have never doubted, and that is that she loves Daniel with a deep and passionate emotion, and — with the memory of that strange conversation still in my mind — that she is terrified of her first husband. That anything could possibly compel her to leave Daniel and take two of the children with her, is entirely baffling.

Daniel turned up rather earlier than he said. He stormed into my flat and made straight for the whisky bottle. "I've got to have a drink," he said. He looked wild and distraught: even the beard, now in its full glory, seemed blown about his face. His shirt was dirty. I noticed this because Daniel has always been something of a dandy, and Vanda is a most careful wife who sees that his clothes are immaculately washed and pressed.

He gulped down his drink then, as if remembering himself, came over to me and kissed me. Then he knelt in front of me, took my hands in his and said, "What the hell am I to do?"

"Well, first," I said, "you could tell me exactly what all this is about. You didn't really explain much on the phone. When did Vanda go? And why? Did you have a row? And what made her take the two children and leave poor little Sophy behind?"

"Oh God," said Daniel, then again, "Oh God," and for a second rested his head against my knee. He is a devout unbeliever. It has always seemed strange to me that unbelievers in crises call upon their maker. Daniel is what he calls a rationalist: he refuses to believe in anything that he cannot explain. I suppose that is why my irrational illness so exasperated him. When I first met him, we used to have endless, unproductive arguments on such details as God and the after-life and the soul. None of them, he said, existed, and then spent entire evenings trying to prove it. It is hard enough to prove that God exists: to prove that he does not is completely impossible. And now he called on God, raised his head again then, sinking back on his heels, stared at me in hopeless shock and dismay.

It is no good being too sympathetic with Daniel: he tends to leap away, he thinks it is unmanly to be comforted. So I resisted the temptation to put my arms around him, and said in an elderly, maternal and sensible way, "Well, let's start at the beginning, shall we? This can't have come completely out of the blue. You must have realised that Vanda was unhappy."

The story came out in bits and pieces. Daniel was too shocked to be coherent and he understood less than I did: yes, Vanda had seemed unhappy and frightened, but he had dismissed this as one of those feminine things, he had not realised she was still brooding on Martin Salvatore.

Had Daniel ever met him?

129

Yes, once. "A bit of a bastard," said Daniel predictably, "and obviously a complete neurotic. I wouldn't say he was mentally deranged, — disturbed, yes, but not certifiable." I could hear the clinical note creeping into his voice, I was relieved to see that Daniel the doctor had not been entirely superseded by Daniel the man. "I admit I found him rather strange. Smarmy and smooth. Quite small. He smiled a lot. It is after all," said Daniel in a puzzled voice, "a bit peculiar to smile at the man who has taken your wife from you. But it was almost as if it didn't matter. I can understand really why Vanda is scared of him. I think he could be a bit sadistic. It wasn't an awfully nice sort of smile."

"But how did you come to meet him at all?"

"He called in at the surgery. I didn't know who he was at first. After all, Vanda was never a patient of mine — " He paused to give me a rather grim little smile. "Just as well, wasn't it? But I always met her outside her home. I never expected to see him. Of course I loathed him, but how could I do anything else? I knew he'd made Vanda hellishly unhappy, and I knew he believed in all sorts of phoney things like witchcraft and black magic and all that boloney, but he didn't seem to me very impressive. It was a peculiar kind of conversation. I didn't know what to say to him. What the hell do you say in such circumstances?"

"But he must have said something to you. What did he say?"

"Oh, how it was all right — "

"What do you mean?"

"Well, that's what he said. He cloaked it all in a lot of words, he's a gabby sort of chap. He said he wouldn't want to stand in Vanda's way, he wanted her to be happy, and he'd give her the divorce and all that. It made me feel rather creepy," said Daniel. "I felt he should be knocking me down, not just sitting there smirking. I was thankful when he went. I know this sounds daft, but I had the kind of feeling that I wanted to scrub the place down."

Vanda had not been well for some time. She had grown very nervous. "She was always dropping and breaking things," said Daniel. "It wasn't like her. She's a careful kind of girl. And she couldn't cope properly with the children. Well, they are difficult. Not Freddy, of course, but Sophy is a terribly over-anxious child, and Mario has always had his impossible moments. We began to quarrel rather a lot. We don't usually quarrel. And then she'd cry and cry, but she wouldn't tell me what was wrong and, when I pushed it, she just told me to leave her alone."

Vanda walked out without warning, taking Mario and the little boy with her. She left Sophy behind because she refused to go. "I think she's terrified of her father. Vanda tried to take her, but she made a scene. One of the neighbours said she heard a child screaming, and it went on for so long that she was about to call in to see what was the matter. I found Sophy huddled in the corner like a frightened kitten. It was when I came back from surgery. It was appalling, Elizabeth," said Daniel. He had grown quite pale. "Of course I didn't realise then that Vanda had left. I just saw this poor kid cowering against the wall, rocking herself to and fro."

"Oh Daniel!"

"She couldn't even speak. I had to hold her in my arms and cuddle her and talk to her for nearly half an hour before she was able to say anything. Then she said, 'Mummy's gone.' That's all. She repeated it several times. I couldn't even go to see what had happened because her arms were almost strangling me. In the end I had to carry her with me." He paused. He gave me a bitter smile, and that smile on the young, hurt face upset me more than anything else, not even the beard could camouflage it: it brought the tears to my eyes and I had to look away. He went on, "There was the customary note. In some ways Vanda is not a particularly original girl. She just said she was sorry, she'd gone back to Martin, she couldn't help it, she would explain later. It wasn't — it wasn't much of a goodbye. We haven't been married that long," said Daniel then, leaping to his feet, "I must have another drink. You don't mind, do you?"

"Darling, you can drink the whole bottle if you feel it will help you, but please don't get drunk because that will just make things worse. I think I'd better have a drink too — Have you heard from her at all?"

"Oh yes," said Daniel, coming back with the drinks. "She rang me the next day. She was crying. She didn't sound like herself at all."

"What did she say?"

"Just that she couldn't help it. She was sorry and — and she loved me." Daniel had walked over to the window so that I

131

could no longer see his face. "I think she's terrified, Elizabeth. I've got to find her somehow. She wouldn't say where she was, but it wasn't a local call. They sold the house in Amersham. I think they had a flat in London, but I expect that's gone too. I don't know where it was anyway. The awful thing," said Daniel, "is that she couldn't confide in me, she had all this stewing inside her and apparently I was the last person she could come to." His voice suddenly rose. "I don't know her, Elizabeth. I think I've never known her. It's so frightful not to know people who are close to you. After all, we're married, we're family, I thought we were happy, I thought if anything upset her she'd tell me all about it. But I was wrong. I see now that I don't know her at all. Do you understand what I mean?"

"Yes, I do. I understand very well."

"Where have I gone wrong? Can't you tell me? You're used to people's problems, I thought you might know. I'm beginning to think," said Daniel with difficulty, "that I'm a bit young for her. Perhaps it was just cheek to think I could take on someone so splendid, with children and everything. I took it all very seriously, you know."

"Oh my darling, I know you did. Don't go on blaming yourself, Daniel. It's not your fault — "

"Of course it's my fault. It must be. I think," said Daniel savagely, falling into the platitudes of disaster, "I've been living in a fool's paradise. It was so wonderful and I adored the children, even that little devil of a Mario, and it was such fun being a father. I don't know if you know what I mean — "

"I do," I said. "I haven't been a father, but I do understand. After all, I took on a ready-made son too, if you remember."

"You didn't make too bad a job of it," said Daniel, looking for the moment almost like his old self. Then he said, "But it is odd, isn't it? People, I mean. One thinks one knows them, and then suddenly one discovers — Oh, it's almost as if they're complete strangers whom one just never knew at all."

"Yes. Yes, Daniel."

"Meanwhile," he said more briskly, "there's the practical side of things. I'm landed with Sophy, and she's really in rather a bad way, she wants to be with me all the time, and of course I've got the surgery and I can't tote her around with me. She doesn't eat properly, and she has nightmares, and if she's left alone she starts this confounded rocking again. I've got Mrs. Lennox there in the day, she's a nice woman who's cleaned for us before, and Sophy's very fond of her, but — well — Elizabeth — "

"All right, Daniel. I'll come down. That's what you want, isn't it?"

"Only for a few days, of course. You are a darling — "

"I am, aren't I?"

He grinned at me. He really did look much better. Daniel is always good on practical matters. Something he does not understand knocks him instantly, but once he gets things organised, he is on his own ground. He said, "It really will be only for a few days. Perhaps just the weekend. I have a feeling Vanda will be back soon. In the meantime I'm going to look for her."

I didn't see how he could possibly do this, but I was glad to see him so purposeful. I said, "I'm sure you're right. I don't think she can stay away long. She loves you too much for one thing."

"Well, she's a funny way of showing it," said Daniel.

I could see that he was veering round from the shocked to the angry. I didn't think this would last either, but it seemed to me healthier than grieving, reproaching himself and drinking himself to death. He went on, a little doubtfully, "But look — this won't be too much for you, will it?"

I was a little disturbed about this myself, but this was no moment for the vapours. I assured him that I could manage perfectly well, I liked Sophy and believed she liked me: the cooking would present no problem, and perhaps Mrs. Lennox would see to the general household things and the shopping.

"I'll collect you tomorrow," said Daniel with a sigh of relief. "It'll be marvellous having you there." Then, "Why do you think Vanda walked out on me like that? You ought to know. You're a writer. You're always coping with people's problems."

I think that deep in his heart Daniel does not think much of my writing. He respects me for earning my own living, and he reads my articles when he thinks about it, even occasionally my column, and listens encouragingly when from time to time I talk about writing the novel that will probably never get written. But sometimes I suspect he regards it all as a nice feminine little occupation, rather like sewing samplers, and certainly this idea that, as a writer, I understand the human

133

soul, is normally entirely alien to him. And quite right too. Writers understand neither more nor less than anyone else, only they have a knack of expressing their opinions with a clarity that covers up the omissions beneath. Their own characters they do of course understand, but since they have created them, that is in no way remarkable. However, there is a fixed set of remarks that are delivered to all writers, especially in moments of crisis, and this is one of them: it was only surprising that Daniel should make it.

In this case I could only answer, "I don't know any more than you do. You said yourself she was frightened. Perhaps that is the reason."

"But of what? Not of me, surely. How could she be frightened of me?"

She could, Daniel. She is older than you, and she has three children. She is not secure. You think you're too young for her, she thinks she is too old. You will grow better-looking in ten years' time, and she will not. And you will eventually want your own children, and perhaps she is frightened of having any more. And you are from a different class and background, you are far better educated, and you will do well in your career, she might feel she is holding you back.

"Oh, I don't know. You can be a little alarming sometimes. Perhaps it's something Martin, her husband, said to her. He sounds quite a sinister man."

"He just looked like a creep to me. If I hadn't known he was her husband, I would have thought he was queer."

"Well, he might be. It happens. Perhaps he threatened to do something to you."

"Oh, what nonsense. As if I'd give a damn. I'm perfectly capable of looking after myself," said Daniel with angry dignity.

I did not answer this. Young men who are tall and well-built, with strong muscles, always think they are capable of looking after themselves. This is not, however, a Paul Ducane planet, and a swift left to the jaw is not always the answer to the world's problems. I had never met Martin Salvatore, and Daniel's description of him was too prejudiced to be enlightening, but I somehow saw him, I visualised him as a quiet, small, pale man whose methods of fighting would be the kind of thing that Daniel would never understand. I hoped that the two of them would never meet again head-on: if they did, I would not have backed Daniel. I left the matter, and went on to discuss what I should bring with me to Amersham and what little gift Sophy would like to cheer her up. And at last Daniel went, saying that he felt much better, and indeed he looked more his old self as he strode towards the door.

I did my small bit of packing. I was a little apprehensive. I still tire very easily and my balance is insecure, but I could not leave Daniel to cope alone with such a crisis, and my heart broke for the little girl, always the most sensitive and vulnerable of Vanda's children. I pushed aside my own stupid weakness, made myself some supper, and reflected as I did so on Daniel's remarks about not knowing people which, if he had realised it, followed so closely on my own situation.

I tried not to think too much of Steve. I had already decided that there must be no more exploration into the past: Count Magnus for me would stay securely bolted in his vault, and if the reason for this were largely a black apprehension of what I might discover, I chose to ignore this. Poor Daniel, Daniel who thought his youth a disadvantage, while everyone believed it to be the other way round. In a way he too had made a fantasy of his marriage, yet it seemed to be based on a deep and genuine love, and I was sure that in the end it would survive, perhaps be stronger for what had happened. He might not know Vanda, but now she was gone, and he was battered and bereft. I could not tell him of the conversation I had had with her, but I was sure that Martin must have put some appalling pressure on her, and she was in some ways an ignorant girl, she would believe everything he said. It was surely the only thing that would bring her back to a man who had ill-used and terrified her, and I was convinced that the threat in some way concerned Daniel or the children.

It all seemed such a waste, and I found myself growing cross and uneasy, with my own problems still knocking at my mind. However tomorrow there would be no time for brooding, I would leave my ghosts behind me, and there was always the possibility that Vanda might suddenly return. I could not really believe that anything would keep her away from Daniel for long. I left my half-packed suitcase open for the last minute things, then early next morning took myself out shopping to buy presents for Sophy.

I have bought her a doll, with some clothes so that she can dress and undress it. She is a maternal, anxious little girl, and I am sure she likes dolls, to cosset, to scold, to worry about. I had quite a time finding one I liked. Dolls nowadays belong to the permsoc., they look like cute little scrubbers, with over-painted faces, long curling lashes and frizzy hair. I did not care much either for the more practical ones that wet themselves and cry, Mama. In the end I found quite a cheap little affair that somehow looked cosy: Sophy could cuddle this doll without offending it. I also threw in a little necklace and a hair-slide of that bright vulgarity that very little girls adore: I do not know when they acquire any kind of taste, but it certainly isn't at the age of five. Then I came home to gather up my papers and the portable typewriter I have had for twenty years: I suspected there would be no time for work, but it looked efficient and I might as well be prepared.

Daniel collected me at twelve o'clock. "I've got a locum," he said. "After all, it's just for one day." He still looked exhausted and drawn, but obviously he had sorted things out in his medical mind, and he spoke quite cheerfully of Sophy who was apparently dancing with excitement at the prospect of seeing her gran, for so she calls me. It makes me feel as old as the hills, but it is rather agreeable all the same. No, there was no further word of Vanda, but then he had not really expected it. He did not mention her again, but I had to see the brief flash of rage and longing that flickered across his face.

He took me out to lunch in a pub not far from his home, which is just outside Amersham. We did not talk very much. He was plainly resolved not to go on discussing his problems, but they were the only thing in his mind, and in my mind too, so we just made desultory conversation.

Only as we were driving up to the house which stands in a little isolated street where homes and gardens and garages all match, I said, "You were going to try to find out where she is. Have you had any luck?"

His face grew grim and resentful. "Not a blind monkey," he said, then, "How can I? I told you they sold the place in Amersham. I've no idea who's got it now. They'll have sold the London flat too. Why should they keep it on now the family's split up?"

I thought that Martin Salvatore might well keep it on, London flats being so impossible to find these days, but I did not say so. I suspected that Daniel, for some unhappy, distorted reason of his own did not really want to find out at all: he was waiting for Vanda to return ashamed and penitent so that he could roar her into the ground. There is something very Victorian about Daniel. He claims to hold the most emancipated views on women but secretly believes their place is in the kitchen and the bed — not the church, for that would be against his agnostic principles.

He went on, "Besides, the bastard doesn't work. Well, I know he's got a business, but that's in Milan or somewhere. I mean, if he had a job, it would be much easier. But I gather he's one of those chaps who sit in the study all day, reading up about witchcraft and all that mumbo-jumbo. It must create a most unhealthy atmosphere. I think he's got a screw loose, myself."

God knows, there was nothing funny about the situation, but poor Daniel's picture of Martin, presumably in a peaked hat with cabalistic signs on it, and wearing a long, black cloak, was a little comic. How strange that Vanda should marry two such dissimilar men. I could not imagine Martin and Daniel having one thing in common, except of course Vanda herself. Perhaps that extraordinary difference is the reason why Vanda fell in love with Daniel. This time she has chosen sensibly, even if she has not behaved so. For all that I have become embroiled in so many things that I do not understand, I am developing a marked revulsion against the occult. I could see that if one lived for a while in so strange and esoteric an atmosphere, someone like Daniel, who would not know a black mass if he saw one, and who has a healthy, English loathing of everything that he cannot immediately understand, must seem like cold, fresh sea-air after joss-sticks and stifling heat.

Yet I am to some extent fascinated by the occult, while struggling to profess a disbelief, though anything on the black, destructive side terrifies me. Nothing would drag me to a coven, however silly it might seem; I may have my horoscope told and sometimes glance furtively at the newspaper star-charts, but I would not go to a seance and, as I had said to Daniel, no reward, however enormous and however broke my finances, would persuade me to sleep in a haunted room. It is strange, therefore, that at this period of my life when I am no longer young, the other world is somehow impinging on me, through Steve, and, unwillingly, through Daniel himself.

Sometimes I feel as if that absurd ghost town stirred something up, made the bolts begin to fall.

Chapter 6

DANIEL'S HOUSE IS SMALL, JERRY-BUILT AND OPEN-PLANNED, AND has the thinnest of walls between itself and its neighbour. Inside it is well-set-out, clean and trim, but the little garden, though delightful for the children, is uncared for and full of weeds. Vanda's life is centred on her kitchen, and neither she nor Daniel is interested in gardens, though occasionally he digs away when he feels he needs some exercise, then forgets to plant anything. There are a few straggling rosebushes, left there by the former occupant, the grass grows high and there is a fine crop of dandelions. Only the mark of the children is still to be seen, and this distresses me. I wish Daniel did not have to see it. Vanda must have taken very little with her: indeed, from all accounts, she left in a desperate hurry. The baby's push-chair is still by the shed, there is a mud-covered football half hidden in the grass, and the swing, put up by Daniel a few months ago, rocks sadly in the breeze.

The house, however, is perfectly in order, and so is Mrs. Lennox, who is Scottish, brisk and no-nonsense. I can see that she has no time whatsoever for wives who suddenly walk out, leaving a little girl behind. It is obvious from the very look of her that she supports hanging and flogging, and would have both applied to errant wives: she radiates that curious violence that is so often found in the irreproachably genteel. But she approves of me, presumably because I am doing my duty, and to my relief does not burst out with the whole story: she would probably think that this was not her place. Sophy, I see at once, is very fond of her, but the child looks so peaked and frail that I am a little shocked.

She always was the odd one out of the three, and the most

sensitive. Mario may put Daz in Daniel's soup, but I am sure he does it quite openly, with no pretence at concealment, just to make it quite clear that he is not accepting this new father. He is a tough little boy, not really a delinquent, just something of a bully. I found out earlier on that, despite his Mafia-like appearance — he is very dark and Italian, with huge eyes, and can look quite sinister — one could always make him laugh, even if against his will, and once he laughs he becomes instantly what he really is, a bewildered if sometimes naughty little boy. As for Freddy, Freddy is still almost a baby, and nothing much affects him providing he is loved and played with and fed.

But Sophy worries. I imagine she always worries. She is only five but sometimes she resembles an old woman. She worries about Freddy if he is out of her sight for more than a few moments, and she plays the little mother with Mario who accepts this with perfect calm and bullies the life out of her. Vanda, as I have said, is not a particularly maternal woman, though she loves being pregnant: I am sure she is devoted to her children in her own way, but it is Sophy who, at this ridiculous age, takes on all the maternal responsibilities. She is not a pretty child. I understand that she is like her paternal grandmother, not that that means anything to me, I have never met the Salvatore family.· She now looks utterly distraught and bereft. No child should look like that. She is pale and thin, with black hair. I have seldom seen her smile and her face, before she realises who I am, is twisted with anxiety. Then she runs to me and bursts into tears, and it is all a bit much for someone who cries at the drop of a hat, and as I fling my arms round her, I can see Mrs. Lennox looking with fierce disapproval at this abandoned continental scene, with everybody so out of control, even Daniel. Daniel does not of course cry, I have never seen him cry, even at his father's death, but he too picks the little girl up and hugs her with abandon, instead of being brisk and friendly as an Englishman should be.

The doll is a roaring success. Sophy is plainly baby-starved. If a doll can be ruined with love, this one will have a very short life. The clothes are instantly put on, taken off again, put on once more; the slide I bought for Sophy is fitted on the doll's wispy hair, and the necklace put round her neck, from which it instantly falls off. Sophy now looks happy again, and Daniel seeing this looks happier too.

We all sit down for drinks at the brilliantly polished table with its spotless white mats: this is plainly Mrs. Lennox's work, and I see that the net curtains have been washed, everything is dusted, and there is not a speck on the carpet.

Daniel says, "Come on, Mrs. Lennox, join us."

"I seldom touch the stuff," says Mrs. Lennox with Calvinist ferocity. But we notice the "seldom" and there is a faint glint in her eye, so Daniel presses it. She says grudgingly, "Well, just a spot, only a spot now. I've better things to do with my time than get myself tipsy, you know."

She will not sit down. She stands there almost at attention: not only does she seem to know her place in an alarming manner, but somehow she makes us know ours. Daniel, winking at me, pours her out a generous dram which she drains at a gulp as if it were vodka, not perceptibly turning a hair. Then she wipes her hands on her apron, glances once at Sophy who is crooning to her new baby, then addresses Daniel.

"I'll be away now," she says, untying her apron. Only Mrs. Lennox could wear such an old-fashioned apron. "I'll be back tomorrow. I've washed and ironed your shirts, doctor, and the wee girl's clothes are laid out on her bed. I'll bring the meat in with me. I've ordered a chicken. I thought madam would like it."

Madam is awed by such efficiency, but I can see that Mrs. Lennox is what they used to call a treasure, and it is wonderful for Daniel and Sophy that she is around. It is wonderful for me too, for I am not an efficient housekeeper, and terrible at ironing shirts. We say goodbye to Mrs. Lennox, and I see her trotting briskly down the path.

Sophy is still playing raptly with her doll, whom she has now called Doris, I cannot imagine why. Daniel, watching her, says, "That was a splendid idea of yours, Elizabeth."

"Well, I thought she might like it. She seems to me a dolly kind of little girl."

And then we look at each other, for this is only the beginning, and neither of us has the least idea how it will end.

I said at last, settling myself comfortably on the sofa by the window, "I don't really understand this, Daniel, any more than you do. But I am still sure that Vanda will be back any day now."

Daniel did not answer this directly. He was pacing up and

140

down the room. It struck me suddenly that he had completely grown up. He did not look like a boy any more. He said, "I wish everyone wasn't so bloody good to me. They are all so sorry for me. Nobody seems to be sorry for Vanda."

I was not at all sure how sorry I was for Vanda myself, but I answered, "People are always sorry for the husband. It's not as if you were on bad terms, quarrelling and ill-treating her. She's just walked out, and the fact that she's left Sophy behind — "

"She couldn't help that, damn it. I told you — "

I noticed that Daniel, who never swore at all, was now swearing quite a lot according to his own standards. But I only said soothingly, "I know, I know. Don't be so cross with me, Daniel. You said you couldn't see any means of finding out where she is. Would you like me to try? Perhaps I could then go and talk to her."

And I could not help thinking as I had thought before that Daniel perhaps did not want to find out, he wanted her to come back on her own accord. After all, the house she had lived in had been sold, and the estate agents must have a record of the transaction. It is difficult to hide yourself these days, and Martin Salvatore was a foreigner. There are consulates and immigration authorities and records of foreign businesses. I may be bad at ironing shirts, but I have sometimes thought that I would not make a bad private detective. However, this induces thoughts that I prefer to ignore, and Daniel was speaking again, answering me as I knew he would.

He said, his face white and tight, "I'm sorry, but I'll do that talking, thank you."

"All right," I said, "all right." Yet it was a pity. It was not that I thought I could handle it so marvellously, it was simply that I was beginning to know Vanda, whom at first I had so much disliked, and I believed I could persuade her to disregard her warlock husband and come back where she belonged. Certainly I would do better than Daniel who, wild with emotion and resentment and frustration, would charge in with the delicacy of Russian cavalry. However, I said none of this, and presently we played a game with Sophy, who was really looking much better, and gave her her supper.

Daniel said, "John's looking in this evening. He's my

neighbour. He and his wife have been marvellous to us, so I suggested he came in for a drink after dinner. Mary reads your magazine column and wants to meet you too, but she has to baby-sit. You'll like John. He's an interesting sort of chap. He's an ex-colonel and he escaped from a German prisoner-of-war camp."

I was by now very tired, and I do not care much for ex-colonels and interesting chaps, chiefly, I suppose, because they do not care much for me. I imagined someone intensely English, with a bluff manner and a little moustache: I thought with passionate longing of my bed. But Daniel, though he is a doctor and a good doctor, tends, as many men do, to disregard his own family. If I had been a patient, he would have noticed at once that I was exhausted; he would have realised that someone just recovered from an illness should not have to take on entertaining as well as responsibility. But he is too used to me. He now seemed to consider that I was completely recovered and, as I did not wish to upset him in any way, I made no protest. After all, ex-colonels are not usually intellectually very demanding, and probably he would spend his time telling me his war memories.

I bathed Sophy and put her to bed. I asked her if she would like me to read her a story. She looked so wan and sad as she lay back on the pillow that it nearly broke my heart: however, Doris, now slightly the worse for wear through so much loving handling, lay beside her, and her face lit up when I said this. Yes, she would like a story, please Gran, and she at once produced the book for it, a small volume of fairy tales in the bookcase by her bed.

I read for a brief while. She obviously knew the book by heart, so I closed it at last and said, "I'll tell you a story of my own, Sophy, and then you're going to go to sleep like a good girl."

"I want to say good night to Daddy."

So Daniel was Daddy now. I said, "Of course. He'll be up in a moment. Shall I tell you the story first? What would you like it to be about?"

Sophy, after deliberation, wanted the story to be about an elephant, an umbrella, Doris and a piece of garlic. It was not the mixture that worried me, for I am quite accustomed to this and five-year-olds are not very particular, but the mention of the garlic jarred me, made me think again of Steve who during the turmoil had been almost out of my mind. But after all I had decided not to think of Steve, he was like Count Magnus, securely shut away in his vault, so I pushed him back yet once more, wished Sophy had not said this, and told my foolish little story, only realising at the end that Daniel had come in and was silently listening too.

Sophy cried out, "Daddy, Daddy!" and I swung round rather crossly, to see that he was laughing to himself.

"This wasn't meant for you," I protested. "It was specially for Sophy. You had no right to gatecrash. You're not old enough for such stories."

But he only grinned at me, and came to sit on the bed. It was plain that once Daniel was there, Sophy had no time for me, so I went downstairs to see if the vegetables were cooked, and presently Daniel came down too, and we ate our dinner.

I did not say this to Daniel, but it was very strange to me that Sophy did not mention her mother. I was preparing myself with some apprehension for questions such as, When is Mummy coming back, but there was not one word about Vanda, yet Sophy had always been very much her mother's child.

But we did not talk of this nor of Vanda, we discussed a variety of minor things during the dinner, which Mrs. Lennox had made ready, and we talked a little of Mrs. Lennox herself who, despite her fierce manner, was very sweet with the children and told them horrific Scottish stories about clan warfare that Mario enjoyed very much.

The phone went twice while we were eating, and each time Daniel leapt to his feet, his face suddenly taut and drawn. But it was not Vanda only in one case an urgent call from a patient, which meant that Daniel had to go out again and that I would be left alone with the colonel.

However, I liked the colonel much better than I expected. He was an elderly man, no moustache, and the baby-sitting done by his wife was for grandchildren. He had a quiet, friendly manner, and was not at all the bluff soldier I had expected. We sat there talking until Daniel came back, and I left the door open in case Sophy had one of her nightmares.

I said, as I poured out some more coffee, "Daniel tells me you were a prisoner-of-war, and managed to escape. Where were you exactly when this happened, and what did you do? Was this the wooden horse kind of thing?"

No, it had not been the wooden horse. It had been, he said, in a place known as Oflag VI B, outside the small town of Warburg in Westphalia. I do not have a particularly good memory, except for things that interest me, but this unimpressive name was not something I could ever forget, and I was so taken aback that I disgraced myself by dropping and breaking one of Vanda's precious coffee cups, spilling the contents all over Mrs. Lennox's spotless carpet.

The colonel was rather astonished, but I managed to apologise, saying that I had been ill and my hands were still shaky. Indeed, they were shaking like aspens, and he was quite concerned, getting up instantly to bring me over a drink.

Fortunately he knew his way about the kitchen, for I had to let him clean up for me: at that moment I was incapable of doing anything. When he came back we both looked wryly at the large stain on the carpet, then laughed.

"I don't think Mrs. Lennox will ever forgive me," I said. "She'll certainly be far angrier than Daniel." We did not mention Vanda, either of us. "What a clumsy idiot I am. I'm so sorry."

"You don't have to apologise to me," said the colonel, "and I think Mrs. Lennox's bark is a great deal worse than her bite."

We were sitting, fortunately, in the lamplight. Daniel like me does not care for a glaring light overhead. I do not know what my face looked like, but I think I would have looked very strange indeed, if the soft lamp had not partly hidden me. But the colonel noticed that my hands were still shaking, and said, "Should you really be down here so late? You look to me as if you ought to be in bed."

I said, "Oh, I'm all right really. I'm a bit tired tonight, but there's nothing wrong with me. Anyway I have a doctor on the premises. Do tell me about this. It interest me. When were you in Oflag VI B?"

"The summer of 1942."

Oh Count Magnus, can't you leave me alone? Or is it that I cannot leave you alone? But I saw then very clearly that I was committed now, whether I liked it or not. I had no choice. My resolution had been sensible, but life is not sensible, it was like moving a pointer round to have it swing back always in the same direction.

Once the spray on my shower went wrong: wherever I moved it, it always slid back towards the wall. That is how it is with Steve. You cannot manipulate people like Steve, you cannot manipulate memories.

I said, for it no longer mattered, "I had a friend in that camp. He escaped too. He must have been one of your lot. I wonder if you'd remember his name?"

"There were forty of us. I am not likely to forget any of them. We did have a couple of reunions after the war, but of course these things fall off, and people die and so on. After all, we were none of us so young. But of course I'd remember the name. Who was he?"

"His name was Stephen Olsen." Then I said, "I gather that only three of you succeeded, and he was one of them."

The colonel looked at me for a moment, considered the matter then shook his head. "No. There was no Stephen Olsen. I could tell you the other two names if you liked, but they wouln't mean anything to you. I expect you've got the wrong number. It's probably another camp."

"You're quite sure?"

"Of course. But it's easy enough to confuse the camps. There were after all a great many of us. And they all sound rather alike. I'm glad he escaped. It's quite a business, what with the lights and the perimeter fences and the barbed wire. I couldn't do it now. I'm too old. But it's the kind of thing that becomes a permanent, nagging sort of challenge, whether you succeed or not. It's almost a game."

Steve had said that, almost in the same words, expressing exactly the same sentiment. I remembered so well all the details. He too had talked of the lights that had to be fused, and the barbed wire. Freedom, he said, was a chilly, solitary thing, but he could never stand being confined, even with men who were the staunchest of friends. There was a kind of fuggy comfort in a prison, one had to make a hell of an effort to get away, but in the end it was the only thing to do. I could hear his voice saying this. I could see the expression on his face —

I asked, "Did you ever do an article on it? I'm a journalist myself, so that's the kind of question I automatically ask. I hate to see good material wasted, and it must be a unique story."

"Well, it's funny you should ask that, but yes, I did do an article. I'm not really a writing man, but I was a bit broke at the time, I don't suppose I'd have bothered otherwise. Gave it some high-flown title. The paper, I mean. 'The Chill of

145

Freedom.' Didn't care much for it myself, but it's true enough, there's a kind of fuggy comfort in a prison, surrounded by your mates, it takes one hell of a push to move away." He paused to peer down at me. He was a very tall man. "You understand that, don't you? I can see it in your face. I think you're rather a perceptive person, Mrs. Waterman."

It does not take much to be perceptive when you have heard it all before. I suppose Steve must have read the article: he seemed to have quoted from it almost verbatim. I did not trouble to deny this, only said, "I can understand it very well. But I should love to read that article if I could. Have you kept a copy?"

"I think my wife has. If you really want to — It's pretty old hat by now. I'll ask Mary about it, and drop it in tomorrow."

At that moment I heard Sophy crying out in that thin little wail that signified she was awake and afraid. I said I was sorry but I must go: he nodded, he was after all a grandfather, he must be used to such emergencies. I found myself a little weak: this bloody illness still seems to magnify all crises. It took all the strength I had in me to get up the stairs.

As I came into the bedroom, I heard the slam of the front door: Daniel had returned.

Sophy was sitting up in bed, looking wild and distraught. The black hair streaked over her face, and the tears were pouring down. I knelt beside her and took her into my arms. I could feel the shudders running through her. I held her tightly, made soothing noises and stroked her hair, saying, "What is it, love? Tell me."

"I want Daddy."

Not, I notice, Mummy but definitely Daddy. Daniel may think he has made a poor job of being an adoptive father, but he has succeeded with this little creature beyond all belief. I must tell him when I see him.

I say that I will call Daniel when I go down.

"Was he out on a call?"

"Yes, he was."

Then Sophy says, "He'll be too tired to come and see me. Poor Daddy works so hard."

We talk a little about Daniel, then we discuss Doris who apparently has terrible nightmares. Sophy, shaking her head wisely, says she worries to death about her, so we pat Doris,

146

kiss her, tuck her up on the pillow, making sure the sheet comes up to her chin. And now Sophy's eyes are closing, she sinks back beside Doris, and in a few minutes she is sound asleep again — with luck this time she will sleep the night through.

I do not go down again. Daniel is there now, he and the colonel can talk men's talk, whatever that is, — besides, I am not very well, Daniel will hear all about that and understand, I hope he is not angry about the stain on the carpet. It was dreadfully clumsy of me. I must have a word with Mrs. Lennox in the morning, she is bound to have some ancient Highland remedy that will remove all traces.

I undress and lie down on the bed, without putting on the light. Some time later I hear Daniel coming up the stairs. He taps softly on the door. I do not answer. Then I hear him running his bath, doors opening and shutting, bare feet padding down the corridor. Daniel is going to his wifeless bed, and I wish with all my heart that Vanda were there, I never believed I could feel so strongly about Vanda, but that is the way things have turned out.

I brood a little on Vanda, silly, frightened Vanda. What in God's name can that man have done to her? She has never struck me as a timid girl, partly perhaps because she is so big, but obviously with him she is the proverbial bird before a snake. Then I think of myself and Steve, almost wearily, without much emotion or drama. For now I am hopelessly committed, for a variety of conflicting reasons — and one of those reasons, possibly the main one, does me little credit. It is simply that now I have to know. I am even aware — how ignoble this is — that I resent being diddled. And oh my God, I have been diddled, how much I still do not know, but I am going to know, I am concentrating on finding out. I am, as must by now be plain, a weak person without much stamina, but like all weak people, I have a rebellion point, and this I have reached.

Silly, frightened Steve. Oh why, why, why? He was in so many ways a fine man, a brilliant writer, and he made a considerable success of his career, even when the quality of his books deteriorated. Why did he have to lie to everyone, and above all, to me? There was no need, no point even, in saying that he had escaped from a German prison camp. It did not glorify him in my eyes, it made no difference to my feelings

147

for him. There was no need to say he had been up at Oxford. I did not love him because he was a hero, because he got a double first. I loved him for what he was, and now I no longer knew what he was.

I am beginning to think that nothing of what he told me was true: this is near insanity, it makes no kind of sense at all.

I fall uneasily asleep at last, and in my dreams return to Jericho City and the ghost saloon. Only the man drinking there is no longer Paul Ducane, it is Steve, and Steve says to me, I am a great film star, why won't you believe me? This time it is I who wake up crying, but there is no Doris to comfort me, so I have to drag myself out of bed, and rummage for my cigarettes. When the dawn comes I am huddled in my dressing-gown by the window, half asleep, wakened with a start that sets my heart thudding by the sound of the garden gate.

I look down into the dim grey light. The garden really is a disgrace. I wish I had the strength to do something about it. Nobody has ever troubled to clip or prune or tidy anything, and there is a great clump of what looks remarkably like oats by the kitchen door.

But I move my eyes away from this. I stare down at Vanda and the two children who are coming up the path. They look like something from an old movie. The prodigal wife, returning to the fold, with the two little children there to melt Daddy's heart — They stand for a moment on the path. I think Vanda is trying to summon up her courage. She will need it. Daniel, however much he loves her, perhaps because he loves her, is not going to take this kindly. The sympathy of everyone may be with him, but he has nonetheless been humiliated: unkinder circles might say that he has been made a fool of, he has married a divorced woman older than himself, who after a brief marriage has suddenly decided to return to her first husband, without even saying goodbye. There is, I think, **going** to be one hell of a row, the shouting, screaming kind: Vanda is not Italian for nothing, and in any case it will probably do them good. But I am not going to be there if I can help it. I do not like rows, they upset my stomach, besides, I should simply be in the way. I will pack my things, greet Vanda civilly, and gently disappear later in the morning. I cannot just now cope with buses or trains, but I will ruin myself and hire a car. Daniel will no doubt offer to drive me

148

back, but this I could not bear: in such circumstances he will be an impossible companion.

I cannot take my eyes off Vanda, who is still standing there like a statue. The light is too dim for me to see her clearly — she must have been travelling half the night, what transport has she used? — but she looks gaunter than I remember, and her hair is coming down. She is holding Mario by one hand, and clutching Freddy, who seems fast asleep, in the other against her shoulder. Mario too looks a little grey and wispy: for once he is not jigging about and playing the fool, he seems to me as if he is as scared as his mother.

There is a small suitcase by the gate. Vanda apparently tells Mario to go and fetch it. Then she strides — she moves with big steps but she is a tall girl — up to the front door, and I shoot guiltily away from the window, though I know perfectly well she cannot see me.

I hear the front door open and close. I hear Mario's gruff little voice. Daniel has heard it too. His door is flung open. He runs down the stairs, and at this point I tear in a kind of panic into the bathroom, locking the door as if pursued, and running the water full-blast so that I cannot hear what is being said.

I do not know what happened. When I came out of the bathroom there was nothing to hear but subdued voices, and when at last, much later than usual, I came downstairs, the atmosphere was one of quiet, seething emotion. I saw that my prophecy of a row was only too true, but it had not yet taken place: they would all be waiting for me to go.

Mrs. Lennox, when she arrived, hardly improved matters. I knew from the very beginning that her disapproval of Vanda's behaviour would be monumental. I also suspect that she enjoyed her brief phase of authority: the Mrs. Lennoxes of this world love to be in charge. It was plain that for her wives who behave in such a fashion are flung instantly into boiling oil. The disapproval on her face was so intense that it almost made me want to laugh. However, this was no time for laughter though, as I looked at Daniel and Vanda, the one white with icy rage, the other sullen and trembling with incipient scene, I could not help feeling that a faint sense of the ridiculous would not come amiss. But I always take my own crises with an utterly humourless passion, so there was no reason why other people should behave differently.

I felt badly in the way, but I could hardly cry, Goodbye,

and rush out. We were all, only too obviously, in a state of suppressed tension, and Mrs. Lennox, just forcing herself to say, "Good morning, madam," to poor Vanda, stalked to and fro with the breakfast things as if about to further an execution.

I could not bear to sit in the dining-room, so I followed her back into the kitchen and asked her for a cup of tea. She poured this out in silence, it was very strong and well-mashed, and I could not bear this either. Then I apprehensively broached the subject of the carpet, and to my relief she became quite friendly and, as I suspected, knew exactly the way in which to remove the stain.

I met Daniel just as I was about to go upstairs again. He looked dreadful, but it was mostly temper. Daniel has always had a violent temper, but once it is expended, he recovers instantly, even if the object of his fury does not always follow suit. This is always the way with bad-tempered people: they scream and roar, then are astonished when the recipient remains angry and battered. But I grieved a little as I looked at him. However frightened Vanda was, it seemed to me that she had treated him unfairly: he is fundamentally a good boy, Daniel, and even if he had not fully understood, he would have done his best to help her.

However, by now he was in no mood to help anyone. He said roughly, "Where are you going?"

As I had one foot on the bottom step this seemed unnecessary, but I answered meekly, "Upstairs."

"Why? Vanda wants to talk to you."

"Daniel," I said — after all I was his stepmother, and nothing of what had happened was in any way my fault, I did not see why I should be spoken to as if I were Mario in a paddy — "Daniel, I'd love to talk to Vanda, but first I must finish my packing."

"What do you mean?"

"I'm going home."

"Of course you're not going home — Don't be ridiculous!"

"Don't speak to me like that, please. I know you're in a terrible temper, but you don't have to take it out on me."

I saw him chewing his lower lip, not quite sure whether to blaze at me or capitulate. Then he gave me a shamefaced grin and a pat on the shoulder. He said reluctantly, "I don't see why you have to go."

"Of course I have to go. And I want to go, not because of

you and Vanda, but simply because I've a load of work to do. I came here to help you out, didn't I? Not that I've done much, I'm afraid, but anyway there's no further need for me to be here." Then I decided that all this smooth talk between us was absurd. I said in a more natural voice, "You and Vanda have just got to sort things out. You don't want a third party present, and frankly, I'd feel horribly in the way. Let me just slide out. When this is all settled, I'll come down again. Be sensible, Daniel darling. You must see that I'd be embarrassing everybody, especially myself."

He muttered, "I don't see how I can drive you back. I've got my morning surgery. If you'd wait till the evening — "

"No, I can't wait till the evening. Don't worry about me. I'm quite capable of getting myself home. It isn't so far after all."

I could see that in his heart he wanted me to be away. But he still hesitated, saying, "Vanda really does want to talk to you. And, I'm sorry, Elizabeth, but I would like you to see her. I think you'd be good for her."

"Well, I'm not going to dash out this second. When she's finished with the children's breakfast, ask her to come upstairs."

He said sulkily, "I don't see why you can't stay for lunch."

But I just smiled at him and went up to my room. I could hear that the household was returning to its normal disorganisation. I heard Mario shouting something, then Daniel answered him and he instantly fell silent. He must have realised that his stepfather, however patient with Daz in the soup, was in no mood to take any insubordination. The little one, being very tired, was howling, while Sophy — I was there when she first saw her mother — was behaving with an aloof dignity that made her look like a little old woman. When Vanda stooped to kiss her, she backed away, extending one drooping hand: she said in a small, chill voice, "Oh, how do you do," then instantly returned to Doris who, by now a little battered, had been put against the toast rack.

It was the only time that morning that I saw a flicker of a smile touch Daniel's mouth.

I did not look much at Vanda, so I do not know how she took this. I did see her shrug and turn away. I was truly sorry for her, but I could not help feeling a little angry too, all this somehow seemed so unnecessary. However, when half an hour later she tapped on my door, I managed to turn on a welcoming smile and asked her to come in.

She looked formidably older. I imagine she had not slept a wink that night. The alarming disadvantage of being the older partner, especially if you are a woman, is that violent emotion instantly adds to your age. I still do not know how old she is, but that morning I would have placed her at forty. She was now impeccably neat again — I have seldom seen Vanda disorganised to the degree of being untidy — but she had scraped the dark hair off her forehead, and her face was white and drawn to the bones. She did not return my smile. She sat down on my bed, tucking her feet beneath her. She said, "I couldn't help it."

"It was hard on Daniel," I said, for I couldn't help it either, I could not entirely restrain myself. She had perhaps every right to be sorry for herself, but she had made Daniel suffer, she must have known how much she had made him suffer.

She began to cry. I had never seen Vanda cry before. She sobbed, "You don't understand."

Well, that was true enough, but I could not bear to see her cry, and this was one of the rare times when she showed signs of confiding in me. I decided to be frank with her, and then perhaps we could begin to understand each other.

I said, "No, I don't really. But don't cry, Vanda. Please don't. Why don't you explain it to me? Dear, you must see my point of view too. You leave the poor boy without so much as a goodbye — "

"I left him a note!"

"A note! Good God, what kind of comfort is that? I think — you must forgive me but I've been upset too — I think that was rather cowardly. Surely you could have talked it over with him?"

"He would never have let me go."

I found my good resolutions dissolving in temper — I hadn't slept much either — and I saw that this would not do. Whatever had happened it was going to be a pretty grim day for Vanda. Daniel was plainly spoiling for a fight, Mrs. Lennox was eyeing her with all the sympathetic charm of a Calvinist synod, the children were grossly over-tired, and even the kindest of neighbours was not going to be exactly sympathetic. I do not approve of hunting, whether the quarry is a fox or a woman, and suddenly I no longer felt angry, only distressed and sorry for this silly girl who was snivelling away on my bed as if she were due for a spanking. I gave her a handkerchief, offered her a cigarette, then said in a more reasonable voice, "You could hardly feel very flattered if he had done so. He loves you very much, after all."

"Do you think I don't love him?"

"Of course you love him. No one could doubt that. Love, why did you walk out like that? Can't you tell me? You'll have to tell Daniel. It'll be the first thing he asks you."

"He has already asked me," said Vanda bitterly. She had stopped crying. She looked as if it were the end of the world.

"Well, I imagine he has. And he'll go on and on and on until you tell him something that satisfies him. You must know your Daniel. He always wants to know. To him this will be like a symptom. If you had a haemorrhage or a strange pain or developed a twitch, he would have to find out the cause. He'd be a poor sort of doctor if he didn't. And when his wife, who hasn't been married to him for very long and who obviously loves him, suddenly walks out with two of the children — oh Vanda, he'll never let you rest until he has the whole story out of you. Why did you leave Sophy behind?"

"She wouldn't come," said Vanda. "She's terrified of her father."

"She's a very disturbed little girl."

Vanda raised the great dark eyes briefly, but did not answer this. I had to see that she was a very disturbed young woman. She was silent for a moment, then she said, her voice very deep, "There are things that Daniel can't understand. I could tell him again and again, but he wouldn't know what I was talking about. I think you are the same."

"Well, you haven't really told me anything yet. Why don't you tell me the whole story, and I'll do my best to understand, really I will."

"You don't know Martin."

"Well, no, but what has that got to do with it?"

Then she said to my astonished dismay, "I would like you to go and see him. I will leave you his address."

"Oh no, Vanda, no, I couldn't do that. Daniel would be furious and with perfect justification. If Martin has been terrorising you, it's Daniel who should go to see him, it's his business, he's a man and he's your husband."

She exclaimed, "No, no, no!" and jumped to her feet. She looked at that moment a little mad, her eyes dilated, her mouth open. "No, Elizabeth. I will not have Daniel near him."

"Why? Do you think Daniel would murder him or something? I assure you — "

"He could kill Daniel."

I was about to tell her not to be so absurd, then I fell silent. I did not in my heart believe that Martin — what sort of creature was he? — could kill Daniel or anyone else, but a great many strange things had happened to me recently, and I was in no position to deride poor Vanda who obviously believed that her former husband had demoniac powers. I said at last, "You mustn't believe that. It is simply not true. The days of vampires and witches are over."

She said as she had said before, "You don't know Martin." Then she said, "Perhaps he wouldn't kill him, but he could do him great harm. He is a maker of mischief. He is a rotter."

The incongruous word — Vanda has the strangest vocabulary — almost made me smile, though God knows, there was nothing funny in all this. She must have noticed this, for she said reproachfully, "He can spread dreadful stories."

"Well, that would be actionable. Besides, I don't imagine that Daniel has done anything he could be blackmailed for."

Vanda said with more perception than I would have credited her with, "We all do things we can be blackmailed for. And with a doctor it is always easy to find out something."

"Are you telling me, Vanda, that you left Daniel because Martin threatened to blackmail him?"

She nodded.

I could see very well that she would find it almost impossible to put this over to Daniel: he would begin by laughing at her and end by being bitterly offended. I said, "But you did come back."

"I couldn't bear to stay away any longer. I should never have come."

"Oh yes, you should. I'm so thankful you did. I think if you'd stayed away any longer, you'd have harmed Daniel far more than Martin could ever do."

"If I'd stayed any longer, I should have killed myself," said Vanda.

"Oh come off it, darling. You're being melodramatic." But I think she meant it, and I went on quickly, "If I do go to see Martin, what on earth do you want me to say? For one thing I hardly imagine he'd let me in."

"Oh yes. He would."

154

"Why?"

"He is very curious always. He would want to see you."

"I honestly can't imagine why. Well, suppose I do go. I still don't see what you expect me to say. Do I march in, crying out, Lay off Daniel, lay off Vanda? He'd just laugh at me. Surely he must recognise by now that you love Daniel, that you'll never come back to him, and that all this carry-on is silly and childish. After all, you are legally divorced."

"He doesn't recognise that. He's a Catholic."

"That's too bad. The law recognises it."

"He says I am still his wife."

"Oh tell him to go to hell. There comes a point where you just have to. After all, you do have Daniel to protect you, and I don't think he's too bad as a knight errant."

"And who will protect Daniel?"

I said, trying to make light of this, for Vanda's intensity was beginning to frighten me, "I suppose I will. Can't you see me, armed with a gun? — Well, perhaps not a gun. I'd probably blow my own head off. But I'd do my best for him."

"And the children?" asked Vanda stonily.

"What about the children? Don't tell me he's threatening them."

"He says he will kidnap Mario and Sophy."

I said more boldly than I felt, "That's completely ridiculous. I know Italians go in for kidnapping, but this isn't Italy, and Martin's not a Mafia boss. You can't just kidnap people like that. You're letting him frighten you too much, Vanda. If you are really taking this seriously, you must go to the police."

I saw Vanda's mouth open in agitated protest. I suppose it is only in England that people go to the police: in other countries the police mostly go to them. But before I could voice this unusually patriotic sentiment, the door was flung open and Daniel swept in.

"Well?" he said. "Have you two girls finished?" The voice was normal enough, and he was even smiling, but the fury within him still burned in his eyes, and I could see that though he had almost forced this tête-à-tête upon us, he could not endure it, he was maddened by the sight of the two of us together, discussing private things, keeping him outside the circle, perhaps even banding against him.

I thought that it was time we had finished. I longed to ask Vanda how she had managed to get away, and other things too, but these violent emotions were destructive and exhausting, I felt mostly a passionate wish to be home.

I answered before Vanda could say a word. I said, "Yes, Daniel, we have. I was just going. I wonder if you'd mind ringing me a car? I feel lazy and I'd like to drive back. There was that rather nice little firm I used before."

He said, reverting to his former sulky manner, "If you'd only wait a little, I'd drive you back myself. You could at least have lunch with us. I know Vanda would like you to stay."

She said like a good little girl, "Please stay to lunch, Elizabeth."

But I said firmly that I had to be back, and three quarters of an hour later was on my way. Daniel and Vanda waved goodbye to me at the door, and Sophy dissolved into tears, though I do not think this meant much, it was simply an excess of emotion. I was as sure the tears would stop when my car was out of sight as I was that my smiling host and hostess would at once fall into frenzied battle.

Well, it had to come. Neither Daniel nor Vanda is of a calm temperament. It would do them good. By night-time they would probably be reconciled. And Martin's address, which had been pushed into my hand while Daniel was directing the driver, was in my bag as well as the article that the colonel had dropped in for me: the sight of this last drove out for the moment all thoughts of Martin Salvatore, and I could only think again of that long, dark tunnel, with an unknown Steve at the end of it.

There was of course the cancer. I suppose I wanted to forget it. Now I remembered. It was one of the strangest episodes in our whole acquaintance, only now there seemed to be so many strange things, it was only one of many. It had hurt me dreadfully. It is always inconceivable to be deliberately hurt by someone one loves.

We had our moments. We had many moments, moments of peace and love, laughter and beauty. I think in his own way he loved me, for a time at least, but he was so twisted within himself that he was afraid of loving, terrified of being bound down, and so each brief period of tenderness must be followed by savagery, insult and cruelty. One could never depend on Steve. I would have married him for the asking, but I would have been a fool to have done so: it would have been hell to be married to him. The first wife, whom he so decried, was virtually broken by him, and the second, whom I so hated, was fortunate that he died when he did: the marriage was already on the rocks, there would have been nothing left for her but disaster.

It was towards the end. I knew in my heart that it was the end. But then this is something one seldom admits: one believes what one passionately wants to believe. One says foolish things like, This has happened before and it did not last, or, He always has these moments of hating, or Tomorrow will be different. People talk of pride and self-respect and decency and so on, but none of these trifling things matters when one is enmeshed, and so I hung on in a contemptible fashion, waited for phones to ring, bells to sound, postmen to knock, and meanwhile lived my furtive shadow-life, doing all the things I had to do, even finishing my column for unhappy readers who wanted my advice.

I gave always the best quality advice.

"Dear Elizabeth Ingram, My boy friend says he is still in love with me, but he never writes or rings, and when we do go out together, flirts with other girls even when I'm there. Please, what am I to do? I still love him so very much..."

A boy who treats you so badly when you are engaged is not going to make a very good husband. You are after all very young, you should think carefully before tying yourself down. I suggest that you try not to brood on this too much, go out with other boys from time to time, make your boy friend see that he is not the only pebble on the beach.

"Dear Elizabeth Ingram, My boy-friend is very cruel to me..."

"Dear Elizabeth Ingram, My boy-friend drinks too much..."

"Dear Elizabeth Ingram, I am so miserable I don't know what to do..."

How they would laugh, these girls — or would they, they do not seem to be the laughing kind — if they knew that Elizabeth Ingram is also miserable, does not know what to do, has a boy-friend who is unfaithful, drinks too much and is often cruel. Yet Elizabeth Ingram is human too, and so are her secretaries who type the answers: they too suffer from wandering husbands, unkind boy-friends and families who do not understand them. I remember seeing one of them crying as she wrote her sensible answer, and sometimes I myself have been amazed at the wide, white path that runs between one's own experience and that of other people. Dear Wretched of Wimbledon, you love a man who is persistently unfaithful, leave him, he's no good, finish. Dear Elizabeth Ingram, you love a man who is persistently unfaithful, hang on to him like grim death, assure yourself he will change, suddenly reform. The operative word in both cases is "finish", only the girl in Wimbledon may take the advice and end it herself; Elizabeth Ingram clings, poor sod, and it ends exactly the same way, only despite herself.

I clung, if that is the correct past tense, it looks a little odd. There were no phone calls, no visits, no sign of life. Then he rang at last, after nearly three weeks' silence, and suggested we went out to a local pub, near his flat in Highgate. Some instinct warned me not to go. For one thing I had grown sick of pubs as a rendezvous. I am not really a deep drinker, and this particular place, which had the odd name of "The Cow in Aspic" — heaven knows where that came from — was where all Steve's drinking cronies tended to congregate. For me it was a little like being in a pillory, though I daresay I exaggerate, I doubt if anyone was so interested. I felt branded as Steve's latest, or Steve's cast-off, I thought people laughed at me or were sorry for me. I don't suppose they did, but I would have preferred to go somewhere else.

I should have said no. I said yes, of course. Of course. And I changed my old working shirt into my best blouse, made up my face carefully, and took great trouble over my hair. I might be sick at the stomach, but at least I would make a gallant appearance at my execution. It was to be my execution too, but I do not suppose I consciously realised that and, when Steve drove up, miraculously on time, we set off for "The Cow in Aspic", and to my surprise went into the private bar which normally Steve despised as a haunt of poofs and elderly ladies.

At least it spares me the cronies who are all boozing away in the saloon, but then I see that I am not to be spared entirely, for at the table to which Steve is already making his way, is an elderly woman, large and prosperous-looking, rather hand-some in her own way, who is obviously expect no us. By her side is a spaniel on a leash, which is avidly lapping up beer from a large ashtray.

She greeted me with a faint, unwelcoming smile. Her eyes moved up and down me. Her voice was the voice of well-to-do, middle-class, elderly ladies who were once used to a fleet of servants. You hear it behind desks in welfare offices, schools and institutions: it was a no-nonsense voice, not unpleasing, but clear and firm with authority. Her name was Phoebe. I don't know her surname, I never knew it.

"Hallo, Elizabeth," she said, pulling the spaniel closer to her in case I might kick it then, as she turned to Steve, her face and voice both softened. If Steve had been asking her for public assistance, he would have received every penny: I would have had to wait at home for an unsympathetic visitor.

I saw that he was very gentle and charming with her, all smiles. There was no one who could be more charming than Steve when he chose. At once I was wildly jealous, though she must have been in her early sixties. I had, as I was to discover, every reason to be jealous, but not of Phoebe who was after all only an intermediary, a kind of upper-class bawd.

Steve bought us drinks. I could see that he was very nervous. There was always one thing about Steve: however abominably he behaved he did not do it lightly. It was as if one section of him hated his own brutality. He was very pale and his hands shook. I suppose — indeed I know, I had to know — that this was all set-up, but he was not enjoying it, and he slopped over some of my drink as he set it on the table.

They began to talk across me. I was as eclipsed from the conversation as if I were a small child: indeed, a child would have received more attention. If I had been a more sophisticated person I would have chipped in and somehow swung the conversation round to include myself, but I am no use at this kind of thing, especially when I am emotionally involved, and I simply sat there while they talked with great animation.

It was disgracefully bad manners, but somehow I was made to feel that the ill-breeding was mine.

At first I hardly listened, for I was in too much confusion. This was something new, it had never happened before. Then I realised they were talking about some young woman called Joanna. Then I did listen, and I understood that Steve had met Joanna at Phoebe's house and fallen very much in love with her. I write this down calmly. Even now it seems to me monstrous, but then I was so dazed and bewildered that for a while I did not really take it in.

Phoebe, whose mission seemed to be that of the hammer of God, turned to me and said, "It really was first sight, you know. Like the novels. I am so happy for Joanna. She has had rather a wretched kind of life." Then smiling at Steve, she said, "I must go now, I've got to take this poor little creature to the vet, but we'll be seeing you on Sunday, won't we?"

I did not hear Steve's reply, which was mumbled into his chest. I have to assume that Phoebe was brought in to do the dirty work, and what kind of woman she was to do that, I cannot imagine, but when she gathered up all her possessions — she was one of those people who always carry enormous handbags, shopping baskets and paper carriers — together with the sick spaniel for whom beer hardly seemed the appropriate medicine, she bestowed a final smile on me, an executioner's smile. I have no idea how I responded. I think now that I should have jumped to my feet and walked out, yet sometimes one's instinct, however cowardly it seems at the time, is better than one knows, and the fact that I remained sitting there with apparent calm was probably more effective than a violent exit.

It must have been, for the triumphant smile changed to a look of some astonishment.

Steve did not follow her. He remained sitting at the table for a minute in dead silence, then went over and brought us two more drinks. He was still very pale and shaking, and I realised that he was very drunk, must have been so when he came in: like most people used to a great deal of alcohol he seldom revealed the normal symptoms of unsteady gait or slurred speech until the very end when his reactions became unpredictable.

I said at last, "What is all this, Steve?" My voice did not seem to be my own. I felt strange, oddly isolated, though the bar was full.

He said, "Don't start nagging at me. Can't you see I'm ill?"

"I see you're drunk," I said. "I see you're a bastard."

He repeated sullenly, "I'm ill."

"Who is this girl, Joanna?"

"I don't want to discuss her with you."

"You've been discussing her in front of me. With that old bawd."

"She's a great friend of mine. I've known her for years. I won't have her insulted."

We were neither of us raising our voices. I imagine that to the other people there, if they were interested enough to look at us, we resembled two friends having a quiet chat over our drinks. A few men had overflowed from the saloon, for it was now lunch-time, and one of them greeted Steve and nodded amiably at me.

"I don't care whether I insult her or not," I said. "She's past insulting. She's a tricoteuse. She's one of those who would be knitting at the foot of the guillotine and laugh as the heads fall." My voice was still low and conversational. "You simply got her here to do your stinking work for you. You're a poor, miserable sort of creature, aren't you? Haven't you guts enough to tell me yourself?"

"I tell you," said Steve, "I'm ill. I'm dying."

"Oh, rubbish! What's all this? You'd better ring Joanna to take you home. You're just pissed."

He said in a choked voice, "Will you help me back to the flat, Elizabeth?"

"You're asking me — Of all the bloody cheek!" But then I saw that I must get out, whether Steve did or not, for in a moment I would burst into violent tears, and really this would not do, I could not so disgrace myself in the parlour of "The Cow in Aspic." I pushed my chair back, then I saw that, whatever the cause, Steve really was ill, for he too was on his feet, staggering and looking ghastly.

I found myself — I suppose through sheer force of habit — taking his arm, and we made our way out of the bar and into the street that led to his home. Our progress was disgraceful. I am small, Steve was big, and he was leaning almost his whole weight on me. I could not see how we would ever get there, and there was no sign of a taxi, which in any case would probably have refused to take us. Taxis do not like drunks: they are prone to be sick or pick a quarrel.

I should have left him there. I should have left him collapsed on the pavement. And there I was, with this six-foot bastard holding on to me so hard that I was all but shoved into the gutter. Fortunately, a friend of Steve's drove past and, seeing what was happening, drew up at our side. He got out and came over to me. I had met him before. He was a television producer. He said, "Shall I drive you back to the flat?"

"Oh, please. I just can't cope."

He took hold of Steve's arm, saying, "There, there, old chap, this way," levered him into the car and held the door open for me. I got in. Don't ask me why. This was the moment to make my exit with such dignity as remained to me. We arrived at the flat, Steve was helped out and I followed him in.

The producer said, "Will you be all right?"

"Oh, I think so."

"Make him a strong coffee. Poor chap. He's been like that since the war, you know. I think he had a very bad time in the camp, it upset his whole system."

I did not make the coffee. When the friend had gone, I simply stood there, looking at Steve who was shambling about the room, then suddenly he went down on his knees before me.

I still stood there. I thought he had simply fallen down. I was not going to help him up, indeed I was incapable of doing so. I was a little out of my mind. I found myself looking round the room. I did not think consciously that this was the last time I would see it, though of course it was — but in this extraordinarily unreal situation it held a kind of desperate reality, I was compelled to cling on to it, it was the only support I had in such monstrous circumstances.

I had been happy here. I had been unhappy too, though nothing like this had ever happened. It was a plain, character-less kind of room. Some men enjoy creating a cosy atmosphere, but Steve was not one of them. There was his typing table: the machine, an old portable, had a page in it, and there was a small pile of typescript at the side. There was a television — he was a great sports addict — and a record player. There were a few books here and there, surprisingly few. It was all very tidy and completely impersonal. It would have been impossible to tell what sort of person Steve was from looking at his room. On the windowsill was some dilapidated plant that needed watering, and a couple of chrysanthemums were stuck in a jam-jar on the mantelpiece. There was not one single photograph. The bedroom led out of it, and the bathroom, which he shared with another tenant, was on the next floor. The telephone, also shared, was on the landing. That was all, but it was too much, much too much, and it was my legs now that would not bear me. I sat down suddenly in the only armchair, and Steve still ludicrously on his knees, crawled towards me, his hand going out for mine.

I said, "No!"

He said, "You must listen. I know I shouldn't have done it that way, but I just didn't know how to tell you."

"I'm going home."

162

"No, you must stay. You needn't worry, you know. I'll never marry Joanna. I shan't be alive to do so."

"What on earth are you talking about now?"

He raised his head to look full at me. He was still on his knees. He looked ridiculous. He said at last, "I didn't mean to tell you, but you'd better know. I've got cancer."

Should I not have believed him? Should I have laughed in his lying face? It is somehow the kind of thing you do believe, it does not provoke laughter, and it seems impossible that anyone should lie on such a matter. I only know that I felt as if I too had received a death blow. It was so appalling, so terrible, that it knocked everything else out of me, that wicked, vulgar scene in the pub, Phoebe, my own humiliation.

As it was of course meant to do.

I didn't cry. That came later. We talked about it quite calmly, holding hands. He said that was why he had seen so little of me lately. No, it was nothing to do with Joanna. He did love Joanna, but he loved me too, it was possible to love two people: now he would have neither of us, we would not have him. He told me about Joanna, and I listened without comment. He had known her a long time ago and they had separated, she had married someone else. Now she was divorced, and he had met her again at Phoebe's house. It was Phoebe who said he must tell me, it was not fair to keep it from me. He had had no idea that she would break the news so brutally, but she had not meant to be unkind, it was after all an impossible situation. She knew nothing about the cancer.

Then he said almost frantically, "Don't mention it to her. Promise you won't. I don't want Joanna to know just yet. I want to tell her in my own way."

I said I was unlikely ever to meet Phoebe again, but even if I did, I would never mention it. Perhaps at that moment a small, very small, almost inaudible warning bell rang in my brain, but I was too battered to listen to it, and there was Steve, looking white and anguished, staring up at me: my heart seemed broken, there was nothing left in me but love and horror and grief.

Yet, just before I left, there was one other moment when, if I had had any sense left in me at all, I might have realised that this was all a con, it was neither true nor real.

Steve said, "I don't know how long it will take. I'm pretty

tough, after all. But when it does come, I just want to go away. I shan't tell anyone, not even you, my darling. I'd like to die in peace. I think you'll understand."

And, as he said this, he raised his head, so that the light from the window illuminated his face. It was a scene straight out of a Victorian novel, all it needed was the choir of angels.

Of course I am now looking on this with coldly realistic hindsight. I am no longer torn with emotion, half-mad with desolation and sorrow. I know perfectly well that in this day and age you do not retire to die peacefully anywhere. If you are dying, unless you somehow contrive to hide yourself away, which is virtually impossible, you are taken to hospital. One could say that people are no longer allowed to die in peace: even if you find some remote cottage in the country, there are neighbours and postmen and tradesmen, all panting to interfere, all prepared to lug you off your deathbed so that you can receive proper attention. I believe that even then this grossly lurid melodrama jarred me a little. Even when catastrophe crushes one down, there tends to remain one small section of the mind that reasons and observes. But somehow this small ray of commonsense was extinguished, a ane at last I went home in a taxi that Steve ordered for me, and I cried thoughout the journey which must have been most edifying for the driver. However, I daresay taximen see worse in their time, and I was long past worrying about his reactions, I simply shoved a pound note into his hand and, without waiting for the change, ran upstairs to my flat, to receive there the full impact of the fact that Steve was dying, soon I would never see him again.

However, he was still alive, and I was to see him twice more, the first of these times a fortnight later. Three months after that he married Joanna and went out of my life.

During that fortnight I behaved like someone insane, ranting and roaring against the horror of the world, then so numbed with grief that I could only huddle on my bed, unable to eat or sleep. Only my friends were for the most part suspicious, even incredulous: one of them actually told me that this was a cruel and downright lie. I refused to believe her and was so angry that I swore never to speak to her again. I think that wild anger on my part was symptomatic, I believe that somewhere deep inside me I was beginning to have my doubts, especially as I never mentioned a word of it to Daniel. What he would have said about all this I can imagine only too well, but then at that time he was submerged in his own personal problems and it was easy enough to avoid him.

Only when I met Steve again, after two weeks of misery, it was he who shattered my belief into minute fragments, through a gross piece of overacting that even a stupid innocent like myself could not accept.

He rang me to meet him at my local, not "The Cow in Aspic" which I could not have borne to see again, but the small pub opposite my own flat. I went across. I must have looked more like dying than he did: no sleep, hardly any food and a waterfall of tears do not improve any female looks, and I was not a young girl. He on the other hand looked perfectly normal. We had a beer and talked as if nothing had happened. We did not mention the cancer. It was all a little remote. When we came out about an hour later, I asked if he would like to come up for lunch. We were crossing the road. He looked at me. I could not read his expression very well, but I have no doubt that if I had been able to do so, I would have seen written across his face, *I must not, if I come in we shall only start things again, it is too dangerous, there is always Joanna.* But this was too simple for Steve. He had to turn it to his dramatic advantage. He said in a gasp, "I'm not feeling good." Then, as I turned in sudden alarm, I saw him stiffen as if in a spasm of intolerable pain: when we reached the pavement, he held on for a second to the nearest lamp-post. Then, looking down into my shocked face he gave me a twisted smile. "Okay," he said, "It's nothing. It happens from time to time. I just have to get used to it. It's all over now. I feel fine. But I wouldn't be much company for you, Elizabeth. You can see how it is. I'll just get home and lie down for a bit."

I said, "Would you like me to get you a taxi."

"No. It'll do me good to walk."

I watched him striding off towards the tube station and, presumably, Joanna. I stood in the doorway gazing after him until he disappeared, then I went up to my own flat and cooked myself a proper meal. It tasted like gall and vinegar, but it was virtually the first solid food I had eaten for two weeks. I knew now that my friends were right. It was all a lie. Steve did not have cancer. I had watched him in that spasm. I don't know why he did not make the stage his profession, for it was very well done — the screwed up eyes, the open mouth, the head flung back, the feverish grab at the lamp-post. How to display anguish in one easy lesson — However, I am only silly nor-nor-west, and even the gullible have their perceptive moments. Not only did he not change colour — and he was looking exceptionally well that brisk autumn day — but there was not so much as a glisten of sweat on his brow or upper lip. In acute pain you sweat instantly, and your colour goes. Every motion and gesture was right, but that was something that even Steve could not simulate.

I was still to see him once more, and that was in a pub too, another pub near the B.B.C. I would have been wiser not to go. I did not know, of course, what awaited me, but in the circumstances, when everything was so obviously at an end, I should have accepted the decision, let it lie. I should, I should — The things one should do. I don't even know why I went. I did not want to go. He had lied to me — I still had no idea of the vast extent of the lies — but there was this one savage, cruel lie that had almost killed me, and it was uttered for no better reason than to give himself the excuse of not seeing me any more. It would have been simpler to say, It's finished, I'm in love with someone else, I don't want to see you again. It would have been brutal, but at least it would have been honest, real and direct. But Steve could not do things like that. He had to make it something dramatic, inevitable, with himself as the dying hero, retreating into limbo to save me pain. The fact that in this way he hurt me far more did not concern him: he had to create a situation that put him in the right and at the same time enabled him to be with his Joanna.

Poor Joanna, I imagine she had one hell of a life, after the rhapsody was over.

I felt quite numbed by my discovery. In a way it was more of a shock than the original lie. I did not tell my friends. I felt too ashamed, not so much for my own folly as for Steve's humiliation. I still found it hard to believe that he could tell me such a monstrous lie, and the fact that he had done it so well, made it worse, like that brilliant piece of drama on the pavement. I did my work automatically, tried to lose myself in other people's problems, I lost weight — unhappy love is the only certain weight-reducer — felt old and ill and sick to death of myself.

When the phone went, and Steve said he would collect me to meet some of his friends, I agreed almost outside my own volition, not quite knowing what I was doing, almost not caring.

I will relate that episode later. I cannot bear to write it down now. It still hurts to describe such things. It was of course only one lie in many, but that I did not then know, I still believed in the prison camp, and the double first at Balliol, and the lost, unhappy existence at the minor public school.

Chapter 7

IT WAS THE MATTER OF THE SCHOOL THAT CROPPED UP FIRST. I suppose I could call it an investigation, if that is the right word, but in this case it really fell in front of me, without any effort on my behalf. And perhaps I could hardly call any of this an investigation, for everything I discovered seemed to shrivel up before me, and in the end it was almost as if Steve had not been born at all.

At least Count Magnus was there, to the dreadful destruction of his pursuer. But even there, there is a certain analogy, for I am beginning to think that I represented to Steve a reality that must be crushed: it impinged on his own, to save his own dream he had to destroy me.

However, I could not spend all my time on this. Apart from my own work which suddenly redoubled as if everyone were undergoing a crisis, I had to see Daniel who came up on a brief visit. And then my unhappy prophecy was realised, for Eve, who had promised to ring me, turned up too. I might have known it. The Eves of this world always turn up, accompanied by their little suitcase full of cosmetics or drugs or silk scarves or whatever they happen to be peddling.

Daniel arrived unexpectedly late one afternoon, swooping down on me as I was dealing with the last two letters of my column. I was very busy, but as always was too pleased to see him to grumble. I swung round to look up at him, received the flowers he dutifully brought me, the official kiss on the cheek, and saw that he looked a little better, though still too drawn and preoccupied for my taste.

"Well?" I said, "How are things?"

I saw the shutter come down on his face. Obviously things

were not yet entirely right. But he said after a pause, "Vanda's better. I am sure she'll never do this again. I think she knows now where her home is. But — Elizabeth, I have to see Martin."

"Why on earth should you have to see him?" It was a silly question, but I was trying to stall: I no more wanted him and Martin to meet again than Vanda did: apart from the fact that it would certainly end in a useless and undignified brawl, it might even get into the gutter press, which was the last thing to be encouraged. It is not a good thing for doctors to be involved in fights with their wife's former husband, and Daniel, usually so self-controlled, was by now in such a state that anything could have happened.

Daniel said, the temper crackling in his voice, "Oh don't be so silly. You must know that I have to see him. For one thing he seems to have been threatening her. She won't go into details — I really don't know what's the matter with her these days — but it's obvious that he's been trying to frighten her. I want to see him to tell him that if it goes on like that, I shall inform the police. That'll scare the pants off him. These foreigners are always scared to death of the police. Besides, it'll do him good to see I'm backing her."

I did not comment on this. It was true that I knew nothing of Martin Salvatore beyond what Vanda had told me, but I had the idea that his pants would not drop so easily. I said, "Well, how are you going to get to him?" I fiddled with the papers on my desk. Martin's address lay in the top drawer. Needless to say, I had no intention whatsoever of letting Daniel see it.

Daniel said more uncertainly, "Well, I thought you might have his address. Vanda just won't give it me. I've asked her and asked her, but the more I go on about it, the more obstinate she gets. Sometimes I just don't understand her. Mind you, I daresay I'll wear her down in time, but you two girls seemed to be confiding in each other, and I thought she might have told you."

"Why on earth should she?"

"Oh, I don't know, Elizabeth. Don't you start getting difficult too. She could have mentioned it. After all, she was there, wasn't she?"

I am too hemmed in by lies to enjoy lying, and I am anyway a remarkably poor liar, except in acute emergencies. This

169

seemed to me an acute emergency. "I didn't ask her," I said, which was true enough, then I added something that was not true at all. "I don't have his address," I said.

Daniel said, "Oh, damn." Then, "Couldn't you ask Vanda for it? You could say — Oh, I don't know. You could make up some excuse. After all, you are — "

"I am a writer. True. You do hold a funny view of my profession, darling. I certainly couldn't ask her. You know I couldn't. She'd say with perfect reason that it's none of my business. Besides, she's no fool and she'd know at once that it came via you. If she doesn't want you to call on Martin, she must have her reasons, and if she gave me the address she'd know I'd hand it over to you immediately."

"That's what I was hoping," said Daniel with a half-grin.

"No, love, I can't, and that's final. It's not that I don't want to help you, but truly I can't see that your meeting him would do any good. I expect he won't do anything more. After all, she came back to you. He must see now that she doesn't take his threats seriously."

That beastly slip of paper was blazing so luridly in my mind that I half expected Daniel to push me aside and open the drawer. But of course he did nothing of the kind and, when he had gone, in rather a bad temper, I saw that perhaps I ought to visit this abominable and alarming man after all. It was not something I looked forward to and, having told myself that I must do it, I pushed it out of my mind and again forgot, in the way that one always forgets things one does not want to do.

Eve rang me the next day.

I recognised the bright, sweet voice immediately. My first reaction was one of sheer exasperation. I did not see why I had to be pursued by a little cosmetician who was so resolved to paint on me a face that was not my own. But I am weak, I am always bad at a direct confrontation. Afterwards I thought of all the decent excuses I could have made, but in actual fact what I said was, "Of course. Do come round for a drink. How long are you going to be over here?"

She answered, to my dismay, "Oh for several months. I want to start a small clientèle here. You will let your friends know about me, won't you?"

My friends are not really the type to wear elaborate make-up and stock their bathrooms with little tubes and jars, but I promised to do so. Besides, it seemed a little unkind to loose Eve on innocent women who might be seduced by the thought of a free facial: it was obvious from my own experience that she would never let go and they would be deaved for months afterwards with ardent phone-calls promising them kissproof lipsticks and cheap perfume.

I suggested that she came round that evening, if she was free, and she agreed happily and arrived on the dot. I suppose that was her professional training. She looked much as she did in the El Saddle, except that the suit was now tweed, and she wore a neat little hat. She was more made-up than I remembered, and she had on a great deal of expensive perfume. She carried a suitcase from which I carefully averted my eyes.

We exchanged cordial greetings. I found that I was quite pleased to see her. She was a nice little woman, and it was not her fault that I preferred to be plain and unpainted. We sipped at our drinks, she said I looked much better, and I said I was quite recovered now and back at work.

"What a lovely apartment!"

"I'm glad you like it. It's fairly new still, but it still excites me. I get quite a lift of the heart when I walk through it."

Eve said, "I see you are not using my make-up, you naughty girl. Would you like me to show you how to apply it?"

"Oh no. Thank you very much, but you know, really, I don't go in for make-up."

"You should. It helps to preserve the skin."

This made me feel like a mummy. I suppose Nefertiti painted her face, but then she was so beautiful that it could hardly matter one way or another. I just laughed and did not answer. If she went into my bathroom she would see her bottles on the shelf. I kept them there because they were pretty and looked so expensive. I never used any of them except occasionally the moisturising cream, which I put on my hands when they were chapped. They were a depressing waste of money.

I saw her bright eyes moving over my room, noting everything, including no doubt the fact that the table was not properly dusted, that a silver decanter needed cleaning, and that the cushions had not been plumped up. If Vanda's children had been to see me, she would have found the floor covered in biscuit crumbs. But I expect she forgave me all this because I was an artist. I am not an artist, but to Eve anyone who can type probably is, and we all know what artists are, the untidy, immoral, fascinating creatures.

She remarked suddenly, lowering her voice, "So terrible about poor darling Paul."

I had forgotten about Paul Ducane, but these words stirred my memory, and I saw once again that mock saloon bar, with Paul, dressed as a cowboy, drinking his scotch and calling me doll. I looked at her in surprise. I said, "Why? What's happened to him?"

She fixed her eyes on me. The lids were blue and the lashes false. They made me think of a Disney cow. She said, "But surely, darling, you read your papers."

I was a little taken aback. I do read my papers, I have always done so, but lately so much has happened that sometimes I just look at the headlines and read the leader. This is very bad, I hold no brief for myself. I must certainly read them properly in future. I said, "Well, I have been very busy. I must have missed it. Please tell me."

"He's dead."

"Oh no!"

"It's so terrible. I still haven't recovered from the shock." Then her voice sank right down so that I could only just hear it. People tend to do this when they are speaking of death. "He shot himself."

I was shocked too, though perhaps for different reasons. I thought of the eternal cowboy, cocooned in his stage setting, riding always into the sunset, walking always down the empty street, leaping on and off his horse, administering chaste kisses at the end of a film. There must for all of us, including Steve, be moments of harsh reality, but to shoot himself — I knew that Eve would spare me none of the details. She lived a life of proxy drama, making up faces more beautiful than her own. enmeshed in the loves and hates of her stars. And at once she started to tell me everything, so that I was spared the necessity of exclaiming in horror.

"It's inexplicable," she said, "Inexplicable!" The syllables rolled off her tongue. "I mean, darling, he was a bit of a has-been, we all know that, he wasn't exactly a young man any more, and of course fashions change in films like everything else — but to shoot himself! Do you know, he put the muzzle of the gun in his mouth — In his mouth! Can you believe it? It must have been a dreadful sight for his poor wife when she came into his study."

172

"Oh my God!"

"Can you imagine it?"

Unfortunately, I could, but I did not answer this: Eve by now was in full spate.

"I just couldn't believe it. It's not as if he's short of money. He's got this lovely ranch and the cutest little wife — Did you ever meet her?"

"No."

"And all those precious children. Of course he didn't get the leading roles any more, but he was always appearing in television Westerns, and the last time I spoke to him he was so pleased, he had just been offered a part in — oh, 'The Virginian' I think it was — you must have seen it, I know you have it over here, and I mean, darling, there was no question of him starving in a garret or anything like that. In fact I know one shouldn't speak ill of the dead, but in the strictest confidence, he was just a wee bit tight with money. And to shoot himself like that, and in such a dreadful way — "

I was beginning to find her rather ghoulish. I noticed that in moments of excitement she sounded quite American, for all she was English, but I suppose that was due to working with Hollywood film stars. I had to see that all this had made her day. It was rather like small children who take such an intense interest in their own mishaps. I remember that when Sophy scratched herself once — and you could hardly see it with a magnifying glass — she told us all about it for weeks.

I said, "I don't think the way he did it matters. The only thing that's extraordinary is that he had to kill himself at all."

Eve did not like this very much. She said a little coldly, "But think of his poor wife."

"Well, of course, it must have been ghastly for her, but then I don't know her. I wonder why he killed himself."

I could see that Eve thought me entirely heartless. She said, "He was a very dear friend of mine."

I do not suppose for one moment she was a very dear friend, or she might have had more idea of why this happened. I wondered what the obituaries had made of him. Obituaries are seldom kind to faded stars: they would probably not give him more than a couple of lines, and perhaps he only had that because his ending was so dramatic. He had never really been celebrated like Gary Cooper or Spencer Tracy: he had simply

173

been popular with ordinary people and young children. But something in Eve's censorious face, drawn together under the make-up, forced a remark out of me that I had not had the least intention of making. I said in what must have seemed to her a savage kind of way, "I had a friend who died in a ditch."

There is a weekly political paper that runs competitions, and one of them recently was for the best party-stopping remark. I feel that this should have won a prize, and the moment it was out, I was bitterly ashamed of having said it, not for Eve, who did not matter a damn to me, but for Steve who did.

She rallied remarkably well. Working in a film studio must toughen one against bad taste, and she was no doubt surrounded by crudities, not to mention four-letter words. She was silenced for a second by this extraordinary statement, then said in a richly emotional voice, "Oh my dear, how terrible for you."

I think I deserved that. We did not talk much more of Paul. I am afraid that Eve found me unsympathetic. She did tell me, however, that the suicide occurred about three weeks after I met him in Jericho City. Nobody, she said over and over again, could understand it. He came home, he seemed perfectly normal, he had had the good news about the part, and then in the morning, when he was cleaning his gun, his wife heard the shot. It could not in the circumstances be called an accident. It caused a great deal of local talk, and the El Saddle Hotel was full of reporters. The post mortem had found no sign of any mortal disease. The ranch was now up for sale, and his widow had moved to New York.

Then shaking her head, sighing and touching her lips delicately with a lace-trimmed handdkerchief, Eve returned to the one subject that wholly absorbed her, and opened up the suitcase. It was full of bottles, tubes, jars and assorted cosmetics. "I knew," she said, "you would be interested, and some of these are new and really marvellous. You're quite privileged, darling, I haven't shown them to anyone else. And they aren't expensive. Most firms would charge twice what I do."

I thought they were very expensive, but could not help being fascinated by row upon row of sweet-smelling nonsense that would remove wrinkles, shadows under the eyes, blot out blemishes and hide that scraggy neck. It was a giant camouflage, a monumental con, it was like being drowned in scent. I listened to the spiel, which she did very well, and of course in the end was weak enough to buy a lipstick and a small atomiser of perfume that Eve delicately sprayed upon my wrist.

"Now," she said smiling, and snapping the case to as she prepared to go, "you must ring me when you are going to some fascinating lunch with your editor, and I'll come along and give you a marvellous facial and make-up. It will make all the difference, you'll see."

The editor who sometimes takes me out to lunch is a woman and an old friend. She wears no make-up herself, and would be frightened to death if I turned up bedaubed and painted. I also lunch occasionally with publishers and agents, but it was no good explaining to Eve that in my profession no one really gives a damn how you look, provided you are not actually dirty: the only thing that matters is how you write, and if your writing is not up to standard, neither lipstick nor eye-shadow is going to help you. However, I assured her that I would let her know at once, and she departed quite gaily, saying as I saw her to the door, "And don't forget now to tell all your friends about me."

I said I would not forget, and she promised to get in touch with me. I am sure she will. I am beginning to think I will never be rid of her. I saw her patter towards the lift, waving her free hand at me, then came back into my flat, which still smelt of her, and thought about Paul Ducane.

So Paul had crossed the Great Divide. One could almost say that he had shot his way through. Eve would have been astonished, though possibly gratified, to know that this news chilled me very much. But then of course Paul Ducane was beginning to merge a little with Steve Olsen, for both of them had specialised in unreality. I wondered, shivering, where and when reality had begun to seep through. Perhaps it is not possible to go on living a phoney life. One cannot spend one's whole existence in a hardboard saloon bar with its swinging doors, wearing a stetson and pointed boots, carrying a gun upon one's hip and saying, Howdy, stranger, to everyone. And then go home to a dude ranch, to his third, fourth, fifth wife, I've forgotten the number, eat a good American meal and go out to watch the Arizona sunset, with nothing much ahead but another small part, where one would play again a cowboy, an ageing cowboy, with stetson, boots and gun.

175

It must have been a sudden impulse. Paul Ducane did not seem to me the kind to plan ahead. Of course I did not know him at all, I knew nothing about him except from the films I had seen, and when we spoke together it was simply an extension of a B-feature, with slight modifications as a concession to reality. Perhaps that was what hit him suddenly so that in a flash of a moment he picked up the gun he was cleaning, shoved it down his throat and pulled the trigger.

But, do you know, I believe he never meant to do it at all. I think he was once again playing a part, and he simply over-acted as he frequently had done in his films. He was after all for the most part nothing, he was as human as the imitation cowboy who used to stand — still does for all I know — above the skyline in the Las Vegas Strip, speaking the same mechanical words at regular intervals. I think for a second he saw himself for the cardboard man he was, and thought in a sudden fit of rage, I'll show 'em, I'll prove I'm human as the best of them. I am somehow sure that as he pulled the trigger, he realised what he was doing and would have changed his mind, but then it was too late, and his wife would come running in to see, poor wretch, a human mess of blood and brains.

I wonder if Steve when he died — and his death was not of his choosing — faced reality in that final second. I hope it was too quick, I pray he did not have time.

Poor Paul Olsen. Poor Steve Ducane — Oh Christ, I'm going nuts. But never mind, tomorrow I shall go to Somerset House, for that after all must be true, he was born, he lived in a house, he had parents. I am beginning to feel that if I can find nothing real to hold on to, Steve Olsen does not exist, did not exist, was a figment of my own imagination.

Even the school — Now this is odd, because this was something I had entirely forgotten, and I am sure the lapse of memory was subconsciously deliberate. I had forgotten it, and now I remembered it, and for the first time since Steve's death I took out the file where I had kept all the things that pertained to him, the odd notes, one bad press photo, reviews of his books and the accounts of his death.

I never looked at it after he died. I do not really know why I kept it. Perhaps I deal with so many of other people's letters that I never, with this one exception, keep any of my own. I have none of Daniel's and he, when he was a boy, used to write wonderful letters, amusing and copiously illustrated. It may be because my father was a solicitor, who sometimes declared that indiscreet correspondence provided him with a large part of his business. But then, for all I am now scavenging in the past, I have never been one to collect the faded pressed flower, I have always torn up rather than shove into the bottom drawer.

Once in my career — for I have done an odd variety of jobs in my time — I took evening classes in what was rather pompously called "The Art of Writing". As a class it was pure Kafka, and seldom could there have been an odder collection of neurotics, mostly escaping — from mother, an unhappy marriage, sexual complications, nervous breakdowns. It would have provided any psychiatrist with the most interesting studies, and in the end, weighed down by impossible confidences, I was reduced to such a neurotic state myself that I decided teaching was not my metier. One of the things we did in this class was to have compositions read out, and very good and very disconcerting some of them were too, especially when the class discovered that no holds were barred and they could write as they pleased. We had one well-known poet in that class, and one successful novelist. But there was a small, well-defined group who had attended the same class long before I arrived, and who would no doubt continue with the next lecturer, which produced manuscripts from the bottom drawer, carefully treasured, and written, God knows how many years ago. I grew to recognise these scripts after the first term, for they wore an unmistakably corpselike air, they were yellow and dusty with age, and once or twice I had to notice that the reader knew his composition by heart, for he read it so dramatically and without looking at the page. There was nothing of course that I could do about it, and it really hardly mattered: if I had had no compositions to discuss the whole class would have packed up. Sometimes I suggested it might be fun to try something new, and occasionally when I grew a little cross at being expected to discuss something discussed so many times before, I set a specific subject. But it made no difference, for the hoarders just wrote nothing, and next time happily produced yet another manuscript ten or twenty years old.

I think this influenced me in my determined resolve to tear anything and everything up. It may have been inborn, but certainly I refuse to keep anything, even my own work. There are hardly any sentimental knick-knacks around my place, except from children: I do keep paper flowers made by Sophy, and I have a variety of artwork from Mario: he is not really an artistic child. I have children's photos, of course, and as Daniel and Vanda are the only family I am likely to have, I have the odd photo of them too, including a wedding picture which like everything of its kind comes straight from the twenties. But other photos, no; letters, no — and as for theatre programmes and suchlike, they go straight into the wastepaper basket. Even Harry's letters — and he was no writer, he wrote briefly and lovingly, rather like a child — are gone now. I cannot live out my life in a pot-pourri jar.

I do not know why I kept Steve's things. In such matters he was the least sentimental of men. But I did keep them and, being trained to work in an office — though now of course I do most of my work at home — I put everything in an orange file, and tucked it away in a cupboard with my stationery.

I went over to my stationery cupboard, and there among the flimsy, carbons and shorthand notebooks, was the file. I felt strange touching it, it was a little like disinterring something in the dust. Not Count Magnus this time, for the old gentleman was after all actively malevolent, and that Steve was not, but it was a little like a ghost story too: I had the feeling that I was moving something that would be better undisturbed.

I took it out and laid it open on my desk. I found that my hand was shaking. And after all there was nothing there. Until I came to the business of the school — What made me keep that? At that time I still believed in most of what Steve had told me, there were lies of course, but then there are always lies, we are human, we cannot in self-defence tell the truth all the time. Apart from that there was so little. The photo was lamentable. He was not at the best a photogenic man. Such looks as he possessed were mobile looks. He could look heavy and ugly then, when he smiled, give out such charm that the snows would have melted before him. He hated press photos, and it looked in this instance as if he hated the photographer. It was unsigned. Steve would have walked straight out of my flat if I had suggested his signing it. I looked at that sullen gangster face, but I did not immediately tear it up, only put it at the bottom of the file. There was the odd note. He never wrote letters. Perhaps, as a man with many women, he was

178

wary, agreed with my father that he might land himself in legal trouble. There were reviews of his books. There was a brief autobiographical note in a literary periodical. There was one full-dress interview, with the same photo as the one I had just put away.

And there was this extraordinary letter from an angry headmaster, which appeared in one of the Sunday newspapers just after Steve's death.

Steve talked a great deal about that school. He always spoke of it with a kind of suppressed horror. He hated it. I found that easy to believe: I imagine that someone so self-centred and eccentric would have been unhappy at any boarding school. He had plenty of friends and, unlike some womanisers, got on excellently with his own sex, but he had, as far as I could see, few intimates, and he had long phases of being solitary and alone. Perhaps that was why he could not establish a lasting relationship with any woman. He was, so he told me, dumped in the school at the age of ten, while his parents were abroad. The only relatives he had, lived in London: an aunt and her two children, both girls. These did exist, I suppose they could have resolved my problems for me if I were ever able to contact them. I met one of the cousins once, a wary, hard-faced woman of forty-odd, who eyed me up and down contemptuously, as if to say, Here's another one.

Steve was desperately unhappy at the school: he was then rather small, and he had the life bullied out of him. He ran away five times, and each time he arrived on his aunt's doorstep, a wretched, shivering little boy, scared out of his wits. She always took him in, but I suppose she had to let the school know, and then he was collected and taken back. It used to make me sick to think of it. She was always kind to him in her own way. He spoke of her with genuine affection: it is possible that she was the only person he continued to love till the end of his life. She died a couple of years before he did, and for the last few months of her life was out of her mind, not violently insane, but foolish and rambling and lost within herself. Steve always went to see her, and during her hospital periods — for from time to time she was taken away for psychiatric treatment — visited her every week, though the hospital was out in the suburbs.

It was a well-known school. I am no admirer of public schools, I do not care much for what they produce, and I have

179

a deep-rooted mistrust of anything that caters for an elite. I have argued fiercely with Daniel on this. Daniel, I think, would have fitted in very well in a public school: he did not go to one because Harry could not afford it, but he went to a day school that is very well known indeed, and which certainly has its own elite, though of a more intellectual kind.

"You and your elite!" he used to say. "What do you think you are? You were up at Oxford, weren't you? That's a snob thing if ever there was one."

"Oh, nonsense!"

"Of course it is. My university is way down below it. You can afford to look down on me."

"You really are talking the most terrible stuff, Daniel. I don't know what's the matter with you. I admit that Oxbridge has a certain mystique attached to it, but the education there is no different from any other university. Your college is probably much more modern, and they say that its medical training school is one of the best in the world."

"If I have a son," said Daniel — this was before he met Vanda — "I shall send him to Harrow."

"Why?"

"Well, Churchill was there. And there's still something about a public school education. I only wish I had had it."

And away he went, on how one learnt to mix with everyone, what a wide outlook one had, what a splendid background, how all our great men were at such places, and so on at such length that by the time he had finished, he sounded like some poor little slum boy who had been to a council school and gone to work at fourteen.

This still crops up occasionally. Mario, if he is not careful, will one day find himself landed at a public school where I suspect he will be as unhappy as Steve. I only hope he will not put arsenic in the headmaster's soup.

I did wonder occasionally why Steve was bullied so much. He told me hair-raising stories straight out of *Stalky & Co.* I knew he was small, but I thought he must have been a fairly tough little boy, despite his description of himself, for he was over six foot when I knew him, and broad to match. He was also surely good at games, which seems to be the traditional password. He played a great deal of amateur sport, especially cricket, though he admitted that he was not very good at it. "I play like a peasant," he informed me — and God knows what that meant — "but I love it." However, sport did not seem to save him, and sometimes, when he got carried away by the subject, he almost broke my heart. I cannot endure the thought of a bullied child: if I had been his aunt, I would have whisked him away, whatever his parents said, and found him a day school near by.

But I accepted everything he said. Why not? It all fitted in. He must have told other people the same story for, when he died, one of the obituaries referred to this particular school and said he had been there for five years. This happened to appear in the daily that I read myself, and it also mentioned that he had been up at Balliol. Balliol did not trouble to contradict this, but the school did. The headmaster wrote an extremely indignant letter — I do not quite know why he was so angry, for the lie was in a way a compliment, and Steve was a well-known man — pointing out that Stephen Olsen had never attended this school, there was no record of his name.

I was utterly bewildered when I read this letter. It seemed incomprehensible to me. I remembered all the detailed stories Steve had told me, even the names of the masters, the description of the few boys who had been his personal friends. I could almost see the school, so vividly had he described the surroundings. But I was too unhappy to brood much on this, and indeed until now, when everything Steve had told me, was vanishing into the distance, had almost forgotten about it.

I reread the headmaster's letter now. He seemed completely outraged that Steve should have foisted himself upon him. However, there was nothing he could do about it except protest, and no one bothered to answer him, so that was the end of the matter.

I suppose I just pushed it out of my mind, like the cancer episode — like that moment of apparent paralysis that somehow communicated itself to me.

Like our last meeting

Most love affairs end in an ugly way. Not that we began so romantically either. Meeting at a party, meeting later in my own flat, and becoming lovers after the vast and preposterous party I gave myself, to celebrate the first flat I had ever had on my own, a kind of belated coming of age. It was a mad, wonderful, appalling party to which I asked everyone in the world that I knew. Harry had never liked parties, I do not care for them myself, but then after he died I lived in a series of small flatlets where there was no room for anyone but myself and the occasional couple of guests. This flat, the one I had before my present one, was enormous, with a huge sitting-room, so big that it almost earned that disagreeable name, the "lounge". I think I had nearly a hundred guests. It was a champagne party, and I put the bottles on ice in the bath. For a while I could not understand why all my guests kept running into the bathroom, they could not all have upset stomachs. Then I realised that champagne in the bath fascinated them, it had become pure class distinction. The poor kept coals in the bath, but Elizabeth has champagne. It was in its way a glorious and insane party, filled with ill-assorted people of all ages, with Steve, quite drunk, wandering through it like a kind of ghost, aggressively rude to people he disliked, unexpectedly charming to the shy, lonely and isolated.

He stayed when they had all gone. We met at last in a room that looked as all rooms look after a party, a shambles of dirty glasses, brimming ash-trays, remnants of half-eaten food. It did not matter. We did not see it. I will always remember that untidy, disorganised party with the utmost joy.

And then came the last meeting.

As I said before, I should never have gone. But he called for me. He looked very strange. He did not mention the cancer again. He said he was having a drink with some B.B.C. friends in a pub near Langham Place, he thought I would like to meet them. I was not dressed for any occasion, and I made no effort to remedy this. It hardly seemed to matter. We set off in his ramshackle tank-car, and I was wearing slacks and sweater and no make-up. We arrived at the pub where there was a small party in progress. There was a poet there, a minor poet of little verses but quite well-known. There was the television producer whom I had met before, who had come to my rescue in front of "The Cow in Aspic". He was a quiet little man who made passes at anyone under eighty, he was amusing and, as it turned out, kind. There were two television girls, I do not know what they represented or what they did, but one of them was the other woman typified, attractive, not very young, footloose, unprincipled and out for any man she could get. Any wife would know her. I imagine she specialised in other people's husbands, and other people's lovers. She made a dead set for Steve the moment he appeared, ignoring me altogether. Her clever, avid face grew eager at the sight of him, her predatory hands stretched out for the kill. She was not the kind of woman Steve liked, but she served his purpose which was to demolish me, and he made full use of her.

I do not suppose he ever saw her again, but I still hate her, I will hate her till the day I die. She must by now be more than middle-aged, I doubt she is married, and the men she attracts must be few and far between, but I still hate her, I hope she rots, I hope she dies in hell.

No, that is not true. She is not worth so much hatred. I do not think for one minute she had the least idea of what she was doing. There was no reason why she should. It was after all a fabricated situation.

I sat there with my drink, and Steve studiously ignored me, answering me when I spoke to him with a deliberate rudeness and laughing as he did so, looking at the others for their amused approval. I do not think they approved at all. They were embarrassed. They were for the most part civilised people, and no one really enjoys the spectacle of a woman being pecked to death. Only the television girl enjoyed it, for Steve was flirting with her as hard as he could, shamelessly propositioning her, saying he would ring her, date her, take her wherever she wanted to go. Once he turned to me, saying across his shoulder, "Shall I get you a taxi to go home?" And at this the television producer got up and sat beside me, talking to me, ignoring the tears that were already in my eyes, buying me another drink, discussing the new play he had in mind. I did not meet him again, but I am eternally grateful to him.

At last I managed to summon up the strength to go. Before that I could not force myself to get to my feet. I asked Steve to get me a taxi, for he was obviously going to be there till closing time, and the young woman was by now well away, convinced she had made a conquest, glancing at me occasionally with triumph and delight.

Not many women realise that a man who treats one female badly will probably do the same with the next. That is why well-meaning ladies who are convinced they can reform a rakish husband are usually in the end so disillusioned. I doubt if Steve ever kept his date with this girl, and in any case there was Joanna whom he was soon to marry, but she plainly believed she had snatched him from me, and she was almost proprietory now, so sure was she of her triumph.

Steve followed me out into the street. He said nothing. He looked up and down the road for a taxi. There was no taxi. There never is in an emergency. I too was silent, and we stood there, barely a yard apart, for what seemed to me an eternity, then at last a taxi drew up.

Steve, not looking at me, said, "Will you be all right now?"

I have never sworn very much, for all I lived with a man who swore as easily as he breathed. Such words as I use in an emergency always shock Daniel — or at least he says they do — but they are not really very fierce, and sometimes I use them simply to arouse that silly, spinsterish look in his eye. I looked at Steve now, and for the first time he met my gaze. His face was twisted with anger, hopelessness and, I think, grief.

I said, "You fucking bastard."

He went dead white. I had never spoken to him like that before, or indeed to anyone, and I meant it, I said it as if I meant it, in a soft, flat voice.

Then I turned away from him and climbed into the taxi. I saw that he was still standing there. He looked ghastly. As the cab turned the corner, I looked out of the rear window. I saw him striding away, God knows where, at an enormous speed. He did not go back into the pub.

That was our farewell. I never saw him again.

I heard about his marriage from my editor. By that time it no longer shocked me: after all, I knew it was happening, it made no difference whether it was now or in a year's time. I felt no animosity against Joanna. It was not her fault. If she had known him before, as Phoebe told me, she must know what kind of man he was: if she still chose to risk marriage with him, that was her affair. I would have risked marriage too. We are most of us idiots, except of course with regard to other people's problems, and dear Elizabeth Ingram was even now answering her letters, telling girls not to be so foolish, not to be so selfish, to go out more, meet other people, try to see the man's point of view, be thankful for small blessings and, If you send me a stamped, addressed envelope, I will reply to you personally, which usually meant sexual difficulties, venereal disease, incest or rape.

My editor, who is an old friend, knew about the affair. I imagine a great many people did. The writer's world is a gossip's world: we talk as much as we write. She gave me a specially nice lunch. She looked at me carefully as I came into the restaurant, then ordered me a large drink. I daresay I looked terrible. I was doing all the normal things, eating, sleeping (with pills) and writing all my letters, but I did not care for my reflection in the mirror, and I had lost weight which at my age always shows first in the face.

She said towards the end of the meal, "I know you'll want to kill me for this, but I think you've had a lucky escape."

"I think I have too."

"What about one of those sweets from the trolley? I think they look gorgeous. Oh go on, Elizabeth, it won't hurt you."

"They look lovely, but I never eat sweet things."

"Well, what about a liqueur then? Oh yes, of course. An apricot brandy. I know that's your favourite."

I realised then that I must look appalling. Editors, however friendly, do not as a rule run up such lavish expenses. I accepted the apricot brandy. It made no difference, one way or another, for I was by now in the state of not caring what happened to me. This is usually the first step to recovery or suicide, but even that did not interest me, it did not seem to matter if I recovered or killed myself.

She had told me about the wedding. This was both kind and sensible, it would have been insulting to ignore the subject. She knew about it because there was a local reporter there who was a friend of hers. Joanna, she said, was a nice, gentle girl: she did not sound as if she could stand up to Steve. There was a child, a little girl. I did not know about this. "Nobody ever mentions it, but she's the dead image of Steve."

Then, as I made no comment, she said, "Did you ever meet the first wife?"

"No. How could I? She's American. She lives somewhere in Wisconsin. They were divorced long before I met him. How do you come to know about her?"

"I don't know her personally. But I met someone the other day who knew both the Olsens. She married Steve when she was very young. I don't think she ever quite knew what hit her. Apparently he was unfaithful from the very beginning. Oh Elizabeth, I'm so thankful you didn't marry him. He's a perfectly awful man."

"No. He's not that. Just lost and damned."

"Oh don't be ridiculous. This is carrying Christian charity too far. Why should he be so lost? He's been very successful. His books sell. I don't like them much myself, but that's nothing to do with it. And he's a good journalist. I think he's a better journalist than a writer."

Then we drank our liqueurs and talked of other things, and I went home. I remember this now as I sit there, with the orange file in front of me. It's the same colour as the apricot brandy. I remember everything, down to the most minute detail in that pub, and somehow it hurts me no longer, it was a kind of logical ending. Steve could never have ended an affair with elegance, he had to batter it down. What still hurts is the lack of reason behind it; the lack of truth. I think he was lost and damned, but like my friend I have to ask why. I suppose we are all to some degree schizophrenic, we all show different facets of our personality, but Steve could be kind and gentle, then suddenly become so savage, brutal and cruel that it was almost as if one were dealing with a madman.

It is a little like that hotel in Copenhagen.

I spent a week there once. I didn't like it very much. I always prefer the south, I find Scandinavia antiseptic and cold. In any case I was on a business trip, which I find tedious, with the possibility of running a series of articles in a Danish magazine. I spent most of my time lunching with people, being taken around, with the odd excursion thrown in. I had no time to make any new friends. I saw Copenhagen mostly from the official angle. I was taken once to a theatre. It was a play about death, it must have been boring even for the Danes, and I hardly knew how to sit through it. I was put up in a very grand hotel, which I enjoyed, ate too much rich Danish food, and retired early most nights to read English thrillers in my room.

The main entrance to the hotel led out on to a fashionable square, with little restaurants, expensive shops and luxury flats. It was like everything else in Denmark, dazzlingly clean, and the people too were clean, with in many cases those bright speedwell blue eyes that I suppose come from the Vikings. One day I was actually on my own for lunch, it was the first time, and I was quite excited at the prospect of going out all by myself. Instead of coming out through the main foyer I chose to take the side entrance which I had not so far explored.

It led into a long wide street. In that street were porn shops, obscene books, skin-flicks, brothels and clubs that dealt with every possible kind of perversion. It was a kind of Danish Reeperbahn. It was an alphabet of sex. And like the square on

186

the other side it was spotlessly clean and open: the girls waited, the boys waited, the proprietors of the sex shops smiled at me, as if it were the most natural thing in the world for a respectable, middle-aged Englishwoman to come strolling by. It was another world, and it was only a few yards away.

Two entrances for the same hotel. Two divergent sides to the same man.

Well, that is not so original, yet it is strange, it is like walking from the light into the dark, it is like the coming of an African night when one moment there is brilliant sunshine and the next pitch blackness. There is no transition. Only with Steve it seemed sometimes as if he were living more and more in his fantasy-dark, as if the light in him were eluding me completely: soon the dark would envelop him, and then there would be nothing, for me or for him.

I still sit there, looking at that file. Soon, tomorrow perhaps, I shall go to Somerset House. It has now become an obsession. I must know, I must. I know the exact date of his birth. I always gave him presents. Once I gave him a small eighteenth-century engraving that I discovered in a back-street, other times I gave him books. I never gave him records because our musical taste was utterly different. He had a great love of Gilbert and Sullivan, which I do not share, and in our better times we argued amiably when he insisted on playing *The Pirates of Penzance* over and over again. But I know that date, it was June 2nd, 1921. I know the house where he was born. Of course I went to see it, though I never told him. He resented that kind of thing, he said it was spying. I suppose in a way it was, though there was no malice behind it. It is sad and ironic that now I really am spying, spying in desperation to find something real as a support.

I remember that house very well. It was an ugly, chipped little place off the Fulham Road, with a small front garden and six steps up to the door. I walked there and stood on the opposite side so that I could have a full view of it. It is no longer a private house. Like most such places it has been turned into flats and, from the dowdy look of it, cheap flats, perhaps for the medical students there, Fulham Road being full of hospitals. There were dirty net curtains at the windows, the house had not been painted, I should imagine, since Steve's family left it, the garden was just a yard, and the steps leading down to the basement were enough to break a neck. As

I stood there the door opened, and for a second I had the sensation that the little boy Steve would come running out, and I knew just what he would look like, a square little boy with a lick of hair across his forehead. But it was only a young man who, as he stepped on to the pavement, gave me a brief look, half smiled, then walked away. He must have thought I had been stood up, standing there with my handbag under my arm.

Steve spoke with an American accent, but it was true he had been born here, he was British whether he liked it or not. Mostly he professed to dislike it. But he was British, and I know this because I once caught a glimpse of his passport. He would never have permitted me to look inside, which is only too understandable. So that at least was true, and surely it was also true that he had been born in June, and that his parents lived in that house off the Fulham Road, It was not an attractive district, and I had always understood that the parents were well off, but then districts go down, and probably in those days it was more presentable.

I knew nothing of his father except that he was in the diplomatic service. I always imagined him as a kind of minor ambassador, for Steve on the rare occasions when he mentioned him, always indicated that this was so, but the diplomatic service covers a great deal more than this, and maybe Olsen senior was a courier or even employed at the Embassy as a minor secretary.

But he talked of his mother who, I believe, is still alive. He hated her. He hated her with passion. He spoke of her a great deal. She lives in New York. She is, I gather, the possessive vampire mother. But there was something more than hate, for he always sent her copies of his books. I used to think of her as the kind of mother sometimes portrayed in American films, who lived an idle, luxurious life, never bothering about the wretched little boy being bullied at his boarding school, who longed for her love and never forgave her for withholding it.

And now of course I do not know. I know nothing. His mother may be a dear, kindly old lady, mourning for her strange, perverse son. I feel that if I knew the mother I might understand everything, but this of course is the result of modern psychology, too much Strindberg and Peter Pan.

The matter, however, of the date and address must be true. Whatever reason Steve had to lie, this could provide no possible excuse. We are all born, damn it, there is no shame in that, we all have parents, we all have an address, even if it is a jail. Tomorrow I will definitely go to Somerset House so that I can tot up one small positive fact.

Then, with the odd feeling that I was murdering someone, I tear up the file. It is a pity for the drama of the situation that things are so impossible to tear. I am not one of those girls who can rend telephone directories with their teeth. I sit there, cursing, fighting with a tough orange folder that bends and will not tear: in the end I have to take a pair of scissors to it. The letters tear easily, so do the reviews. The photo I take in my hands to look at for the last time. Goodbye, Steve. Fine. It is a rotten photo, there should be no sentimentality attached to it. But there is, there is, there always bloody is, and suddenly I close my eyes and — the scissors are still in my grasp — cut it right across, and then down so that it falls into four pieces. I do not look at them again. I pick up the whole mess of it and drop it in the rubbish bin. I am out of my mind to have kept this junk for so long.

And I come back to my desk and burst into tears.

Then Vanda rings. I hastily blow my nose and answer the phone. Daniel would know at once from my choked voice that something is wrong, but Vanda never notices things like that, I doubt she would notice if she actually found me crying. She is not interested in people: they only concern her in so much as they touch her.

"Hallo, Elizabeth. This is Vanda speaking."

"Hallo, Vanda. How nice to hear from you. How are things?"

She does not answer this. She says, "I am coming up to London tomorrow for a little shopping. The sales are on and I want some things for the children. I thought perhaps I could look in and you would give me a little lunch."

I had made up my mind to go to Somerset House. I was unreasonably irritated. But if Vanda makes a gesture of friendship, I never like to refuse it, I remember the days when our relationship could only be described as armed neutrality. Now we seem to be on good terms and we must stay so, I cannot possibly say no. After all there is no urgency, I can always go the next day.

"I'd love that, Vanda. I'll make an omelette or something quick that I can do while you're here, so if you get caught up in some gorgeous shop you needn't worry."

189

"I will try to be punctual," says Vanda. "I am only buying useful things."

"Buy yourself some pretty thing too. Make it a little gift from me."

"Oh no. I will not be so extravagant."

It is not so much that Vanda has no sense of humour whatsoever, it is also that there is no lightness to her. She is a heavy girl. She would bore me to death if I were married to her. But then Daniel has not much sense of humour either, so I daresay they suit each other very well.

Have I any sense of humour left? Perhaps it is better not to go into that.

We settle on one o'clock. We talk for a little of the children. Daniel's name is not mentioned, and somehow I dare not so much as ask for him. I have the feeling in any case that there are going to be confidences, so I plan a cosy little meal, try to forget about Somerset House, and at last settle down to some work.

Vanda arrived very late, laden down with packages.

She looked rather distraught, as might be expected from someone shopping in the sales. I personally always avoid sales: they seem to me the nearest thing to a revolutionary mob outside a revolution. Her little fur hat was well on one side, and some wisps of dark hair hung over her cheeks. She had the appearance of one who had bought up all Oxford Street. I had never seen so many parcels. Knowing Vanda I was sure they were full of vests and pants and socks and woollies with not so much as a pair of tights for herself. She is always like this, it is very noble and irritates me unduly.

She flopped down on the settee with a gasping sigh and kicked her shoes off. She gave me a wan smile, and I hastily poured her out some sherry.

"You must be absolutely dead-beat," I said. "You'd better relax for a few minutes, then I'll see to the omelette. It's a new recipe. I saw it in the paper. It sounds rather good."

Vanda accepted this without comment. She is a good cook, both she and Daniel like their food. She makes the best pasta I know, and her chicken casserole is out of this world. I always enjoy cooking for her. There is nothing more infuriating than making a meal for people who are not interested in what they eat. Leni — God rest her memory — was one of these. She would put away magnificent steaks and well-stuffed chicken without any comment except to say, as she held her plate out for a second helping, "I don't mind what I eat. There are so many other things to think of. I think it's greedy to go on about food."

Vanda, drinking her sherry down like a thirsty man in the desert, said, "I've been so looking forward to coming, Elizabeth. We can have a nice womanly talk."

She does at times use the strangest phrases. A womanly talk to me suggests pregnancies and sanitary towels, the kind of talk I seldom hold. Once I remember I did hold it, with a young man who was illustrating one of my rare short stories. He was a nice boy, a homosexual who made no pretence of being anything else, and we talked for a good hour on clothes and perfume and make-up. It would have gladdened Eve's heart. It was only when he had gone that it struck me how odd it was.

However, I prepared myself for the womanly talk and wondered what on earth it was going to be about. It did not come at once. We both had another drink, and we talked again about the children: Mario was behaving himself these days and he had taken to following Daniel everywhere, Sophy was much less nervous and played incessantly with Doris, whose hair had fallen out from over-combing. Then we looked at the parcels. There were, as I suspected, all essentials, with the exception of one small package, and Vanda, holding this hesitantly in her hands, suddenly to my surprise flushed a deep and lovely pink, looking at me furtively then away. This made me laugh. "Oh Vanda," I said, "what have you done? You've bought yourself a diamond necklace."

"It is very wicked of me. I am a naughty girl."

"I am delighted to hear it. Do let me see."

She opened the package quite timidly. It was a pair of ear-rings, a simple little costume affair that could not have cost more than fifty pence. She put them on, — her ears are pierced — holding her head on one side and giggling a little: this for some reason touched me so that I suddenly gave her a kiss. I said, "You're a silly girl, aren't you? They look lovely. Why shouldn't you buy something for yourself?"

"Daniel will be angry."

"I really don't believe that, but if he says just one word, you put him on to me. You mustn't let him bully you. No one could call you an extravagant girl, and it's good for the feminine morale to buy a pretty from time to time."

And if that was not womanly talk, I do not know what is, but then I saw that this kind of frivolity was in the circumstances a little dangerous, and Vanda saw it too: she glanced at me once then took the ear-rings off and put them in her handbag.

We ate the omelette which was as good as it sounded, I gave Vanda the recipe and we made a big pot of coffee. There was no point in postponing it any longer and I could see that Vanda was going to go round and round the subject if I let her, so I asked bluntly, "Well, how are things? Have you two made it up?"

She sat there, playing with the fastener of her bag. She looked old and unhappy. At last, without answering me, she said in a gasp, "I must ask you something, Elizabeth."

"Of course, love. Anything."

"I gave you Martin's address."

"Yes. I haven't had time to go yet, but — "

"I don't want you to go."

"Why not? You were so keen on it. That's why you gave me the address after all."

"I don't want you to go. You must not go."

"But at least tell me why you've changed your mind."

"He is a bad man. He is dangerous."

We are mostly unreasonable, inconsistent creatures. Up till then I really had not wanted to see Martin Salvatore, but Vanda's words made me realise that I would go on this visit if it were the last thing I did. But I did not say this. I only said, "If I'm being over-inquisitive, please forgive me, but I just have to ask you this. Why did you really go back to him? Oh yes, I remember what you told me. But it still doesn't make sense to me. It must have hurt Daniel terribly, and it was not as if you were going to stay with him, you must have known you had to come back."

"I couldn't help it. He made threats about the children."

"So you've already told me. Dear, he can't do anything. You are legally divorced. You have the custody of the children. What can he do? We don't look kindly on kidnapping in this country, he would be put in prison, and in any case why should he want to take the children from you? I always understood he wasn't interested in them at all. You told me so yourself. You said he was unkind to them, he beat Mario and Sophy is plainly terrified of him. You're not telling me the whole story, are you? Why don't you talk it over with me? I give you my word I won't tell Daniel."

She only said, almost hopelessly, "You don't understand."

"No, that's true. But you're not helping me very much, are you? Can't you explain a little more? He frightens you terribly, doesn't he?"

"Oh yes, yes."

It was true, she was shivering, and this began to frighten me, so I poured her out a brandy and insisted on her drinking it. At last, when she had quietened down, I said with some difficulty, for this was interfering with a vengeance, this was the kind of thing I warned my correspondents about, "Is this really not going to happen again? For truly, Vanda, you must believe me, Daniel won't stand for it. He is a very obstinate man, he doesn't like being made a fool of, and this must have been extraordinarily humiliating for him, with neighbours and his patients and his friends. If you want to keep your marriage, you must never, never again run back to Martin, whatever he says or does."

She raised her head at this. The tears were running down her face. She gave me a long look. She said in a choked voice, "It won't happen again."

"I'm so very glad. Are things all right now between you?"

"No. Not really." Her voice was wretched, and the tears were still trickling down.

I said quickly, "Well, it's bound to take time. It must have been such a shock — And you know better than I do that Daniel is the most kindhearted man imaginable, but he is very easily hurt, and he does rather brood on things. You couldn't expect him to accept such an intolerable situation without some reaction. But he'll get over it. He does love you, you know. I imagine his anger is mostly fright. You must have given him the fright of his life. Don't blame him for being unforgiving. I expect in his heart he thinks all this is partly his own fault."

"I don't blame him for anything." Then Vanda began to speak at great speed. "You don't know what it was like. Martin is a terrible man. He believes in horrid things, and he has power, and he used to be so unkind to me, he always made fun of me in front of people and — oh, I can't tell you the things he did to me. And he rang me up when Daniel was in the surgery, and he said if I didn't come to talk things over with him, he would take the children from me and — and smash up my marriage. He said I had no right to keep his children from him, and that is not true, Elizabeth, because I would always let them see him, but they don't want to go, even Mario, who loves his papa very much, is afraid of him. And I went to see him, and he locked us up, he wouldn't let us go — I never meant to stay, but what could I do?"

"Vanda!"

"And I had to climb out of the window at night, with the children. I was so frightened, and we had nowhere to go, and I had so little money on me."

"It never struck you to come to me?"

"No!" She looked quite astonished and then I lost my temper, I was so upset by all this that all my efforts to remain calm and detached vanished. I shouted at her, "You bloody silly girl! Martin lives quite near here, and it never entered your idiotic head to come round — "

"It was the middle of the night."

"Do you think I'd have given a damn in the circumstances?"

"I don't know why you are so angry with me. There is no need to shout." She was crying again, and I was instantly ashamed: Elizabeth Ingram had better sell her typewriter for all the good she was with other people's problems.

I said more quietly, "Oh I'm sorry, darling, I really am Please forgive me. But it really hurts me to think that there you were, marooned with little Freddy on a cold night, and you could just have taken a taxi here. I'd have paid for it, and I would have been so relieved and happy to see you. We were all sick with worry about you. Oh Vanda — No, I'm not shouting, at least I don't mean to, but you are a complete and utter imbecile, I can hardly believe what I'm hearing. Where did you go, my poor silly girl?"

"We went to Baker Street Station. We got there just before they shut."

"Ten minutes away from me!"

"It is no good being so cross with me, Elizabeth. I did what I thought was best," said Vanda flatly, and I saw that indeed there was no good being cross with her, no good in Daniel's being cross with her either, for there was a kind of immovable stolidity to her, even in this appalling crisis. I could just see Vanda as a refugee, sitting on her suitcase and waiting patiently for the train that might or might not come to save her: if it did not come she would gather up her belongings and her children and trudge for weary miles, God knows where, to repeat this if necessary over and over again.

What an extraordinary girl for Daniel to marry.

What an extraordinary girl period.

I said quite faintly, "You just sat in the station then."

"Yes. We took the first train. I had return tickets," said Vanda.

"And what about Freddy? He must have grizzled the place down."

She looked at me, surprised by what to her was obviously a foolish question. "He was all right. I fed both of them."

"What with?"

"I took some chocolate from a machine. And there was half a bottle of wine in my room, I brought this with me. I gave him some. It made him a little drunk, but then he went to sleep."

"And Mario?"

"I gave him the rest of the wine. He slept too."

"Does Daniel know all this?"

She hesitated. "A little. Not quite all. He thinks I stayed because I wanted to. If I told him I was locked up, he would be so terribly angry." She added, her eyes moving away from mine, "I did not tell him about the wine. He is so English, he would not understand."

I could only say, "You'd rather Daniel were angry with you than with Martin."

She again looked surprised. It was all so plain to her that she could not understand my own obtuseness. "Of course. If he knew, he would go and murder Martin. I would not want that," said Vanda.

"Of course."

We were both silent for a while, then Vanda began to gather up her parcels. The womanly talk was over. I said, "Would you like to ring Daniel to tell him you're on your way home?"

But she only said, "Of course I'm on my way home. It would be a waste of a call. Besides, he is in the surgery and he does not like to be disturbed."

There seemed nothing more to say. Only just as she was leaving, she repeated, "You must not go to Martin."

"I wish you'd tell me why. Yes, I know he is a bad man, but you can't really believe he'll harm me. This is the twentieth century after all, not the time of the Medicis. Let me talk to him, love. I am sure I could make him understand how silly and unnecessary all this melodrama is."

Vanda said with an unexpected shrewdness, "You just want to see what he is like."

This made me laugh. I said, "Well, I expect that's true. He sounds like no one I've ever met in my life. But I still think it would be a good idea. I agree that it would be disastrous if Daniel went — "

"Oh no, no!"

"Well, we both agree on that. But it might be quite a good thing if someone from the family went, and the fact that I'm a middle-aged woman and Daniel's stepmother might make him see that you're not just on your own and unprotected. It might make him think twice about threatening you again."

"You must not go, Elizabeth," said Vanda.

I imagine she spoke to the children in just that tone. You must not touch, you must not put that in your mouth — Sometimes of course she screamed at them, I have heard her doing so, but mostly she was a patient mother, only losing her temper when exasperated beyond endurance: then she would burst into a high-pitched torrent of Italian, following up the torrent with generous slaps that Mario at least invariably dodged. I don't think it harmed them. Children do not mind screams and slaps, provided there is plenty of love and care, and that certainly was not lacking.

I did not answer her last remark, for I was resolved to go and did not wish to provoke any further scene. I only said, "What will you do if he rings you again?"

She hesitated, dropped one of her parcels and stooped to pick it up. She said, "I won't go back. I couldn't go back. He is not my husband any more. Daniel is my husband. It is my duty to be with him."

I knew how much she loved Daniel, so I paid no attention to the pompous tone of these remarks, except to think rather crossly that she might have thought of all this before. I was sure that under the apparent calm she was horrified and appalled by Daniel's violent reaction. She is a girl who lives in the present: she does not have the imagination to see what the result of her actions might be. If he had beaten her she would have understood very well, but Daniel will never beat her, he is not capable of it. I daresay she expected it: the frenzied scene that I am certain took place, followed by resentful sulks and brooding, is beyond her comprehension.

But she will tide it over in her own way, and she will tide it over, I know that. She will accept the anger as something she deserves, she will cook especially nice meals, and at night she will lie patiently beside him in the double bed, waiting until he decides to make love to her. I don't think Daniel has a chance. Besides, there is a deep love there, however submerged, and I am beginning to see that this strange peasant girl is what Daniel needs, something solid and faithful and acceptant to moor him down.

I said to her at the door, "I wonder if you and I will ever really understand each other."

She gave me a half-smile. She smiles far too seldom, but when she does, she becomes beautiful. "We both love Daniel," she said.

"Yes, we both love Daniel. Goodbye, Vanda. And don't be so silly again, will you? If ever you're in any kind of trouble and you think I can help you, for God's sake let me know. After all, I am a kind of mother-in-law, and mothers-in-law aren't just dirty jokes, they do have their uses."

I could see from her face that she had no idea what I was talking about, but then Vanda and I tend to sail on a vast sea of misapprehension. But I think she is beginning to like me, which is the most important thing, and I am beginning to like her. Within her own family a mother-in-law would be something one had to endure, living no doubt with the young couple, telling them how to bring up their children, and generally ruling the roost. Thank God I do not have to live with Daniel and Vanda: the very thought of it fills me with horror.

The eventide home will suit me much better.

When Vanda had gone — "Put those ear-rings on for Daniel, they are so pretty," — and, "You are better, I hope, Elizabeth, I have not yet asked," — I brooded on all this as I cleared up the lunch things. I was, as Vanda had seen, far too curious about Martin Salvatore to miss the chance of seeing him, but even as I thought this, a faint apprehension stirred within me. He sounded so evil a man, and I do not believe in evil, at least not the kind that brings Count Magnus up from his vault and stirs the dust on tomb-stones. I would not have thought of Vanda as a timid person, but obviously he terrorised her, it was almost as if he had to beckon and she came, however unwillingly. I wondered what he looked like. I could not picture him at all, and she never actually described his physical appearance. It was Daniel who described him as a little, insignificant man, but then Daniel is over six foot, and would be jealous enough to despise a man smaller than himself whom Vanda had once loved.

I knew now that when I went — it would be the day after tomorrow — I would go by minicab, and ask the driver to wait for me, to call for me after an hour. This was cowardly, but my flesh crept a little at the thought of the strange creature who could threaten his own children, and lock up his former wife. The prospect of going entirely on my own frankly terrified me: never mind if it seemed silly, I was going to be very careful.

I hope Daniel and Vanda will soon be friends and lovers again. I cannot see this quarrel continuing much longer: surely the *convenances de nuit* will bring them together again. Daniel has always been inclined to brood, but she is his wife, she is there, and I suspect that one day he will suddenly forget, laugh at something, behave in his normal fashion: by the time he realises that he is supposed to be aggrieved, it will be too late, to return to the quarrel will make him look ridiculous.

But I wish I could rid my mind of that stupid girl sitting with Mario and Freddy on a draughty station platform. She must have hidden somewhere while they were closing the gates, and slipped out later. And my flat so near, she only had to phone me or simply come and ring the bell. I swear at her and at myself, and I still see her sitting there, putting chocolate in the children's mouths and making them drowsy with wine.

And this is the strange young woman who has first married a psychopath and then my dear, pigheaded Daniel who, younger than she is, has chosen to take to himself a peasant wife and three children by another man.

It is true what I said: I shall never understand Vanda.

Chapter 8

It was all quite brief. I think in the ranges of my mind I knew what was going to happen. I have been to Somerset House before on more normal errands. I jotted down the date — I was unlikely to forget it, but it seemed somehow more business-like — and found easily enough the volume I was looking for, though the books are so big and it was difficult to manage. The people who organise museum catalogues and records of births and deaths seem to imagine we are all weight-lifters. I am still a little uncertain in my balance, and these particular volumes almost defeated me.

However, I found it and took it out. There was no reference to Steve's name at all. No Stephen Olsen had been born in the British Isles on June 2nd, 1921. In a way I was expecting this, yet it was a shock if only for its sheer absurdity. Then I did what I had done in the Reading Room. I looked up three years before and three years after. There was nothing. Olsen is an unusual name in this country, so it did not take me long.

When I had finished, for there was no point in continuing, Steve after all was not an old man or a young boy, I felt sick, exhausted and a little faint. The effort of lifting up those heavy volumes was too much, especially as it now seemed that Stephen Olsen did not exist at all. I came out, tottering a little, and fortunately found myself a taxi, for I had no strength left in me and might well have subsided on to the pavement.

I muttered to myself in the taxi, It's not possible, it's ridiculous. And so I kept on saying after I had arrived home. It was a couple of hours before I could settle down to any work. And even then, typing away, I found that my mind wandered through Jericho City, and the El Saddle Hotel, to that B.B.C. pub where our whole relationship crumbled in a stench of ugliness and cruelty. I thought of Eve, with her little case of lotions and make-up, living her bright life in painting on unreal masks, turning bushy eyebrows into a neat pencilled line, covering up blemishes, making mouths unkissable painted arcs, obliterating the marks of living. You must be careful with white collars, she said to me once, because the liquid foundation does come off a wee bit, however careful you are. You must not rub your eyes because the eye shadow will blur, and of course you must never cry because the mascara will run. But then Eve's painted ladies surely shed little but glycerine tears: crying is ugly, it ruins hours of artistry. Always and eternally young, Eve's ladies, yet somehow so very, very old, with their masklike faces that must never stretch beyond a faint, thin smile. There is a celebrated film actress who has had her face lifted and lifted until there is no real face at all: she looks like a beautiful clown, she must represent Eve's ultimate effort.

And Paul, poor Paul, who ended up a mess of brains and blood, who lived his life on mythical plains, riding for ever into painted sunsets, shooting down well-paid extras in rehabilitated ghost towns. His death was as real and ugly as the life he chose to ignore: it was a strange yet inevitable ending for one who must at the end have forgotten what reality is.

And Steve — Steve did not exist. Steve never existed. He had made a ghost life for himself: a wife who, poor girl, had slept with a ghost beside her, who must have felt that she was holding on to nothing. Balliol College with its double first, earthy barmaids with big breasts, willing to comfort at all hours of the day or night. The public school, where a wretched little boy was bullied until he ran away, then dragged back, beaten and bullied again. The prison camp and the brilliantly organised escape. I had read the colonel's article. Steve had read it too. He had quoted it to me, almost word for word. It was dreadful to read that article. It was like listening to the voice of a ghost, only the voice spoke lies: it had happened but not to Steve.

And the Normandy beaches. That at least was true, that was the one thing to hold on to, the one truth in a wilderness of lies. The only time when Steve had really existed.

Did he live for me? The end came with a crash as ends do, but it had really ended a long time before. The cancer ended it, the quarrels ended it, the neglect ended it. Neglect ends love and friendship more than anything else. One may still hang on the phone, wait in pubs and restaurants and at street corners, listen for the front door-bell, but the very fact of waiting and listening cracks love across so that the image is blurred and distorted.

There was one moment of truth, No, there were two. That, like Paul's suicide, which I am more and more sure was never meant to be suicide at all, was true. He died in reality. I wonder if in his dying the fantasies faded, if for those few moments the pictures vanished like Eve's make-up before a cleansing lotion, the blemishes reappeared, and the real face showed through again, with all its real shadows and lines. No more bullied little boys, no more brilliant Oxford graduates, no more brave, skilful escapes, only death which no one can escape, reality lying in a ditch to be discovered the next morning.

But there was one other moment of truth, and that moment, for no reason that I can yet understand, nearly engulfed me too.

I could see him still. The crucified image on the bed. *I'm paralysed, I think I'm dying.* And then the scream of, *For Jesus' fucking Christ's sake, don't you see I'm dying?* —

And it was nothing. There was nothing wrong with him that a hangover pill could not cure. But there was something wrong with him. Reality was wrong with him. For the first time he was caught up in something that he believed he could not escape. It was more than drink, it had nothing to do with drink. I think that at that moment the fantasies had pinned him down so that he could no longer run away: he saw himself hopelessly entrapped, no more schools, colleges, barmaids, prison camps, no more mortal illness to give a vulgar brush-off glamour — That was why he screamed.

That was why he screamed.

As for me, I do not know, it is Steve who has pinioned me down, if it had not happened, I would never have known the truth, perhaps he wanted me to know the truth.

Daniel would kill me for all this nonsense. He would be rushing to the phone to book me an appointment with a psychiatrist, or perhaps an analyst who would take out small pieces of my mind and lay them before me. I once went to an analyst, I do not really know why, except I am always dabbling in things that frighten me. I only saw him once. He had never met me before, and he asked me questions of such impertinence that I could not answer him. I wanted to quote *Hamlet* at him, to say "You would play upon me; you would seem to know my stops; you would pluck out the heart of my mystery."

Perhaps I had no right to complain. I am trying to pluck out the heart of Steve's mystery, it serves me right that the tables have been turned on me.

However, this plainly will not do, so I shove Steve aside, and return to Dear Elizabeth Ingram and the only too real problems of my correspondents.

I think that in so many cases these appalling difficulties are, like the Pinter play, a lack of communication. Mothers and daughters do not understand each other, sweethearts, lovers, husbands and wives.

He goes out every evening and leaves me alone. My mother always wants to know where I'm going and insists on waiting up for me. My daughter-in-law doesn't like me, she never lets me see the children. I went to a party and drank too much, now I'm pregnant, I don't know what to do, my father will kill me. I have been married for two years and we've been very happy, but now a former boy-friend has come back into my life, and I find I still love him, what am I to do?

I type out the incontrovertible commonsense. Talk things over with your husband, I'm sure he doesn't mean to hurt you. You must see that you are still very young, and your mother worries about you, but do have a talk with her, I'm sure she'll understand that you must have some independence. I'm afraid there is not much you can do, but make a point of asking your son and daughter-in-law, round at regular intervals with the children, don't let her see you're resentful, if the day is made really friendly and pleasant, she'll want to come back. I suggest you get in touch with the Unmarried Mothers' society, I enclose the address, but do try to talk things over with your mother, she may understand better than you think. Don't be silly, grow up, you're happily married and any boy-friend who tries to break up a marriage is no use to you.

Oh God, such stuff — Go on, divorce him, leave home, tell your daughter-in-law to go to hell, you're a bloody silly girl, you should learn to hold your liquor, and as for you, madam, you are an utter idiot.

Dear E.I., I'm an ass of a middle-aged woman, I've had a disastrous love affair, my stepson and his wife are behaving like lunatics, and I think it's time I gave up and retired to my eventide home.

Dear E.I., I think you ought to be certified, yours sincerely, E.I.

And now at last I will meet Martin Salvatore, Count Magnus to you. It is interfering to the n'th degree, it is absolutely none of my business, what Daniel would say I cannot begin to imagine, and Vanda came to see me with the express purpose of asking me not to go. I do not even ring to make an appointment. I am totally convinced that he will be there, somehow — I cannot explain why I feel this — this is the last link in the chain.

I ordered my mini. I asked for a driver whom I know quite well. I have become too dependent on the minicab service, even now when I no longer really need them, I have had most of their drivers in my time, and some of them have become my friends.

But this time it is essential.

They are strange people, mini-men. They are independent, they work when they choose, most of them are middle-aged, a great many are retired and Jewish and were once in the rag-trade. On Yom Kippur the firm must go mad, for three quarters of their drivers are not available. There is Lou, whose wife walked out on him, and who has since walked out on life: he lives with his married sister, does no other work and will never marry again. There is Denis, who once dealt in skin-flicks and obscene books, who is upright and dependable and who would knock down anyone who insulted me. There is old Len, cussed working-class of the old regime, who has the cheek of the devil and who would probably park in the courtyard of Buckingham Palace and get away with it. And there is young Desmond who is charming and queer, who claims bastardy with a well-known family, and who fervently reads my column.

They are all oddly unmoored. Sometimes they vanish for weeks on end. Then they reappear, charming as ever, and get on with their job.

I ask for Victor. The woman who runs the car service does not approve if one asks for a specific driver. She probably thinks the customer hopes to get jobs done privately without paying the commission, and I daresay this frequently happens.

However, I am a regular customer, I do not try to cheat the firm, so she agrees, and Victor turns up as he always does, on the dot. It is largely Steve's doing that I become irritable and nervous if kept waiting, even when as in this case it does not really matter.

Victor is also Jewish and a Cockney East-Ender. He is very much a lady's man, and flirts mildly with me, always addressing me as "young lady", and once offering to kiss me goodnight. This is not normally part of the minicab service. However, I am now old enough to accept this kind of thing with calm, and Victor flirts as easily as he breathes, it means nothing. He loves to talk about London, which he knows very well: in the summer he takes American tourists around, and fills them up with information that is mostly correct and sometimes downright fabrication. On Sunday mornings he runs a stall in Petticoat Lane, just by the alleyway where Jack the Ripper committed his final murder. I have seen that alleyway. It looks dreadful, nothing would persuade me to walk down it, even in daylight. He sells what he terms "schmatters": carrier bags with Union Jacks on them, plates embossed with London views, and quite appalling souvenir spoons and brooches and paper knives, all geared for the tourist market. He does extremely well, and I am sure his patter is marvellous.

He greets me in his usual way. "Well, young lady," he says, "and how are we today? You're looking better, if I may say so. And where are we going?"

I have already composed my story, which has just enough truth in it to be excusable. I am visiting an ex-patient of Daniel's. Victor knows all about Daniel. He drove me down for the wedding: it was the first time I met him. I have not met the old boy before, I tell Victor, but I know he is a hypochondriac and becoming a great nuisance. He wants Daniel to come up and see him every week from Amersham, which is simply not possible, and Daniel has asked me to go and explain and provide him with the name of a good specialist. Now I come to think of it, the truth in all this would about cover a teaspoon, and it is really quite unnecessary to tell Victor such a story at all, but everybody seems to be making things up these days, so why shouldn't I?

Then I come to the crux of the matter.

"I don't want to stay for more than an hour," I tell Victor.

"And you know what these hypochondriacs are, they do go on and on. If I don't come out in an hour, will you please call at the flat for me and remind me that I have another apppointment?"

Victor assures me he will do this, and when Victor says he will do something, he does it, which is why I was so determined to have him as my driver. He says he will wait outside the flats — he knows them and there is a parking place provided — and then he looks at his watch, a magnificent gold watch that is certainly not the kind of thing he sells on his stall, and says, "We'll be there about ten past eleven. At twelve fifteen I'll be banging at the door."

I feel comforted. This is all quite absurd because Martin, however diabolical he may be, is unlikely to lock me up as he did Vanda, but I like to think of Victor's calling for me, and I do not think he will be easily turned away.

It is one of those monumental warrens of flats. It is also obviously expensive and in the wealthy part of Highgate, so Martin must be a rich man. This is not something that Vanda ever mentioned to me. As I walk towards the entrance, Victor waves goodbye to me and winks. I always attract familiarity: it must be because in my heart I rather like it. Certainly the porter who comes forward to greet me, cap, uniform, gold braid and all, would never be familiar.

"I'm looking for Mr. Salvatore. The number of the flat is 46."

"That is on the fourth floor, madam, if you'll kindly come this way."

He leads me to the lift and takes me up. He insists on accompanying me to the flat door. We walk along endless corridors, and I feel more and more like a battery hen. The carpet is dung-coloured plush, the doors are all alike: the only individuality is in the rubbish that is neatly stacked outside a few of the flats, and I cannot help glancing at the bottles and newspapers there, to get some idea of the owner.

I would go mad living in such a place. I too live in a block, but there are only a few flats on each floor: it is the long walk that is so alarming, it must be horrid at night.

Outside Number 46 I hesitated, but the porter was still standing there, so I rang and waited.

Martin Salvatore was in. He opened the door. He looked at me in some surprise, and then I found myself shaking almost uncontrollably, my hands were damp with sweat and I was so dizzy I had to hold on to the wall. I could say that the damnable illness which seized me had left me far more vulnerable than I used to be, made my physical reactions more violent, but I do not think this was the trouble at all. The truth was that I was frightened to death of Martin, he was to me Count Magnus, and the first sight of him was such a shock that, absurd as it may seem, I hardly saw him at all.

Fortunately this passed as quickly as it came, and I managed to say in a reasonably normal voice, "Mr. Salvatore?"

"That is my name, yes."

I still could not focus my eyes properly upon him, but the voice was calm and thin, the voice of an old man. There was scarcely any accent at all, only the intonation: it was mainly the pronunciation of the vowel "o" that revealed he was not English. It is strange with that one vowel: all foreigners, without exception, however beautifully they speak English, give it a faintly precious, full value that betrays them.

I say, "May I come in? My name is Elizabeth Waterman. I am Daniel Waterman's stepmother. I have come to see you about Vanda."

He answered with the same calm, "I have heard of you. How uncivil of me to keep you standing in the doorway. Do come in, Mrs. Waterman. I fear you may find the flat a trifle disorganised, but I have been packing, I am going away in a few days."

We all excuse ourselves by saying, when people come, that our flat is untidy. The only thing about me is that it is perfectly true, whether I am packing or not. My vision had cleared entirely now, and I stepped into the most beautiful flat I have ever seen, with to my eyes not a thing out of place. It was like an interior from the Victoria and Albert Museum. We came into the sitting room, a large, long, light room, with books almost from ceiling to floor, except for a couple of pictures which seemed to me good and certainly originals. There were rare books too: I am not an expert on such things, but some of them were very old, and I would dearly have loved to take a look at the titles.

However, one cannot walk into a stranger's flat and immediately make for the bookcases, so I looked at Martin Salvatore instead: for the first time I really saw him. He was smiling a little as if he knew how afraid I was, and motioned me to an armchair.

He was in no way the old warlock I had begun to believe him to be, nor was he the strange, smiling little man described by Daniel. Indeed, he was almost negligibly ordinary. Despite his voice I would have placed his age as the mid-forties, perhaps a little younger than myself. It is always difficult to tell with a man. With a woman the neck and hands give her away. He was of medium height, with receding dark brown hair cut unfashionably short. He was neatly and expensively dressed in conventional style, suit, silk shirt, a tie that I think was a Paris model, and it was hard to imagine him performing strange rites, invoking the devil or doing anything necromantic at all. He now watched me gravely as I sat down, then suggested that I might like a sherry.

And so we sat, with only a couple of yards between us, and it was only then that I grew aware of the amusement bubbling within him. I saw that he knew perfectly well how embarrassed I was and that I did not know how to begin: this delighted him, he was in no way going to help me.

And then I said something I did not mean to say. It was nothing to do with Vanda. It simply popped out like the toad in the fairy story. I said, "I understand you are like Count Magnus. I hear you do terrible things. Are black magic and witchcraft and all those things one reads about — are they real to you?"

He was understandably a little disconcerted. It is after all as a conversational gambit a trifle unusual from a woman you have never met, who has come uninvited to your flat. His smile vanished. He looked away and out of the window. His flat faced the back of the block where there was a small private square: the foliage of the trees almost touched the pane. He must look down on a beautiful view. In the summer there would be the song of thrushes and blackbirds. Then he swivelled round to look at me again. God knows what he saw. I had made no attempt to dress up, I had lost weight and grown pale.

His eyes, which were very dark, moved up and down me. Then he said quietly, "That of course is Vanda."

"Naturally. Who else could I hear it from?"

"Black magic and witchcraft — I have never done such things. They are for stupid children."

"You've frightened Vanda with them."

His lip curled. People's lips do curl, and not only in romantic novels. It was displeasing, almost a sneer. He said, "Vanda frightens easily. She is a peasant girl, she is superstitious and very stupid."

I would not have called Vanda stupid. She is uneducated and primitive, but there is considerable intelligence there. I do not think Daniel would have fallen in love with her if she had had no brains. Where this incredible conversation was going I had no idea, but already we were away, it was now out of my control. I exclaimed indignantly, "You married her after all."

"Yes. I married her. It was the greatest mistake of my life. But one does not. always marry for intelligence. She was very beautiful then. She looked like a cinquecentist madonna. I believed I could make something of her. I saw her as more adaptable than she was."

"You were playing Pygmalion!"

"Perhaps I was. It was foolish of me. I thought that once she was away from her appalling family, she might be a credit to me."

I said, almost in a whisper, "I think that's the most arrogant thing I have ever heard."

"But, my dear lady, I am an arrogant man." The eyes raised themselves to mine. I would like to say they were strange, compelling eyes, but they were not, they were simply considering. "I should say that you are a most intelligent woman."

"I don't see what that has to do with anything. I don't think I am intelligent at all." And I could not help thinking that if I were, I would not be here. I said, "You haven't really answered my question."

"I hope the sherry is to your liking? Perhaps you would like a biscuit."

"No, thank you. But I would like an answer."

"I am interested in the occult, yes. Oh I know what Vanda will have told you. She will have indicated that I am in the habit of raising the devil twice nightly, that Beelzebub and Azrael darken the windows with their black wings, that I talk with the un-dead and perform strange, disgusting ceremonies. None of that is true. Only fools do such things. But I am interested in your question which you worded in an unusual manner. You asked if these things were real to me. That's what you said, isn't it?"

I could see now what was happening. I should have known. If something envelops one's mind to such a degree, it is inevitable that a sensitive person will pick it up, as if from a radio. I looked at Martin Salvatore. I did not like him. He might not be the fiend that I had imagined, he looked like an Italian businessman, which of course he was, and perhaps his avowed interest in the occult was simply a matter of intellectual curiosity, but I could understand very well Vanda's fear of him. It seemed to me that here was someone who would dispassionately watch torture, if he considered it necessary: he would in no way be moved by the fear and anguish and cries of his victim. I believe he would not perform it unless he felt there was no alternative, because such physical excess would be distasteful to him, but if he did, there would be no mercy or pity in him, because human beings with all their frailty did not interest him.

I would hate to be married to him. I am not as simple as Vanda but I am more imaginative. He must have fascinated Vanda, no doubt offered her the earth, taken her to good restaurants, perhaps bought her clothes and jewellery. Poor little rabbit, it must have been a sad awakening when she was married to him, and he no longer found her attractive. I was growing a little afraid too. This smallish man — I suppose he was about five foot six — was in some way reading my mind, he was touching on my obsession. But I only answered as calmly as I could, "Yes. That is what I asked you."

"Are they real to me? If I answered yes, would you not go away and instantly surround yourself with garlic and silver?"

So he knew about that — How did he know? What had Vanda said to him? I said sharply, "No. What good would that do? That's pure superstition."

And I could see the cob of garlic on my windowsill, and suddenly I flushed, and I knew that he noticed this.

He said, "I can see that such things are not real for you. Shall we leave for the moment the question of magic? The word to you will not mean what it does to me, so we would be talking at cross-purposes. I have told you that I am interested in it, it exists but not in the form that my silly wife — my silly ex-wife — believes. It is a good thing we are apart from each other. She has now, I see, married precisely the kind of man she needs, an English middle-class blockhead who calls himself a doctor, who will beget half a dozen stupid children, and whose imagination is circumscribed by the rules of his so-called profession. I have seen him. Six foot of wood. No doubt he is proficient with his fists, it is a pity the brain is lacking."

I saw that Martin Salvatore was human after all: this display of what one could only call jealous temper was somehow reassuring. Not even the black arts could entirely destroy natural feeling. I was only thankful that I was here, not Daniel: my gloomy prophecies of the straight left might well have been realised. But the remarks made me angry, and there was no point in my losing my temper too. I said, "I should prefer not to discuss Daniel. You are quite wrong about him, but that does not matter. Only he does happen to be my stepson, and I am very fond of him. Shall we leave him out of it? I assure you, he wouldn't like you any more than you do him. One could hardly expect it in the circumstances, however dispassionate a view you take of life."

He inclined his head with a little smile. "You are so right, Mrs. Waterman. It is very rude of me to talk of your stepson in such a manner. Fortunately we are never likely to meet again, so it does not matter. I saw him once, and that, I fancy, was enough for both of us. Now let me consider your question again, without being sidetracked. I have admitted that these things you mention are real to me, though I do not practise them in the way I believe you imagine. I could only play with them if I thought they were fundamentally unreal. But I do not believe for one moment that you are concerned with magic. You are concerned with reality, Mrs. Waterman, only you no longer know what it is. Is that not so?"

I looked at him without answering. I thought in a bemused way, what a person to confide in, I do not like him, I do not trust him, I think he is evil. Yet why not, for it would be entirely impersonal, in a strange way it would not matter, and in an even stranger way I thought he might understand.

He said, "Why do you not tell me what is in your mind? Let us play at being strangers on the train."

I said, almost in surprise, "I play at little else. For a vast number of people that is all I am."

I do not see how he could have understood this, but he accepted it as if he read my column regularly. He said, "Then in a moment you will tell·me about it. But I will say one thing more. You have come mainly because of Vanda. I don't know why such a stupid, common girl interests you, but she is lucky to have so gallant a protector. If you are frightened for her, you need not be. I never want to see her again. She disgusts me." Then he smiled at my expression. "I gather that I have offended you again?"

I said a little wearily, "It's not the prettiest of remarks."

"Ah well, strangers on the train can afford to offend each other for they will never meet again. I told you I was going away. I am going back to my own country. I don't imagine I shall be returning here for a long time. Your strange industrial situation does not encourage me to open a business here. You can tell Vanda that. She is safe from me."

"And the children?" The words slipped out before I could stop them. But then the whole conversation was already so extraordinary that it did not seem to matter.

His face changed for a moment. But he answered calmly, "And the children."

"I hope you mean that, Mr. Salvatore. It is the one thing that really worries me. They are nice children and my stepson, you will be surprised to hear, loves them. I couldn't bear them to be hurt."

He said a little savagely, "How sentimental you English are over children. You have the worst record in the world for ill-treating them, but you still slobber over them as you batter them. I think we'll leave that. I prefer to return to the subject of reality. I think it is time you told me about it. After all, that is why you have come."

"What do you mean?"

"Of course it is. You are not interested in Vanda, or if you are, not to that extent. You are unhappy. I can see that. You have the idea that the wicked Martin Salvatore out of his experience of the occult arts will be able to help you. It is possible. Why do you look like that? Do you think I will harm you?"

"How do you know all this?"

"Because I am a magician. I repeat, do you think I will harm you?"

I said, "No. I don't think you are interested enough."

His eyebrows shot up at this. I do not think anyone had ever spoken to him like that before. But he said quite pleasantly, "I think that remark deserves another sherry. Now Mrs. Waterman, why don't you tell me what has happened to you? You talk of ghosts. I have the impression that you have been raising them, yourself."

I could have asked him what he meant by that and then, how did he know. It would have been both stupid and unnecessary. I knew exactly what he meant and, as to how he knew, I do not believe there was anything magic in that at all. I am convinced that he was an unusually telepathic man, and that was his real magic. Perhaps it was a gift he had cultivated, or perhaps he had been born with it. Certainly he had been born with a talent for a deep and cynical summing up of other human beings. But he spoke the truth. I had been raising the devil, and I fancy that if you raise the devil there is not necessarily a smell of fire and brimstone, nor the black sound of beating wings, but there is a look that comes upon you, and certainly it was upon me.

So I neither denied this nor exclaimed in horror. I simply said, "You are quite right."

"Then you had better tell me about it. According to your view of me, I should understand very well. It may seem disturbing to raise ghosts but ghosts are immaterial things, they can only harm you through your own imagination."

"I have a great deal of imagination."

"So I gather. You have already turned it on to me. You are too emotional, Mrs. Waterman. Emotion erodes into one's individuality, it destroys reality. I have learnt to control it. You should do the same." He added thoughtfully, pouring himself out another sherry — I had hardly touched mine — "However, I do not think you are as susceptible as Vanda. I could without much effort make Vanda believe that Satan himself was standing in front of her, complete with hooves and tail."

"I imagine it would amuse you to do so."

He did not answer this, though his mouth twitched. He only said, almost apologetically, "I am human. I am human, after all. You must know that fear automatically produces cruelty. You no doubt count yourself as a humane person, but if you had to rebuke someone, and that person were plainly terrified of you, you would be far harsher than with someone who did not give a damn. Vanda is scared to death of me. I suppose she told you that I locked her in?"

I could feel the weight of his personality like a heavy eiderdown. It almost crushed me, stifled me. I felt I would never condemn Vanda again: she would have no defence against someone like Martin Salvatore. What he must have been like to be married to, I shudder to think. I only hoped that I had sufficient defences, and I prayed that Victor would not forget to call for me, for I was beginning to think I would never have the strength to leave this flat on my own. I took a mouthful of the sherry — I am not a connoisseur on wine, but I think it was a very good sherry indeed — and said a little indignantly, "I don't think it matters what she told me. Do you think it does?"

"No, of course not. But you might as well know that I never locked her in. I simply told her I had done so. She was so afraid that she never even tried the door. But I left the window open for her. The window at the back leads on to the fire escape. It was very simple. My only alarm was that she would be too paralysed with fear to move, and then I suppose I would have had to do something about it. I do not want her here. She could never fit in with this flat — "

"She's not a piece of furniture!"

"Precisely. You could not put it more accurately. I wanted to see her and the children for the last time, to make sure that there was no mistake. That is why I told her to come. The moment I saw her, I knew it was quite useless. She has changed. She never had anything but beauty, and now that is gone. She has become so vulgar and middle-class, I could never endure it. I got rid of her as soon as I could, but I wanted to punish her a little. After all, she walked out on me. I kept her here as long as it amused me, then as she showed no signs of going, I said goodbye in my own way. She did not suffer any harm."

"You could have opened the door and said goodbye."

"Oh, that would have been very boring."

I said, "I think you're mad." And I think he was mad, as well as being both conceited and affected. Madness is not just mopping and mowing. When Daniel summed him up as neurotic, he was perfectly right, only I would have gone one stage further and said that he was virtually certifiable. He was a complete and utter egotist, and that after all is a form of insanity. Yet oddly enough I was no longer afraid of him. When he laughed at my comment, which no doubt flattered him, I paid no attention, only said, "I suppose I have been a little mad too. I think I might as well tell you. As one lunatic to another, I should like to have your opinion."

213

He waited without speaking, and I told him the story. He was the first person I ever told it to. He will be the last. I have very good friends in whom I can confide almost anything, I do not need to write to Elizabeth Ingram, but this was not only my story, it was also Steve's. You cannot say to people, My lover was a fraud and a liar, he was cruel without reason, he tried to destroy everyone, including myself. Only with Martin Salvatore it somehow did not seem to matter. It was not only that this would be our last meeting. I knew I would never see him again. I think it was because this whole story was something that he would instinctively appreciate and understand. I do not know him, but I know that he too is a destroyer, and a far more vicious one than Steve could ever be. When poor Vanda said he had power and did terrible things, she was perfectly right, but this did not mean that he invoked the devil, performed secret rites or worshipped at a black mass: he would despise such childish things. I cannot frankly see him robbing a grave at midnight or doing any of the silly things that would-be satanists do. He had no need to do them. The devil lay within him, that was his power, and it was a power that I myself could feel, even though at that moment I was not afraid of him.

And so I told him, more or less without omissions: if I missed out some of the more personal things, that was simply because they did not concern him.

He listened in a professorial attitude, his chin resting on his touching fingers. He did not look at me. I told him of the lies, the fabrications, the fantasies, my long journey back to nothing through that dark, twisting tunnel, I could see that tunnel as I talked, only I could not see Steve at the end of it, I wished I could see Steve at the end of it.

He remained silent for a while after I had finished. It was a very silent flat. We could have been alone in the world. I lay back in the chair, exhausted. I had at last shed the burden I had been carrying for so long: I felt weak with relief, though my father-confessor was not the kind I would ever have believed I could have chosen.

He said at last in a rather spinsterish voice, "I really don't find this so unusual. Does it seem extraordinary to you?"

"Why, yes. Of course it's extraordinary. How could it seem anything else? I am not saying he was a brilliant writer, a genius, but he was good and, what is more, he was successful.

Why should he feel he had to do this? It makes no sense to me. I could understand it a little if he never sold anything or if he was poor and ill, or if he could not get on with women. But he was none of these things. He was a person in his own right. Why should he have to obliterate himself with senseless lies? Do you imagine it made the least difference to me if he was up at Oxford or not, if he went to a public school or some council school, if his parents were people he was ashamed of? I am not that kind of person. He should have known that. He must have known that."

Martin Salvatore said, as if he were a professor explaining matters to a slow and dim-witted pupil, "There are a number of things that come to mind. The question of reality, of course — But never mind that. This is obviously partly a matter of class."

"Class?"

"Oh, certainly."

"But I — "

"If you would let me finish, Mrs. Waterman. Class is so important in this country."

"Like battering babies, I suppose!"

"If you wish. It always amuses me in this so-called permissive age that we talk so much of sex and so little of class, yet neither has in any way changed. You are just as class conscious as you ever were, and just as inhibited about sex, for all you so display it."

I was beginning to find Martin Salvatore extremely pompous, but this time I did not interrupt him. He went on, "I am certain that this gentleman of yours came from a poor and working-class background. You say it doesn't matter. You can afford to say it. I judge that you come from what is termed the professional middle-class, which is reasonably classless — not so much as it thinks, perhaps, because of course it is intellectually snobbish — so naturally you are broad-minded. He would not be. To him the business of a good school and college and diplomatic service and so on was vitally important. As for the cancer, that was simply to break off your relationship without hurting his own self-esteem, it seems to me very much taking a hammer to a mouse, but I daresay it was all he could think of at the time. He would not want to seem a cad — is that not your English word?"

"It was a generation ago," I said, more sharply than I intended, for his words were hurting me.

215

"I thought you still used it. My apologies. But I don't really find any of this very interesting. What I do find interesting is your own shock and horror."

"To find out that someone you knew and loved virtually did not exist at all! — "

"But of course he existed. Only you are egotistic enough to resent it that he did not exist as you chose to see him. You say it makes no sense to you. Why should it? It's none of your business." Then he smiled at me, that odd, secretive smile, rose to his feet and propped himself up against a bookcase. It was perhaps coincidence that he now stood with his back to the light. Certainly he could see me with the utmost clarity.

"You and your reality," he said, quite crossly. "I find you very arrogant, Mrs. Waterman. Reality! I told you that I put Vanda in my back room. I informed her that I was locking her in. She believed me. To her it was real. But it was not. She was not locked in at all. She could have opened that door any time she liked. Which was real then? The locked door or the unlocked door? Your friend chose to lead what you call a fantasy life. He came of a good family, his parents were in the diplomatic service, he lived in London, he took a double first at — what did you say? — Balliol, and he slept with a barmaid with large breasts — "

"I didn't mean to tell you that."

"Ah no. That is where your reality impinges. But for him it must have been entirely real. And why not? I myself," said Martin Salvatore idly, "prefer a different kind of woman, but I can see that to someone like that, who is lost and angry and disillusioned, the idea must have been very comforting. And of course the escape from prison — That really should have told you the whole story. So there he was, creating the kind of life he had always wanted to lead, making a mess and muddle of it as most of us do, then dying peacefully by himself. After all, a ditch is not real, it doesn't affect death, who cares? In the act of dying it surely makes no difference where one is. One is alone, that is all there is to it. Then you come along. You choose to look on all this through your eyes, not his. You say, 'Do you imagine it would have made any difference if — ' and, 'I am not that kind of person,' and so on. You charge in, you interfere, you chase him back to his very birth, you would doubtless do so to his conception, if you could. And then you have the effrontery to be horrified because he was nothing of

216

what you imagined." He stared into my outraged face, then laughed, one brief, harsh, unamused laugh. "What has all this got to do with you? You say you were in love with him. Does that give you the right to investigate him? I see nothing unreal in your friend. It is you I find unreal. He simply chose to live his life on the plane of his own imagination. It is like a beautiful woman who makes up her face, dresses her hair, puts on a new gown. When she is alone at night, the make-up goes, the gown falls to the floor, the hair is out of curl. Which is real? Both are real, but to her lover and her maid she is two different people."

The description was oddly old-fashioned but then so in his way was Martin Salvatore. I only said, "Has no one the right to know about other people?"

"No."

"Do you not find it strange that wherever I looked there was nothing?"

"No. I find it strange that you looked. There was no reason for you to do so. You are denying him the one inalienable human right, to be private. Everybody tells us what to do, asks us why, criticises, disapproves. It is none of their business, none at all."

"You talk as if we all live separate lives. We do sometimes touch each other after all. We cannot always live in isolation."

And as I said this, I was aware of a kind of prudish withdrawal. I knew then that there are people who live in isolation, not poor Steve, who grabbed with one hand what he hurled away with the other, but Martin Salvatore: to me at that moment it was as if he lived on some remote, ice-bound shore, away from humanity, analysing us all, watching, observing, computing, never once drawn into a personal warmth.

He did not answer, and I could not see his face. I said, "What about the war?"

"What do you mean, what about the war?"

"Steve's war. That was real. But you won't let me say that, will you?"

He held out his hands. It was the first foreign gesture I had seen him make. "How stupid you are," he said. He sounded almost waspish. The friendliness between us was gone. "You seem to think the war was the focal point of his reality. Of course it was not. It was the war he was escaping from. How he must have hated it, the smells, the sounds, the blood, the beastliness. He called it a prison camp. He rationalised it. But it was the war itself. If you have any sensitivity, you should understand."

I said, I do not know why, "Were you in the war?"

He stiffened in an affected way, as if I had spoken some obscenity. "Dear lady," he said like a ham actor, "do not be so foolish. Can you imagine it? All kinds of violence are distasteful to me. I am not interested in such things. I live in my mind."

It was true, I could by no stretch of imagination visualise Martin Salvatore in the war. I was silent, thinking a vast confusion of thoughts in which Eve and Paul and Steve somehow merged. I said at last, "And why do you think his hysterical paralysis should affect me, after he died?"

He answered indifferently, "It is you who are frightened of reality. You forced that on yourself. It was nothing to do with him. You believed you had suffered more than you could endure. It was your way of getting rid of him. You remembered his paralysis subconciously and I can only asssume that you too wished to escape. You prefer not to recognise that, of course. That is why you have tried so hard to track him down."

"I don't think that makes much sense."

"If you think it over dispassionately, you will find it does. I daresay this — this love affair of yours was quite a traumatic experience."

"You use such jargon!"

"It is the language of our time. Too much to take, a trick of memory — Shall we leave the subject? I am beginning to find it boring, Mrs. Waterman. I am going away in three days' time. I am tired of this country. I want to be home again. I have a business in Milan."

I wondered what the business was. I visualised something to do with antiques, fine jewellery, period furniture. I could not imagine this cold, isolated, fastidious man in anything else. But his next words startled me so that I felt hot and dizzy, with a weakness in my legs that frightened me.

"Come with me." He must have seen the horror in my face. Most men would have been offended, affronted, but he was delighted, it was what he wanted.

I whispered, "You're joking."

He said pleasantly, "Why should I be joking? I am perfectly serious. I am not suggesting anything permanent. Come with me. For a holiday. It will at least be a kind of reality."

I could not see his eyes but I felt that they were fixed on me. I felt the purpose in him, he was willing me to say yes. I tried to get up, to say I must go, but believed for that second I could not. He said again, with great force, "Come!" — and at that moment the front door-bell rang.

Oh, God bless Victor! On the dot as always. But it broke the spell. I think Martin Salvatore was both disconcerted and angry, but muttering something under his breath he went to the door and opened it.

I heard Victor saying, "I'm sorry, sir, but this is to remind madam — " (Madam! He has never called me madam in my life) " — that she has another appointment in twenty minutes."

I at last managed to get up. I was light-headed with relief. I walked towards the door. I said, "Thank you, Victor. I'd quite forgotten." I turned towards Martin Salvatore and held out my hand. "Goodbye, Mr. Salvatore. I hope you have a good journey home."

He took my hand, bent his head and kissed it. I did not like the feel of his hand or his lips. As I stepped out into the corridor, he spoke once more in his thin, dry voice, his eyes following me.

He said, " 'We are such stuff as dreams are made on; and our little life is rounded with a sleep.' "

The door closed behind him.

Victor said, "What's that all about then? What's he talking about?"

"It's a quotation, Victor. From *The tempest*."

"Oh. Highbrow stuff. I'm not a reading chap," said Victor, "don't know about that kind of thing. How did it go?" Then before I could answer, he said abruptly, "I don't think that's a very nice man, young lady. You don't want to get tied up with the likes of him."

"I think you're quite right."

"I don't know what your son was thinking of. You get him to do his own dirty work next time."

He always calls Daniel my son. But I only smiled at him, loving him for his normality, his ordinariness, his decency. I wished that Martin Salvatore had not quoted those lines.

219

They are so beautiful, and I think he is a sad and evil man: sad and evil men should not speak poetry with such feeling.

When I came home, I rounded off a crazy day by becoming crazy myself. I sat in front of my mirror, I picked up Eve's little tubes and bottles, and very carefully I made up my face. I looked at the result, the shaded eyelids, the pencilled brows, the lipsticked mouth. It was not myself. It was not real. It was not even attractive. Then I washed it all off, with common soap and water. And I looked into the face of a plain, ordinary middle-aged woman, and I knew myself, I felt for the first time for longer than I can remember, at peace.

Daniel and Vanda turned up unexpectedly three days later with the children. I could see that everything was all right again. It was like a second honeymoon. Vanda was smiling and beautiful, and Daniel had completely lost the savage, defensive expression that has been on his face the past few weeks.

I think that Vanda is pregnant. No one says a word, but there is a kind of glow to her: she is a girl who is happy in pregnancy, who enjoys the process of having a baby. It is the best thing that could happen, nothing will bind her and Daniel together better. I daresay they cannot afford another child, but then one never can, babies always arrive at the wrong moment. She is a sane and sensible girl, and I love her very much. Martin Salvatore will never touch her again. I am sure it will be a lovely child.

I did not of course mention my visit, it is something I will never talk about to a living soul. But it was Vanda herself who mentioned Martin. I suppose he rang or sent a little note. "He's gone," she said in her deep voice. "He's gone back to Milan. He says he will never return to England. He has his business there, of course."

I expressed a most heartfelt satisfaction, and Daniel grinned at me over her shoulder. I said idly — after all, it was a quite normal question — "What is his business?"

Vanda looked surprised as if she thought I ought to know. "He makes toilet paper," she said, then seeing the expression on my face, "It is very profitable, Elizabeth. He makes a lot of money. He is a very, very rich man."

She will never understand why I burst out laughing. I think Daniel thought I was hysterical: I saw the professional look appear in his eye. The children were delighted and laughed with me. We made quite a noise. But of course it was not hysteria. It was relief and joy at the magnificent incongruity of it. The strange man who lectured me, who spoke truth to me — it was truth, I know it was truth — who lived in such an elegant flat, who was too fastidious for war, too fastidious for Vanda, made his living by manufacturing one of the most mundane essentials of our civilised life.

I like that. I like that very much. It shoots things back into proportion. Martin Salvatore is no Count Magnus. He is an ordinary businessman who dabbles in the occult, who must by his nature be hideously alone. And he makes toilet paper.

At least toilet paper is real.

I say, when they go, "Are you all right, Daniel?"

He gives me a hug. "Oh yes. Yes indeed — Are you all right, Elizabeth? You're looking quite chippy."

"I'm fine."

I'm fine. And after all, what is all this about? Steve is real for me, he will always be real for me, beside me, in bed with me, in my heart. All these lies and fantasies do not matter, he is as I knew him, and in time the stupidities and cruelties and ugliness will vanish. They never were important. I have been foolish even to consider them.

We all live in a ghost town. We are hemmed in by ambitions, money, power, lust and pride, they are all fantasies. We ride into painted sunsets, we smudge the face that living has given us, we entangle ourselves in every kind of muddle and confusion.

Dear Elizabeth Ingram, —

Dear Steve.

"We are such stuff as dreams are made on; and our little life is rounded with a sleep."